José Builds a Woman

José Builds a Woman

a novel by

Jan Baross

Ooligan Press
Portland, Oregon

JOSÉ BUILDS A WOMAN

OOLIGAN PRESS, PO BOX 751, PORTLAND, OREGON 97207

OOLIGAN@PDX.EDU/WWW.OOLIGAN.PDX.EDU

FRONT COVER PAINTING BY JAN BAROSS.

COVER DESIGN BY MARK INSALACO.

INTERIOR DESIGN BY SHERRY GREEN.

12 11 10 09 08 07 06 1 2 3 4 5 6

ISBN10: 1-932010-14-9

ISBN13: 978-1-932010-14-5

LIBRARY OF CONGRESS CATALOGING-IN-PUBLICATION DATA

[AVAILABLE FROM THE PUBLISHER]

PRINTED IN THE UNITED STATES OF AMERICA.

For a great storyteller

Bertha Seiferth Bannett

Part One

You come into existence
each morning when
your eyes open to
the jacaranda's bloom,
your lips sweet as bread
are baked anew
by an astounded sun.

PROLOGUE

IN THE SHADE of the purple jacaranda in the jungle by the sea, my son José builds a woman.

José makes adobe bricks in the hot morning sun with red clay from the River Rojo and straw from our fields. He rolls his hands over the wet earth. The bricks form to the shapes he will need. Rounded for the buttocks, curved for the breasts, sturdy for the flat toes.

While the bricks dry in the sun, José clears a knoll of pepper trees and builds tall scaffolding from the branches. In the center of the scaffolding, he lays dry adobe bricks, as deep and wide as five beds. On top of the base, José builds the woman's feet. Her ankles are strong and slender, her shins straight, her thighs thick with being a woman, her mound gently curved. Her torso, small breasts, and strong neck rise gradually toward the top of the canopied trees. Creamy, wet clay between the bricks weds them like the layers of a cake.

José pauses to inhale the female landscape of the jungle, the hard-perfumed blossoms of orchids, the soft scent of tendriled trees and the rich tunnels of moist undergrowth.

He inhales all this and breathes it into the woman he is building.

As the woman reaches a great height, José grows until he reaches a great height as well. He no longer needs the scaffolding.

I look up at José's wide back.

"My son, your brown body grows as the woman grows."

José pours a gruel of wet clay over her body and polishes her skin until it looks as smooth as the sweat on his cheeks.

"My son, the woman is as high as one home on top of another, yet her body is headless."

José strides to the bank of the Río Rojo, kneels, and scoops clay into the shape of a head. He molds the deep inset of the woman's eyes, the slight droop of sleepy lids set close to a strong nose. His strong arms knot and unknot in light and shadow until he completes the woman's face.

José picks up the woman's head and carries it to her body in the jungle clearing. He is the height of his creation.

He places the woman's head on her neck. She opens her eyes, though her feet do not move from the foundation. Her wide face above the treetops startles two cormorants in flight. José raises his mouth to kiss her.

"My son, you have given the woman my face."

José bends over me and casts his giant dark shadow over my body. There is no escape from the consuming fire of his eyes. His fingers, red and cracked with crimson mud, reach for me.

CHAPTER 1

I AM TORTUGINA. They call me little turtle because I am snappish. My mouth has an overbite. Some say I look predatory, but I am good in bed.

I was born in a two-story house by the sea, in the village of El Pulpo, sixteen years before I gave birth to José. The village is called El Pulpo because octopus is the only thing we have to sell in abundance.

All houses in El Pulpo are white, built by the rule of one because one color is good enough for everyone. White homes built with stones from the quarry, white slate roofs, white lye walls of the church and white dust in the breeze from shells shattered by the sea. Our white village, high on a cliff, looks like a many tiered wedding cake with a hundred black doors. To outsiders it may seem edible, but to me, it is stale as old bread.

On the night I was born, Mamá said a white dog howled in the doorway all night and a shattering storm brought hail the size of coconuts that cracked the church bell. When the hail was directly over our house, an albino bird dropped bloody from the sky onto the roof and Mamá grunted like a pig.

I slid out in a rush of liquid, small and pale like an octopus pulled from a dark cave. My bones long to return to the safety of fluids.

"Ayee, another girl!" Papá said, holding my streaked legs apart. "I am going to Ignacio's Tavern to curse in silence."

My two sisters wept with Mamá. I was the last child she could have. No son to bear the burden of Papá's store. But I did not cry.

It was my destiny to make my family weep for not wanting me as I was.

Most of the time I do not live in my white village. I live in my dreams, the only place where there is color. Not smooth legs of rich red topsoil, or yellow cracks of the arroyo, or tilled furrows of dark curled mud. No, my dreams are the colors of the sea, an escape into the weightless veins of manganese, stretches of purple through muscular green currents. A thin membrane separates the sea and the pulsing of my dream to be an octopus diver.

With my head dreaming on a white brocade pillow, the nightly enchantment begins. A plunge into the warm, green sea with Gabito. He is the most beautiful octopus diver in all of El Pulpo. We dive side by side past rocks packed in foam, from clear azure to dim greens, deeper and deeper, to ancient underwater caves. In my hands I hold a net.

"Show me," I whisper into Gabito's perfect ear.

Along the dark base of the cliffs, there are octopus of all sizes and colors. The orange ones are closer to the sun. The green and purple ones live deeper. Their boneless legs straighten and disappear into the sanctuary of small caves. Gabito reaches into a hole, and because this is a dream, the octopus rush into our nets.

"You see, Gabito," I say. "Nothing is a struggle when we hunt together."

Gabito pushes my shoulders back into the white sand. It splits with the weight of my spine and rises in granular puffs on the soft current. My body is trapped between his strong brown legs. He holds my arms above my head. My body is not afraid of the water, of the sea, of liquid of any kind, any more than his is. He slides his hands inside my nightgown.

"I want nothing more than you," says Gabito.

In celebration, my flannelled hips rise off the sand toward the hard muscles inside Gabito's goodluck yellow swim shorts.

"At last," he says.

"At last," I say.

Gabito kisses me. Our lips release two long strands of silver bubbles that become one.

"Little turtle." Mamá's voice is the foghorn of my dreams. "Arise morning glory."

I am caught in the undertow of her voice.

Gabito slips sadly away, riding a dark current to the deeper safety of the sea. Mamá pulls back the quilt. A quick movement like a bird's dry wing. The chilled air shrivels my nipples.

"Mamá," I moan.

Chapter 1

“Hush before you wake your sisters,” whispers Mamá.

She wraps her fat arms around me. Mamá’s blue robe has the sour smell of sleep. She slips her cold hand under my nightgown and pulls off my underwear. She holds it up to the crack of light at the door.

“No blood yet, Tortugina,” says Mamá. “If you delay being a woman this long, you are bound to have bad dreams.”

She pats my cheek too hard. I snap my overbite at her wrist. Mamá shuffles toward the bedroom door in her crushed slippers.

“Hurry, hurry, little turtle,” she says.

Mamá’s world turns too fast for me.

CHAPTER 2

THE BLUE SHUTTERS are half open in Mamá's yellow kitchen. She stands over the tin sink washing her face with rainwater. She rubs her gums and teeth with a slice of lime and spits into the sink. Mamá's blue robe hangs so loose it could be the curtain for a traveling show.

She turns toward me, sweeping her long peppered strands into a big bun, and pierces the bulb of her hair with an abalone comb.

"You are the slowest thing on earth!" she says. "Go!"

I snatch the straw tortilla basket off the table. Since my sleep must be sacrificed, I slap my sandals loudly across the floor to wake my dreaming sisters and snoring father. Jumping down the back stairs, and off the last uneven step, I hear my loud echoes through Papá's store. His open barrels of grains and stacks of dried roots smell like old people's shoes. I skip past the cellar door where Papá makes his intoxicating aguardiente, fire water, that burns the throat with happiness.

I grab a stem of red licorice from the open jar on the counter. Stolen candy is the taste of morning.

My last revenge is to slam the front door shut so hard it rattles our neighbors' shutters. Villagers sleeping in the white buildings lining our quiet Plaza de Allende know when Tortugina has been unbedded.

Calle del Mar is my street. Anything named "street of the sea" should have gray waves curling down the cobblestones, sweeping the youngest ones who run for morning tortillas into a quiet place where dreams are never interrupted.

Gabito's white shirt is a distant sail across the plaza. The heavy leather of his sandals rudders by habit toward the soft chugging of the tortilleria.

I have loved Gabito since I was six and he was eight and he beat me senseless on the black sand when I stole a kiss. I would willingly follow him through the most dangerous shoals.

He passes the small church with one white spire. Saint Assisi by the Sea, administered and swept by fat Padre Abstensia and horse-faced Mother Mary Inmaculada, who runs the nunnery that was once a stable. When Gabito and I marry, it will be in this white church.

At this hour, the plaza is barren of footsteps and covered in a light mist. Fat grackles chirp in the trees trimmed square as green boxes. Curled at the base, Salsa, the three-legged street dog, raises his patient brown head that is white from the birds' night droppings.

Gabito sees me coming and sprints past wooden shutters closed as sleep. It is our running game. I have always chased him, believing that I could catch him. We fly past the cast-iron bandstand covered in flaking black curls from centuries of painting and repainting. Magicians, fat políticos, troubadours, all left their echoes under the pointed roof. Here the village band plays the same sour notes every Saturday. The old tunes inspired generations of calloused feet to dance, to court, to wed. I am the result of so much footwork.

I follow Gabito through the vegetable market, dodging between the empty stalls sheltered from the sun by bolts of colored canvas. In an hour, the vendors will be shouting their poems of produce.

"Caaa-caaaa-hueee-te! Peanuts! Naaaraaanjaaa! Oranges!"

Up ahead, Gabito runs past Señora Grosera. Under her faded red umbrella, the tiny vendor waves first at Gabito then at me. Her family has a lifetime claim to the coveted space in front of the Office of All Public Concerns.

"Carne caliente! Hot meat!" shouts toothless Señora Grosera.

The old witch divines weather and predicts who should marry. She winks at us.

"Gabito! Tortugina! Hot meat!"

Señora Grosera shoves a slender stick into a marinated strip of beef. She drops it onto the grill. Her frying rooster-chilies sting my eyes. I hold my breath and hurry past her stand.

Outside the Chicken Palace, Señor Aves picks up the buckets of marigolds he feeds to the chickens so the yolks of their eggs will be bright yellow.

"Tortugina, what plague have you brought today?" he says.

Chapter 2

Señor Aves has never forgiven me for accidentally killing his rooster with my slingshot.

I hurry past him up the winding street.

"Assassin!" he shouts after me.

As I follow Gabito around the last winding corner of upper Calle de Serpiente, his broad shoulders fill the street in front of Señora Porción's tortilleria. Our hearts beat from the morning run, faster than the chugging of the old tortilla machine inside.

A breeze ruffles Gabito's hair, and I wish it were my fingers in his curls. Gabito is not the youngest and does not need to run for tortillas every morning. He is here so that we may stand side by side, arms barely touching in the tortilla line. As he enters through the low door of the tortilleria, he looks back over his shoulder and smiles at me. I slap the straw basket against my hip so he will notice my figure and follow Gabito into the dim warmth. In line, we stand close, elbow to elbow, and I breathe in the sweetness of baking corn and his diver's sea scent. It is my shame that at fifteen years of age my blood has not come so we cannot marry.

CHAPTER 3

IT IS ALWAYS windy along the crushed lava trail of the Forbidden Cliffs. This is where the color of my day begins, a big blue bowl of sky over an emerald sea. Hundreds of feet below are the ragged lava rocks. Humpbacked waves curl toward shore and shatter on the volcanic spears.

My job is to fill an empty burlap sack with mussels kidnapped from their seaweed ledge. I speed through this job so fast that Mamá would be astounded. It leaves me enough time to sneak up to the Forbidden Cliffs where my half-naked Gabito and the other divers do their dangerous work.

Gabito's black dog, Coriander, guards the switchback trail down the sheer cliffs to the divers' ledge. Under penalty of banishment, a woman must never approach the cliffs, for she might distract a pulpo diver from his dive. But that will all change when I am a diver.

Chapter 3

Coriander shakes his wet jowls to warn me. Bubbled spit flies into the dust. When I bare my teeth, he snaps the air close enough for me to smell the fishy odor of his breakfast.

There is a secret way to Gabito, a crevice that snakes down the cliff. Leaving Coriander to growl at shadows, I climb down the deep, battered trail. Two curtains of stone hide the entrance to my cave. My shawl blots dampness from the rough edges as I squeeze inside. Light pours into the cave from a large window in the jagged rock that frames the horizon of the sea. A browning banana from yesterday's lunch spreads its rotting perfume. I take a small notebook from my painted tin box and a brass telescope I found washed ashore on the black sands.

Slipping under a large black cotton cloth with eyeholes, I become one of the cave's broken shadows. My camouflaged body presses against the edge of the jagged window. I adjust the rusted eyepiece of the telescope until I am focused on Gabito in his goodluck yellow swim shorts. Fifty feet below, the forbidden divers' ledge is a dark rock that sticks out over the waves like a rude tongue. Gabito, his curly hair shifting in the wind, sits close to a small campfire and shoves a whole candy bar into his mouth. He works his face around it until even my eyes taste his chocolate.

Smiling Tomás, Gabito's brother, pulls a torn jacket up around his hairy neck. He is wiry and dark, with monkey-quick movements. His dark eyebrows creep up his short forehead into a thatch of black hair. If he were not Gabito's brother, I would suspect his line was linked to another species.

Skinny Vicente kneels near the flames in his canvas shorts. He has a tiny ass, and bones of a fowl that poke through his marigold skin. When he dives, he is like a weightless kite in the wind. His father, Señor Aves, worships every splayed step Vicente takes because he is the only son in a five-daughter family.

Big Luis circles the fire in his long dark shorts and beats his arms to keep warm. He may be the mayor's youngest son, but Big Luis has the long, stupid face of a burro. Even his ears droop, though his footing on the cliffs is rock steady.

Gordo, Keeper of the Flame, waddles over and drops a small log on the dying fire. He is lighter skinned than the others, and his hair is wispy. A mother-knit wool sweater climbs up the bulge of his stomach.

Gabito snaps a towel at this vulnerable place on Gordo's body. It is not that Gabito is cruel. Gordo invites pain. He makes himself irresistible because he will bear anything to be close to the divers.

Gabito stands and stretches into the sunlight. He shakes his shoulders and twists an octopus net into a belt around his waist. No loose ends to catch on the lava spears hidden beneath the surface of the sea.

Gabito's first dive of the day starts my own routine. I cross myself.

"Mother Mary, supreme hoarder of hope, let Gabito live another day."

Each prayer is one more layer of armor between his body and the sharp rocks. One week I was sick at home, and he slashed his leg on the rocks. I have kept Gabito alive since he began diving at the age of twelve, and I can say more prayers in a short amount of time than a priest.

"MaryMotherofJesusourLordGodprotectmyGabitoAmen! MotherMarylethimhitthewavessafelyAmen!Spreadyour divinenetofprotectionadlethimcatchmany octopusAmen!"

Chapter 3

I do not pray for the rest of the divers because I want their job.

Gabito's body rocks back and forth. The sun washes his skin in a warm lemon light. He waits for the perfect wave.

His toes grip the edge of the lava stone. He pumps his legs to warm up, bends his knees, and straightens. He slaps the blood awake in his legs, stomach, and chest. His curly head cocks one way then the other, as though he was already shaking water out of his ears. Finally he crosses himself with a prayer. His arms fly back, his knees bend deep. If he does not dive with precision, dive just as the trough settles...

Gabito pushes off the ledge, arms and chest wide, arcing his sea-bird spine.

"MotherMarydoyourjob!MotherMarydoyourjob!"

Under the black cloth my fingers move around my chest in a triangle of prayer for Gabito. God. Jesus. Mother Mary. I may have permanent bruises on my chest from the fast pecking of my fingers. The ritual is sometimes long and complicated, depending on how terrified I am.

Gabito's feet are pointed, hands together, nose down. His yellow shorts ripple against his thighs.

My fingers move faster than Papá's on his abacus. The telescope jiggles against my eye.

Gabito's body knifes between the lava spears. Green waves close over his pointed toes. I exhale my relief.

Then quickly, with one long inhale, I hold my breath. Until Gabito's head breaks the surface, until he breathes, I will not breathe. This is my diving practice.

"One, two, three..."

My mind sinks into Gabito's cold, silent world. I am the

current caressing his brown ankles. I am liquid trapped in his goodluck shorts. I am a part of his graceful strokes downward past the yellow and orange octopus into the deeper crevices where the most tender gray octopus live in dark cliff caves.

Holding my breath. "Twenty-five, twenty-six, twenty-seven…"

I make the first entry of the day in my notebook:

"Monday morning, Oct. 4th, 7 a.m. Gabito's first dive. Perfection. The grace of a bird." Under "Improvements," I write, "ABSOLUTELY NONE."

I have lists of improvements for the other divers. Their faults teach me to be a better diver.

"Forty-three, forty-four…"

I feel the first hint of tightness in my throat. I look down at the waves, watching for Gabito. Only once did a diver die, many years ago. His adoring fiancée threw him a kiss and distracted him. Days later, his crushed body was washed onto the shore.

My chest is tightening. "One hundred, one hundred one…"

I never cheat at this. Some things, yes, but never this. I must prove to myself that I have lungs enough to make my dream come true.

Big Luis pulls his long burro face away from the flames. He places his feet precisely in the diving grooves and watches the waves. Then with a slow, deliberate inhale, Big Luis leans forward, swings his arms back, and dives head first. He always waits until the last moment to stretch his arms out in front of him, like a dare, and so far it has worked.

Chapter 3

I make my entry in the book. "Arms scary as always. And no grace."

Smiling Tomás pulls up his black shorts and gives his balls a squeeze. He bends his monkey head over the ledge to see if either boy is in his way. Then he dives quickly, almost carelessly, as though his jungle body has a mind of its own and will take care of the details.

In the notebook I enter, "Idiot."

Holding my breath. "Two hundred, two hundred and one..."

My nose feels hot. The pressure building in my lungs might cause a nosebleed. I sniff and hold the new air.

Skinny Vicente turns the ledge into a one-man circus for Gordo. He wiggles his bottom, a flat crack where a rounded ball of muscle should be. Then he dives into an updraft that suspends him for a second before it drops him down the side of the cliff to the sea. At least there is no blood, which is the best sign.

In the notebook under Vicente, I try but I can no longer write. Eyes water, chest hurts.

"Three hundred and one..."

It is too hot under the black cloth. I rip it off my head.

"Three hundred and fifteen..."

I am dizzy. My skin is too tight. Gabito has never been this late.

"Three hundred ninety-one, three hundred ninety-two..."

My lungs plead for air. Weaklings!

"Three hundred ninety-three."

The air hardens inside my chest. Enough! I look over the ledge. He cannot stay down any longer!

"Three hundred ninety-six."

My lungs shriek, "Gabito! Hurry!"

I feel a hundred pulses in my head.

"Give me three more seconds!" I say to myself.

"Three hundred ninety-seven. Ninety-eight! Ninety-nine!"

Gabito's black curls break through the foam. His chest is high in the waves.

One more count!

"Four hundred!"

I gasp, and my lungs drag the salty air deep. I lay my face on the damp rocks to cool my skin.

Four hundred! I did it! I did it, Gabito! I beat you!

I crouch in the dark with my victory while Gabito climbs up the cliff with a heavy net of octopus strapped to his waist and the sun shining on his back. It should be me hauling the catch up the cliff. I have proven that I have the lungs of a boy.

Tortugina, girl diver!

Tomorrow, I will move toward Gabito the way the women in the taverna walk, stopping just out of reach. They make the men rise and come to them. I will walk like that tomorrow morning at the tortilleria, and he will not be able to resist my request.

Let me dive!

CHAPTER 4

MAMÁ SCRAPES HER worn slippers to my bed and pulls back the quilt. She stares down at me because I am wide awake, fully dressed in my new red skirt and smiling up at her.

"Good morning, my lovely Mamá," I whisper.

She rubs the sleep out of her eyes. "Have I got the wrong bed?"

I slide off the sheets without an argument and slip my feet into my best sandals, though they are not best for running. In the morning's dim light I hear the echo of Gabito's words that came in my dream last night.

"Tortugina, you are my diving partner. We will marry underwater and all our children will swim like fish."

Ten more minutes to the tortilleria, and I will be able to tell Gabito that I held four hundred breaths. How can he say no in the face of such an accomplishment?

"Tortugina," whispers Mamá. "Why are you smiling? Did you get your blood?"

Chapter 4

Her hand reaches for my skirt. I slip around the bed and pull my best knitted wool shawl from the closet. Holding the short shawl out like wings, I dance silently through the bedroom door and beat Mamá's quick steps to the kitchen. I flip the empty tortilla basket, catch it, and twirl to the door.

"Tortugina, what has happened to you?"

I run silently down the stairs so as not to wake the rest of the family, and do not slam the front door. After all, divers are considerate of others.

Gabito races ahead of me as always, and for the last time, I let him beat me. He is waiting, as always, in front of the tortilleria. I walk toward him like the tavern women, holding onto my little shawl, and swing my hips as far left and right as they will go. As I come closer, Gabito's eyes fill with a sense of our new game. His silky lips swell and he steps close to me. The aroma of limes rises from his hands. Gabito cocks his head left and right as though shaking water out of his ears.

"Tortugina," he says, "you are different today."

My heart beats faster. I lower my eyes then look up at him with my lashes batting hard. The heat under my skirt will burn my underwear to ash.

Gabito's smile leaves a gentle kiss on my cheek. His hand reaches around my neck and gently tugs on my braid. I lose my practiced words. All I can smell is the sea. I want to be Gabito as much as I love Gabito.

Now I cannot think how to tell him he must make my dream come true.

Gabito coughs and takes polite steps backwards until he slides through the door of Señora Porción's tortilleria.

I move into line with Gabito, hot elbow to hot elbow. El Fuerte, the loud metal tortilla maker, chugs and shudders to a stop. Señora Porción raises her wrench and smashes it against El Fuerte until the gears grind to life again. The heat and the low ceiling, the generator and gasoline, make the room feel like the inside of an old ship putting out to sea.

Children crowd through the door with their baskets and lean against my thighs for comfort like a litter of puppies. Their warmth makes me drowsy. I want to climb back into bed and pull a quilt over Gabito and me.

I poke two fingers under my shawl making pointy breasts where I have none. The children giggle. Gabito leans on the blue tile counter and turns to see my nipple-fingers pointed at him. He turns red.

"Whatever you are doing, Tortugina, stop it," says Señora Porción.

She spins on her peg leg and lurches for the counter. Gabito smiles at her. It is a smile that keeps the women of El Pulpo eager for his octopus. He turns his voice a notch deeper and leans closer to Señora Porción.

"A big basket today, Señora. My uncle arrived last night."

Señora drops a pile of hot corn tortillas into Gabito's basket.

"Gabito, bring your uncle next time. Is he married?"

"Forever," says Gabito.

Señora Porción laughs and grips the counter with one hand so she can receive Gabito's coins with the other.

Many holidays ago, after too many glasses of wine, Señora Porción hacked off her own leg when she decided to machete her sugar cane by the light of the moon.

"Careful," says Señora Porción. The steaming stack of tortillas falls against Gabito's fingers.

Chapter 4

"Oh, they will keep me warm Señora!" says Gabito.

Señora Porción's lips crease at the edges. "You do not need to get any hotter, Gabito."

Gabito blushes and I laugh at him. I cannot stop my own snorts. The smaller children giggle at me.

"Tortugina, you sound like a horse," Gabito teases.

The children laugh harder.

"Tortugina is more like a wild monkey," says Señora Porción.

I put the tortilla basket in front of my face and shut my eyes. I am used to teasing, even humiliation, but today was supposed to be different. I let the basket drop to the counter and blast louder than El Fuerte.

"Gabito," I say, "I can hold four hundred breaths. I could be as good a diver as you!"

Gabito's face turns a terrible shade of purple. He steps away from me. If I measured the distance between us in heartbeats, he would be miles away.

"Tortugina, why can't you just be a girl?" he says.

Señora quickly piles hot tortillas into Mamá's straw basket and shoves them at me. "Take this to your mother, Tortugina, and we will not tell her how badly you behaved."

Gabito's smile slowly returns. "For you to be as good as me, you would have to be a witch."

"Bruja! Bruja! Bruja!" howl the children.

"Are you a witch, Tortugina?" asks Gabito.

Gabito moves so close that I am overwhelmed by the scent of lime, the sweat on his clothes, and the wild wind that clings to the hair of boys. I will faint if he comes any closer.

The children shout, "Bruja! Bruja! Bruja!"

Their screaming gives me a headache. I grab my steaming basket and run into the chill of the street.

If my dream kills Gabito's love, then what have we been carrying in our hearts all our lives?

Gabito's heavy sandals pound the cobblestones behind me. I am tempted to slow down, to let him catch me. But not today. I let my true speed unwind. It carries me down the narrow streets, past Señor Aves and his roasting chickens and the eye-watering chilies of Señora Grosera. My feet are wings sailing across the plaza, faster than the street dogs, faster than the grackles launching skyward. I leap over the buckets of Señora Flora's dried flower bouquets, race past Señor Afilado's knife-sharpening bicycle. The spinning file makes bright metal sparks that jump after my heels.

Ahead, Papá's black door marks the sanctuary of home. I cross Calle del Mer and slap the door to mark my victory. I have outrun Gabito, but what have I won?

Behind me, the sound of his heavy leather sandals. Though he stops on the opposite side of the street, there is no distance between us.

I tuck the basket of tortillas tightly in my shawl and bend to pick up the bundle of firewood Señor Hachete and his white burro left outside our door. I want Gabito to see the shape of my bottom pushing against my new red skirt. I feel his eyes stroking my hips. The muscles in the small of my back tingle. As I stand and turn to him, my body hides again under the folds.

Gabito crosses the street. The heat between us thickens the crotch of his white pants. The mystery in Gabito's pants is something I am told happens to boys and men in the vicinity of women, wine, and some domesticated animals. This is the first time I have seen Gabito like this. I do not ask how he does it.

Chapter 4

When his body is so close that I feel his warmth, I drop the bundle of firewood. He raises his hand and pushes his dark curls off his neck to show me something small and green behind his ear. I lean closer. It is a tattoo of a tiny turtle with the name "Tortugina" at the bottom of the shell.

Until now, no one has ever shown me a picture of love. A turtle cut into human flesh, blood hot below the ink with my name that can never be washed away. We both tremble as I run my finger over the tattoo. He lets his hair fall back into place, hiding our secret.

His brown face is so close I could lick his dark arched eyebrows. Through his sweet lips, the words come very hard, with long pauses between them.

"Tortugina, I know you want to be a diver," says Gabito. "But—"

And here is the longest pause of all.

"—you must be content to be the wife of a diver."

Heat prickles my face, and my heart beats faster than I could ever run.

"You are asking me to be your wife?"

Gabito nods.

Yesterday I would have searched for a handkerchief to dab tears of gratitude. But today I feel like I will die if I do not speak the truth. It is hard to find breath for the words.

"Gabito, I love you. I want to marry you more than anything in the world," I say. "But I must also be a diver. Do you love me that much?"

Gabito slowly turns as white as the chalky houses of El Pulpo. He walks away from me down the cobblestone street, then runs like a sea-bird skimming the tops of the waves.

CHAPTER 5

INSIDE THE HEAVY black door of home is another kind of heat, the heat of family. I pound up the dark stairs to Mamá's kitchen and throw the bundled firewood into the kindling box.

"Tortugina, you are as loud as a man," says Mamá.

She stirs the coals in the wood stove and throws kindling on top of the embers. The sticks burst into flames, feathering Mamá's round face with an orange glow. She seems to expand from the heat to fill the kitchen. There is never enough space when Mamá is in the room.

"Well?" she says. "What new disgrace this morning?"

I am Mamá's entertainment, her partner in the cockfight of her kitchen.

"Gabito asked me to marry him."

"Tortugina," says Mamá. "Do you think a boy like Gabito would give you anything but a bad cold?"

Chapter 5

I sling the basket of corn tortillas onto the flowered oilcloth. It ricochets off the stucco wall and spills tortillas on the floor.

"You only believe the bad about me!" I shout.

I push open the blue wooden shutters and climb onto the window ledge, then onto the slate tiles of the roof. Cold wind shoots up my dress. I kick a tile that slides off the roof and smashes on the street below.

"Tortugina!" yells Mamá. "Get back in here!"

Mamá's fearful eye twitch is my revenge.

"The one who shames you?" I say.

I look beyond my house to the sea, the safety of fluids. Someday I'll abandon these cliffs and build a home on yellow foam.

"Tortugina?" says Mamá. "Little turtle?"

There is concession in her tone.

"Come pick the cat hairs off the tortillas before Papá sees them."

I have softened her eyes with fear.

I crawl back inside. Her pillow arms hug the warmth back into my body.

"My little turtle," Mamá says. "I should kill you before puberty."

Her gentle chide. She lets me go with a small smack on my bottom. As I step back, my sandals crunch soft bones, the daily offering of our spotted cat Gato. I bend quickly to grab a rat's shredded tail and toss the carcass out the window. Mamá shudders.

"Wash your hands, Tortugina!"

I wash in the icy rainwater then brush each tortilla free of cat hair. Without being ordered, I re-stack the tortillas in their basket and put them on the table wrapped in a colorful towel. I wipe the tablecloth with a damp sea sponge and set our places with Mamá's mamá's mamá's old cracked plates painted with red and green flowers. I fill a pot with rainwater from the cistern pipe, put the water pot on the stove for coffee, and shove a fry pan of last night's refried beans onto the heat.

"Tortugina," says Mamá. "I will iron your favorite dress since you are behaving."

I pull my green dress out of the folded laundry. What Mamá irons, I wear. But if she irons something I do not like, I wear something wrinkled. The ways to disgrace her are endless.

Mamá lifts the hot iron off the stove and spreads my green dress on a thin towel. She presses the heat into its wrinkled front, and I feel the warmth on my chest. Starch fuses with the weave. For a single moment, I am in love with Mamá.

A loud crash echoes down the hall. Papá curses from his bedroom.

"Hector, the children!" Mamá shakes her head.

Papá limps barefoot into the kitchen in the brown shirt, brown jacket, and brown pants that he wears every day. His moustache trembles.

"You moved the box of canned beef! Look what you did to my foot, Celia!"

All Papá's wounds are Mamá's fault. Having sired only girls, Papá considers that he is entitled to constant nursing. He sits down and spreads a pair of socks on the kitchen table.

"My socks don't match either!"

Chapter 5

Mamá spits a mouthful of rainwater on my dress and shoves the heavy iron over the damp folds of the skirt. Her voice is gentle but firm.

"Who cares about the color of your socks, Hector?"

Papá and I both look at her.

"Who would want to peek up your leg?" she says.

"Celia!" says Papá. "I buy the same color, brown! There is no question that I will match! Now, I find one brown and one light brown! Are you using bleach on my socks?"

Mamá sighs and retrieves another balled pair of brown socks from her laundry basket.

"Beware, Tortugina," she says. "All love comes down to socks."

She tosses the pair to Papá as gently as she would toss a toy to a puppy. But he is never content.

"My poor feet, Tortugina," says Papá. "My onions, bunions, carrots and tomatoes. Would you like to play in my vegetable garden?"

Papá holds out his foot to me. What choice do I have? With his bony heel in my lap, I massage the icy pads of bunions, bloodless carrot toes, and one tomato-red hammertoe crossed over the big toe. Because of Papá's feet, I cannot eat the sun-warmed vegetables from Mamá's garden.

My eldest sister, Véronica, stands at attention like a stick soldier in the doorway, as though she needed orders to enter.

"Good morning, Mother. Good morning, Father." Never "Good morning, Tortugina."

At seventeen, Véronica could be the most attractive of us three girls. She has a small waist and two perfect porcelain teacup breasts, and below her woman's mound are two long, shapely legs. But she wears too-big dresses so thick with starch that she sounds like paper crushing when she moves. And her hair is pulled in such a tight bun that her skin and eyes look stretched.

Sweet Amanda shuffles into the kitchen rubbing her eyes, and yawns hello. Ten months younger than Véronica, Amanda smiles at each of us, her brown eyes dancing at the pleasure of family. She kisses Mamá then Papá then me. Amanda is so round and soft that other children, animals, and old men like to rub against her. A pale cotton dress balloons over her mushroom belly, and her dimpled chins tuck on years beyond her sixteen.

I gladly give up my place to Véronica and Amanda, who kneel in front of Papá as though he were the Pope. Véronica closes her eyes and moves her thumbs in precise circles over his calluses. Sweet Amanda lays her red cheek on top of one foot and brushes his instep with her soft fist while she sings a little song she made up:

Onions, bunions, carrots and tomatoes—
We play in Papá's garden.
Red, white, pink, and brown—
We dig our fingers in his ground.

Papá has his only laugh of the day and hums along. When he has had enough, he pulls on his brown socks and boots.

Lowering her heaviest iron skillet onto the stove, Mamá flips a thick wad of lard into the center. She unwraps the soft green plantain leaves that hold the pulpo. Garlic, onions, tomatoes, cilantro, and finally the octopus sizzle in lard.

Chapter 5

When the octopus is fried, Mamá cracks a dozen of Señor Aves's eggs over the top and stirs quickly. Véronica serves the red and green plates overflowing with curled octopus legs poking out of yellow egg mounds. We sit in our accustomed seats and bow our heads in prayer.

"Dear God," Papá says. "Thank you for the blessings of food, hard work, and a fine wife. May you find husbands for my three daughters, the sooner the better. Amen."

Papá's lips form words as he eats. He is already rehearsing for his customers, counting his inventory, berating his cans of beets for not selling as well as his cans of Spam.

Véronica keeps track of the family temperature, shifting her eyes right and left. Amanda rolls pulpo and eggs on her tongue to savor the taste. I spread refried beans on my warm tortilla and wash it down with the grainy coffee. Papá, the fastest eater, sucks the last pulpo leg into his mouth.

"Time for work," he says.

None of us ever gets to finish eating. Véronica, Amanda, and Mamá stand to clear the table. While they wash the greasy plates, I dig out a rough cotton towel to dry.

"Véronica," says Papá.

"Yes, Papá," says Véronica.

She brushes Papá's brown woven coat and dark brown pants free of crumbs with a small whisk broom and plucks a brown bowtie off the shelf. With a few swift adjustments, she centers the tie on the collar of Papá's brown shirt as though she were awarding a medal. In perfect uniform, Papá opens the door to the downstairs store and passes into his day with Véronica and Amanda matching his determined steps.

Draping the blue bathrobe off her shoulders, Mamá washes the grit of sleep from her face and her underarms and the smell of Papá from her woman's parts.

I cover my nose with my ironed green dress and inhale the rose starch smell.

"Tortugina," says Mamá.

Her voice that I know so well speaks in a tone I do not know at all.

"Your Papá and I have discussed your future."

The future is something we have never discussed. Mamá pulls the green dress down over my head and fastens the buttons.

"Women in our family begin our blood at twelve," says Mamá. "You are fifteen. Perhaps Papá has been praying too hard that you might turn into a son."

"Mamá, I'm a woman," I say. "I am the fastest woman in this village!"

Her face turns red. "I am grooming you for a husband, not a racetrack! For all the years you have lived, you still act like a child."

Mamá slips into her polka-dot working dress.

"Today you will begin your duties at Papá's store like the rest of us. Papá said, and I say so too."

This is the day I have dreaded beyond all others. The slow death march down to the coffin counters of Papá's store.

"Mamá," I say, "I am in training to be a diver! I must be free to practice!"

I cannot explain to her that if I am not on the cliffs with Gabito, where I am forbidden to be, he could die without my prayers.

"What do you mean practice?" says Mamá.

Chapter 5

"Watch me hold my breath!"

I run to the tin sink and stick my head in the bucket of rainwater up to my neck. The water tickles the inside of my ears. Silently I count. "One, two, three…"

Mamá pulls my head out of the water and rubs my hair with a towel hard enough to hurt. If there is a good time to argue with Mamá, I have not found it.

"As a woman," Mamá says, "I follow your Papá to the store because I must accept my husband's life. It is what keeps this family together!"

The wrinkles around her eyes deepen. For a brief moment Mamá lets me see the full weight of her life, the family balanced on her sturdy shoulders.

"Today," says Mamá, "you will watch how I treat the customers. Some of them, I would rather crush their entrails in a vice, but I smile because they buy from your Papá."

I have seen all the dull brown faces of the village in Papá's dull brown store and Mamá serving them with her tired smile.

"I will die if I have to be you, Mamá," I say.

"Tortugina, you are too old to say whatever is on your mind."

"I am a diver!"

Mamá slaps me so hard that my head snaps back and I stumble against the wall. I cover my head, waiting for another blow, but it does not come.

"In your dreams you are a diver," says Mamá. "In the real world you are a clerk in Papá's store."

Mamá tosses her purple shawl over her shoulders as though she were headed for the stage instead of the village store. She guides me ahead of her toward the stairs. Her hand is firm on my shoulder, but she squeezes gently. What does she want? Forgiveness?

I shut my heart against Mamá and the darkness ahead.

CHAPTER 6

THE HEAVY CHAIN rattles as Papá opens the double doors onto the Plaza de Allende. Stale fumes empty out of the aisle into the morning mist. As the day arcs, a dusty rectangle of light will stretch over the slump of burlap grain sacks and up the wall of canned goods.

I am surrounded by a colorless collection of earth-tinted buckets, barrels, bags, and cans. Where is the adventure in selling dried vanilla beans or gnarled fingers of ginger or the white and purple necklaces of flaking garlic? There is no challenge in black beans, red beans, garbanzo beans, coffee beans, sesame seeds, poppy seeds, scabs of dried beef, or buckets of night crawlers.

Papá curls the stems of his half-moon reading glasses around his ears. He unlocks a drawer, takes out the sales ledger, and reaches for a pencil. He rubs the key to his aguardiente cellar on his jacket and returns it to the drawer. Below the store, in the cool darkness, are hundreds of bottles of the clear, fiery liquid. Though I never tasted it,

Chapter 6

I have watched Papá distill the molasses made from sugar cane and mix it with anise, adding more sugar to make the sweet "burning water" that he sells at high prices.

Mamá harnesses herself into a green canvas apron, pulling the straps tight enough to give her a figure. The embroidered yellow flowers on the apron have been frayed against produce boxes and the sides of dented cans. Mamá stacks brown beer bottles in the glass-door refrigerator because, as she never tires of telling us, cold beer sells faster.

Véronica draws a dull knife through the lid of a cardboard box that holds a dozen cans of tomato sauce. She stacks and spaces the cans so evenly, her concentration could warp labels. She tosses me a brown cloth.

"Tortugina, dust the cans on the lower shelves."

Never before have I cleaned with the idea that it could fill my day. This is a thought that tightens around my chest like Papá's heavy chain. I marvel at the serenity in Amanda's face as she hums, giving herself completely to the gentle arrangement of white toilet paper next to the blue bleach boxes.

The metallic sound of a cane ticking against the floor rouses Papá from his ledger.

Señora Estonia, a bent, frilled wreck, shimmers on the doorstep. Her long, wilted breasts make strange bulges in her expensive silk blouse. Had she been a street dog, her nipples would have left trails in the dust.

Señora Estonia leans on her cane as she shuffles to the counter. Gravity and sex have bowed her brittle legs. Finely crafted shoes support her long flat arches. Her acrid perfume fumigates the far reaches of the store. I sneeze and rub my nose.

Papá bows. "Señora Estonia. My humble shop is yours."

She is taller than Papá by a head.

"Yes, if you do not pay your mortgage, Señor Gomez," says Señora Estonia, "your shop is indeed mine!"

Her dry laugh is more brittle than her bones. Señora Estonia was once the most beautiful madame in the richest whorehouse of Porto Gillo, far north of El Pulpo.

Mamá whispers to me through a smile, since the Señora is nearly deaf.

"See how I smile, Tortugina. Let me see your best effort."

Mamá elbows me toward the old whore. I give her a wide smile with so many teeth showing that I think my lips might split.

"Good day, Señora Estonia," I say.

Her watery gaze finds me. She clicks her ivory dentures into a smile under the twin sunsets of her rouged cheeks. The red wig shakes on her head, not from a sense of rhythm, but from the ravages of a slow sex disease that dances her toward the grave.

"Well, Tortugina, are they letting you work as though you were a normal person?"

"I am pleased to help Papá," I say.

"Aha, Señor Gomez!" says Señora Estonia. "You will have a worker for life. No one marries a loca like Tortugina!"

Mamá pats my shoulder. "Tortugina is very helpful, Señora."

Señora Estonia's filmy cataracts are dull with menace.

"You have invited chaos, Señor Gomez," says Señora Estonia. "Tortugina, if you are not as stupid as you look, you will join my old profession and get paid for it. Everyone knows Gabito and his divers use you like a sheep."

Chapter 6

Papá drops Señora Estonia's fresh coffee beans on the counter.

She says it so convincingly, I am almost persuaded that I am no longer a virgin. Papá looks at me with a narrow squint. His suspicions cut deep like the sharp hatchets he sells.

"Papá! I am a virgin! She is a liar!"

Mamá slaps my head. "Apologize to Señora Estonia!" she says.

Señora Estonia's angry red wig shudders like a cock's comb.

"Señora Gomez, you make wild animals of your children by not punishing them enough!"

Papá's hands have hardened into fists. Mamá does not answer. Instead she calmly scoops the scattered coffee beans off the counter into a piece of paper. She folds the paper and hands it to Señora Estonia with a big smile.

Mamá whispers to me, "See how I smile, Tortugina."

She whispers to Señora Estonia's deaf ears, "Señora Estonia, here are your coffee beans. May you drink too fast and die for insulting my daughter."

Señora Estonia leans closer to Mamá. Phlegm rattles in her throat. "What did you say about your little tramp, Señora Gomez?"

I throw my dust rag across the counter at Señora Estonia's sagging breasts and yell loud enough for her to hear, "You should die, you wingless old bat!"

I burst out of Papá's store into the warmth of the morning sunshine. Sergio, son of the sweets baker, whistles through the wide gaps of his rotten teeth. He moves his mountainous flesh toward the candy in Papá's store and sings, "Puta, puta, you are a whore, Tortugina!"

Why does everyone think Tortugina is a whore! Does Señora Estonia spread rumors?

Then let there be reason for it! I run up against Sergio's big belly and twist his ears toward my face. I open my mouth over his lips. When he tries to scream, I stick my tongue between his lips like the pictures in Señor Duro's back room. Sergio's mouth tastes like chocolate. He struggles, but I hold on to his ears.

A wicked blow from behind knocks me to my knees. Sergio spits my kiss into the dust.

"Tortugina!" says Mamá.

Her thick bristle broom pins me to the cobblestones.

"Sergio called me a whore, Mamá!"

"She attacked me!" yells Sergio. "Hit her again!"

I am already flat on the ground when Amanda runs up behind Mamá and grabs the broom. Her gentle touch always tempers Mamá.

Señora Estonia in her well-built shoes shuffles toward my head. The bright copper tip of her cane stops inches from my nose.

"No need to grovel, Tortugina," says Señora Estonia. "I accept your apology."

Her crackle makes me want to break her thin ankles. Papá clasps Señora Estonia's elbow and steers her toward home.

Humiliating Tortugina in public is nothing new. If Mamá doesn't do it, somehow I do it to myself. Poor Mamá wipes the sweat off her upper lip as I rise in front of her. My freshly ironed green dress is covered in dust. My back aches from the broom.

"Tortugina," says Mamá, "what am I going to do with you?"

Chapter 6

She steps toward me. I step back. For every step Mamá takes toward me, I take one step back. Finally she stops and I stop. Her nostrils flare like two white rings. I wish they would explode and leave a hole in her face.

I cannot help but smile at the thought of Mamá without a nose.

"I do not know what I expected," Mamá sighs with exhaustion.

Quietly, a growling laughter tickles out of her throat. If Mamá or I start laughing, the other cannot resist. My horse-snort breaks into a big field of laughter. Amanda's sweet clucking makes us a crowing barnyard chorus. It has always been like this. Mamá, Amanda, and I lean against each other as our howling weakens us. I am never sure we are laughing for the same reason, but I know the laughing sweeps ugliness away better than Mamá's broom.

Sergio slowly turns his mountainous rage toward Papá's store.

Mamá blows her nose into a small handkerchief, her sign that the respite is over.

"Tortugina," Mamá wipes her eyes, "I cannot stand any more of you today. Go pluck mussels. Tomorrow we start your training again. As a clerk!"

Dark clouds roll across the horizon from the north, as though a shroud was being laid over the sky. A light rain paints the rocks black. In the Forbidden Cliff, I lean against the jagged window ledge of my secret cave and lick the salt from my arm to taste the sea.

Tomás dumps his catch in the small rocky pool of fresh water. He jumps up and down to warm himself by the fire. Skinny Vicente and Big Luis slap each other to stay warm in their threadbare jackets.

Under my black hood, I watch through the old telescope and begin to build layers of protection around Gabito's body with prayers.

He is tensed for the jump. Wind flattens the curls against Gabito's head. The goodluck yellow trunks flutter, thin and threadbare, against his thighs and his lump that the boys call their big dog, burro, stallion, as if it were something they could feed and tame.

With no warning, a sharp pain ricochets above the bones of my woman's mound. It is a deep cramp. I am as bent as old Señora Estonia. It hits again so hard that I drop the telescope and slide to the cave floor. The pain holds me to the damp stones.

Could this be a heart attack like Señor Molino's? Does it start between the legs and gradually strangle everything up to the heart? There is dampness between my thighs. I take the black hood off my head and lift my skirt. My fingers touch a spot that is wet and warm. It is too dark to see anything. I slide my panties down my legs and hold them up to the jagged rim of light. There on the white crotch is a beautiful puddle of my own bright blood. The badge I thought I would never wear!

Oh, Gabito, at last I am honored with the full cup of womanhood! We can marry! I will give birth to our child in the sea so he will keep the talent of breathing underwater.

I hold my panties delicately between my fingertips. The day is a witness to this proud flag! You see, Mamá, I am not the son Papá wanted. I am not a circus freak! I am a woman!

I can barely wait to tell Gabito. I lay the precious panties on the ledge to dry in the breeze and tie the black cloth around my loins to catch my trickling womanhood. At last I pick up the telescope and return to my job.

"MotherMarypleaseprotectmybelovedGabito."

I am well into the fast rhythm of prayer when a strong cold wind whips past the ledge. Dust blinds one eye, but worse, it whisks my underwear off the ledge.

I blink and grab, but the panties are spread like a kite in an updraft. Caught in a narrow shaft of sunlight, the crotch turns as rosy as stained glass. It is as though a holy relic has taken flight.

A whirlwind hovers my panties just above Gabito's head. He looks up from his dive. His body is a horror of imbalance.

"No, Gabito!" I yell.

He whips his arms backward. He is angled too far over the edge of the cliff to stop himself.

Tomás runs up behind Gabito and clamps his hairy fists on the yellow waistband.

"Gabito!" I scream.

Gabito falls over the cliff. Tomás keeps his grip. He falls flat on his belly but holds on to Gabito's hanging body. They are both going over.

Big Luis grabs one of Tomás's thick ankles. Skinny Vicente seizes the other. They brace themselves, their bare feet anchored against stone. The taut rope of Tomás's arm is all that holds Gabito above the lava spears. One, two, three, the boys pull backward on Tomás's ankles.

Tomás roars with pain as his muscles stretch between the hanging body of Gabito and the divers pulling at his heels. Gabito knows to hang limp and not stir. Little by little the divers pull Gabito up the windy cliff.

My fingers hurt from holding on to the lava rock, as though that could help the boys' straining muscles.

A cormorant swoops past. Gabito's head rises. I think he is looking up at me. His face seems to say, "Tortugina. I am safe now."

Through the brass telescope, I watch his body suddenly fall out of frame. Tomás is left holding Gabito's ripped yellow shorts.

"Gabito! Gabito!" I scream.

Gabito's naked brown body flies down the face of the cliff. He straightens his long back as he falls. Hands together, he plunges toward the sea. Gabito tries to shape his body thin as air to fit between the rocks, but this time his perfection does not save him. Blood rises black in the dark gray swirl of waves crushed between the lava spears.

Tomás holds the yellow shorts to his chest. I scream and scream. I cannot stop screaming.

CHAPTER 7

BLACK SUITS, BLACK crepe dresses, black hats, black heads bow over Gabito's grave. All our lives, Gabito and I played in this cemetery behind Saint Assisi by the Sea. We ate fallen pomegranates with goat cheese, slept in the sun on warm marble slabs that cover the village bones. It is a cemetery of cement Virgins, wood crosses, and marble headstones with inlaid portraits of the dead in black and white.

Gabito's headstone is black with the only photograph of him, taken on the day of his First Communion when he had a terrible cold.

Fat Padre Abstensia's wooden teeth rattle Latin over Gabito's coffin. He sprays wet prayers on the Bible. A breeze lifts his words and his cassock, but grief weighs him to the gravesite.

The coffin is closed and empty since Gabito's body was washed out to sea and never found.

Chapter 7

I watched from the shore all day and night in the foolish hope that my prayers would make him return. By now crabs and barracuda have cleaned his bones, but we can stand here and remember his beauty.

I slip a fresh brown egg out of my pocket. It is tradition for a woman to breathe sorrow for a man into an egg and then bury it to be free of the sorrow. I hold it with both hands as though I am praying. A tiny yellow feather flutters, stuck to the shell by a streak of dried hen blood. I blow my heat on the curved surface, fogging the albumen inside, and whisper to the marigold yolk.

"Forgive me, Gabito."

Later I will bury the egg with the prayer that I will reform my selfish, sinful nature, so as not to spend my life scooping eggs into shallow graves.

Amanda, smelling of lemon powder, touches the small of my back. Her forgiveness weakens me almost to tears. Véronica's fingernails pinch my arm. I am grateful for the distraction of this simpler pain. Papá looks down at his black leather funeral shoes. He has not spoken to me since I walked back to the store the afternoon Gabito died and told him, "It was an accident."

Mamá cried in front of Papá's valued customers. Papá hit me once across the face then could not stop. It is Amanda who holds me these nights. I cannot sleep. The dreams are gone.

Tomás, Gordo, Luis, and Vicente lower Gabito's empty coffin into the ground. Tears drop onto their wool jackets as they cover the coffin with red earth. The divers pack the mound, beating the earth with their shovels. If Gabito were in his coffin, he would be holding his ears.

While the grave is being filled, Padre Abstensia sprays his Latin incantations to God. Then the service is as complete as it can be for an unfinished life.

We follow the Padre out of the cemetery over the rocky sea road toward Gabito's home.

Tomás and the divers carry their diver's funeral wreath. It is big as a wagon wheel, made of dried grapevines woven with branches of rosemary. Gabito's torn goodluck shorts are tied into a curved branch. The divers' mothers and fathers, Mother Mary Inmaculada, Señor Aves with his guitar, the mayor, the sheriff, the bandleader, the repairman and his son Gordo, the garbage collector, street cleaner, shopkeepers, all attach notes to the wreath of remembrance.

They wedge objects into the weave. Silver amulets, wooden crosses tied with black string, tiny plaster figures of the Madonna. Señora Grosera shoves in her famous beef and hot chilies on a stick that Gabito loved. Peg-legged Señora Porción catches up to the wreath. Between two silver fish heads she ties a stack of tortillas wrapped in yellow cellophane. She will miss the heat of Gabito's smile over her blue counter.

Señora Estonia, the cheap old whore, leaves one tin amulet rattling on a dry grape branch. She and her cane thump next to me, a sunken smile on her lips. She could not be happier to see me disgraced.

Gabito's brother, Tomás, carries his six-year-old brother, Salvador, and walks next to his father, Señor Emilio. Señor Emilio is a handsome man with a full head of gray hair who was, like Gabito, the best diver of his time. Tomás guides the old man's slumped shoulders toward their home.

Chapter 7

Gabito's stone house sits on a cliff a hundred feet from the sea, a good place to be in a storm. The old house was built by Gabito's great-grandpapá, the first diver in the family. It is the sturdiest house in the village because it has to be. It was large enough for the lives of three boys, a man, and the memory of a dead mother. Now it must make room for another memory.

Señor Emilio stands on the porch in solemn welcome. The villagers file up the stone steps into the house. The muscled butcher helps old Señora Estonia in her shaking red wig.

Papá, Mamá, Véronica, and Amanda, outcasts by association, wait silently with me. If my family is not allowed to share in the village grief, it will be the biggest insult imaginable, worse than not being invited to Padre Abstensia's Christmas party.

When everyone else is inside, Gabito's father puts his hands in the pockets of his wool pants and stares down at us. Finally, he nods consent to Papá. The family climb the stairs and move slowly through the stone portal. A guitar begins inside.

Before I enter, I whisper to Señor Emilio, "It was an accident. I am sorry. I loved Gabito."

Gabito's father hears my apology. He chooses to obey the terms of silent banishment. The old man steps inside and shuts the door in my face.

The porch is cold. For once I will miss the warmth of my family.

I hurry around the side of the house, away from the wind. Big black Coriander growls, guarding the shallow-rooted vegetables: lettuce, tomatoes, radishes, sons of radishes.

Gabito planted them all.

To stay warm, I circle the house so many times that my breath creates a fog. The icy wind is just enough torture that I do not have to think only of Gabito.

A wooden bench sits beneath the kitchen window. I stand on tiptoe, nose pressed against the thick glass, and watch the figures inside. Papá and Mamá are a solid silhouette near the glow of the fireplace. Their hearts have brought them this far together. They are like an octopus, eight limbs between them, welded by good luck and bad luck. Gabito and I will never have eight legs.

Señor Aves plays his guitar and sings the divers' song.

Ai, Ai, Ai, Amigos.
We belong to the sea.
The sea belongs to us.
Faithful mistress is she,
Who gives us oc-to-pus.
We will die in her arms.
We will die in her arms.
Ai, Ai, Ai, Amigos.

Gabito's father cries. His hard stomach has gone soft against his belt. Gabito's belly would have gone soft too, and together we would have grown toward the grave.

I have become frozen, my eyes wide with cold tears, my feet to the icy bench.

The guitars are silent. Thundering waves below the cliff are my funeral song. I lower myself slowly off the bench and count the painful, stiff steps, past the house, one hundred, and one hundred more to reach the edge of the black cliff.

Chapter 7

Icy spray blasts from the mouth of the monster sea. I am wet from my shoes up.

"I am coming, Gabito. My death will pay for yours." I close my eyes and take a step.

CHAPTER 8

STRONG ARMS AROUND my waist lift me back from the edge. When I turn there is a man, naked, except for an immodest loincloth of dripping kelp. He seems either unformed or torn into pieces that hover together. I must be dead or frozen in a dream.

Something is so familiar, the way he cocks his head from side to side as though he were shaking water out of his ears. Above the roar of silence, I hear my heart start to beat.

"Gabito?" I whisper.

Slowly his features come together like a table puzzle.

I did not know beauty like Gabito's could ever change. The right side of his face has a few cuts in his still-perfect jaw. But on the left side, his face and body look like they have been trampled by a herd of horses. Blood drips from his scalp and his split lip. He smooths his wet hair over a hole in his cracked skull the way men try to hide their baldness.

Chapter 8

"Tortugina," says Gabito.

The voice doesn't go through the usual cavities but flows directly from a hole in his throat.

My heart pounds louder than the old tortilla machine.

"Gabito!" I say. "It's true, what the brujas say, that no one really dies."

He looks down at the puddle of seawater forming under him.

"I am some kind of dead," says Gabito.

"Gabito, forgive me," I say.

He shakes his head, and the bones seem to settle closer to their old shape.

"A good diver should never be distracted, Tortugina. It was not your fault."

He watches my eyes adjusting to the new him.

"Do I look that bad?" he asks.

"You will always be you, my Gabito."

I am trembling. I hear the dripping of his kelp loincloth. His torn cheek flutters like a gill.

"Tortugina," he says sweetly.

His fingertips against my cheek are just as solid as if he were alive. They are cold, but not as cold as skin after a dive. This cold feels sore. As he bends to kiss me, his left eyeball loosens from its socket, drops, and dangles on his cheek. He tucks the eye back under his lid.

"Sorry," he says. "It takes some getting used to."

There is nothing more than a membrane to shield the left side of his chest. The muscles and tendons have been torn away. Gabito places my palm on the thin sheet that remains. I feel his tender pulse. If I pressed, my fingers would break through and touch his heart.

Gabito turns his good side toward me, firm, whole with only a few wet gashes. His good eye flirts sweetly. He is a wondrous stranger without being a stranger at all.

"Marry me, Tortugina," says Gabito. "I have earned you with my life."

I want to scream, "Yes." My dream to marry Gabito has come true. But his death, it is hard to know what changes it brings. Can we make love, Gabito? Can we have children? If I keep thinking, the obstacles will mount higher than a funeral pyre.

"Tortugina? Did you hear me?"

Gabito's hair is drying into his old curls. He is so nervous, his left eye slips out of its socket again. He cocks his head and it shifts back into place. A new habit, unconscious, like pushing slipped reading glasses back up the nose.

"There is only one question, Tortugina," whispers Gabito. "Do you love me?"

"With all my heart," I say.

I try to think of the good side to this union. I will be married to the man I love. I do not have to cook or clean for a ghost. And half of him is still handsome. How many women can say that about their husbands?

"Yes, Gabito," I say. "I will marry you."

In front of the steps of his father's house, Gabito solemnly takes my hand. His scarred fingertip circles my wedding finger where a ring would be. His touch leaves a bluish gold band.

"With this ring," says Gabito, "I, Gabito Ramirez, take you, Tortugina Gomez, for my wife. I pledge my love for eternity, though my eternity has begun a little earlier than yours."

Gabito circles his ring finger, leaving a purplish gold ring mark on his skin.

"It looks like a bruise," I say.

His broken lips spread into a smile. "Our courtship has been like that, hasn't it?"

His spread of loose teeth widens into a bigger grin. I suppose it will not be so startling in the morning if I wake up on his good side.

"Now it is your turn to pledge yourself to me."

"Gabito, my beloved," I say. "In heaven or hell, on earth, for eternity and a day, I am your wife."

Tears gather in Gabito's eyes. He blinks at me with the eye that remains steadfast in its socket. I am quickly growing to like his new face. It is more vulnerable in the rearrangement.

Gabito leads me around the side of the house to the wooden bench below the kitchen window. He moves his hands as though he is shutting a curtain, and a thick, luxuriant, warm mist surrounds us. His kelp loincloth drops in a wet heap.

"I do not want to rush our wedding night," says Gabito, "but I must return to the sea."

He gently lifts the black dress up my thighs and removes my white panties. My blood rises to meet Gabito's cool touch.

"I am finished with my first blood!" I say. "It lasted only one day."

Gabito smiles and rubs my white underwear against his cheek. It absorbs his trickling blood.

"Whenever I see your underwear, I will think of death," says Gabito.

We meld together on the glowing bed of mist. With sighs of relief, Gabito takes me apart, inch by inch, with the pleasure of his touch, his tongue damp from the taste of the sea.

There is no sense of his physical weight. Gabito floats on top of me, his hips to my hips. I feel him between my legs, gently rubbing against my wetness. His body moves softly, then harder, pressing. Finally he thrusts deeper, and there is a sharp pain. Virgin skin tears me free into womanhood.

"At last," I sigh.

My diver Gabito plunges again and again as though I were a current of the sea. Our breath is as ragged as Gabito's bones. Something is gathering inside me that his movements have awakened. In my woman's mound an ache grows and cramps until I must scream. And then I do. I scream. The sun releases inside my body. Bursts! The ache releases. I cannot stop screaming until the air is gone from my lungs.

"Tortugina!" Gabito cries with his last thrust.

I hold onto his shoulders and feel his heart beating as though it were in my chest. My woman's mound feels like a hot bowl of honey.

"Gabito," I whisper.

My throat is raw. Our breathing slows together.

"Am I good in bed?" I say.

"You are," he says with a long kiss.

My lips spread in a smile nearly as wide as my legs.

"I love you, Gabito," I say, and I try the new word. "Husband."

"I love you, Tortugina," says Gabito. "My wedding gift to you is this."

Chapter 8

He hands me a scalloped shell with a hole in it like all the divers wear around their necks for luck.

"Someday you and I will dive together," he says. "I will make your dream come true."

I want to scream again, but my throat is too sore. "Yes! I love you, Gabito!"

Gabito kisses me one more time before he floats away naked through the disappearing mist that surrounded us and dives over the cliff.

I curl under my shawl and fall asleep with the shell in my fist.

Over the whine of the wind, I hear the front door slam. Maybe Mamá has come with another shawl for me, or food. I am as hungry for beans as I was for Gabito.

I pull on my pants, adjust my dress, and limp to the corner of the house. Tomás, Gordo, Vicente, and Luis stumble out of the house drunk and into the stony road with their wagon-wheel wreath.

Tomás sees me. "Tortugina!"

He cocks his arm and throws his beer bottle at me. It explodes on the corner of the stone wall. Foam and wet fragments of glass cover my face, hair, and shawl. If his aim were better, I would be wearing the bottle in my brain.

"Go to hell, Tortugina!" yells Tomás.

With his drunken insult, Tomás is the first person outside my family to acknowledge my existence. His words break the code of silent banishment.

"Witch! Witch! Witch!" yells Gordo.

I am surprised how gratifying even bitter recognition is. Their silence was unbearable.

"You whore, puta," screams Vicente.

All I need to do is answer, and we are engaged in conversation.

"Pigs!" I yell. "Drunken pigs!"

I watch the effect of my words on their faces. Dark fury, blacker than the blackest storm cloud. Tomás drops his handhold on the wreath.

"I am going to kill you, Tortugina!" yells Tomás.

I pick up the neck of his broken beer bottle and hold the jagged edges like a sword.

"I do not care if I die!" I mean it with all my heart. "I am not afraid of you!"

I wave the sharp glass. "Go ahead, kill me!"

Tomás grabs my arm and twists the bottle away. He grabs my hair and holds the jagged edge at my throat.

"Die!" screams Tomás.

Vicente grabs his arm. "Tomás! Leave this to God."

Tomás drags the sharp glass across my skin. The cut does not feel deep. Warm blood trickles down my neck.

"Tomás!" I say. "Gabito was here. He gave me a shell like yours. He said I could be a diver."

Tomás shoves me onto my knees.

"I am telling you the truth. Look!"

I show them the shell in my hand, but they do not seem to see it. At a signal from Tomás, the boys pick me up and carry me to the back of the house.

"You want to dive, whore? Then dive!" yells Tomás.

The divers drop me into a horse trough full of green water. Hands push my head under. Hold my breath. Face down into the bottom slime. Struggle to get my head up. Hands push on my back, my legs. Fight! Kick the bastards! I did not get a good breath! My fingers grab the edge of the trough. They cannot kill me! A hard heel crushes my hold. Water leaks into my mouth. Breathing. Breathing water. I cannot fight the floating blackness.

CHAPTER 9

I SINK DEEPER under the dark water, under the waves. Tentacled creatures with transparent bodies swim past my face and become two large hands. And then I see his face.

"Gabito?"

He is wearing an ancient blue navy jacket with large golden epaulettes. His long legs are covered in white tights that follow every curve.

"Tortugina, beloved, I did not expect to see you so soon. Are you all right?"

I push him away as he tries to take me in his arms.

"Your brother tried to kill me," I say.

He frowns and looks up through the waves crashing above our heads.

"He loves me," says Gabito.

His brown hand cups my face.

"I promise," he says, "you will never come to harm as long as I am dead."

Chapter 9

He kisses me. I have developed a taste for his blood, and I kiss him with my tongue. "Am I good?"

"Tortugina," says Gabito, "you are so good that I have something to show you."

He motions for me to follow him and swims away. I swim after him with more of a talent for the water than I knew. He leads me into a shallow cove on the other side of the cliffs. Half hidden by seaweed and sand is a mossy Spanish galleon the size of a large whale. The masts are broken and the hatches are ripped open.

Gabito gathers me in his arms like a bouquet.

"Come!" Gabito disappears through a hatch covered in seaweed and slime. I swim after him through a corridor with trapped, algae-green skeletons. They bump gently against the swollen teak walls. Gabito knocks bones out of my way. He turns at a door and waits for me.

"Mind your head," says Gabito. "This is the captain's cabin. I haven't had time to clean."

The captain's cabin is small, with a table and two chairs in the center. All the surfaces are covered with delicate flags of lime-green algae.

"It needs a good scrub," I say.

"Look, Tortugina."

On one side of the cabin, under mounds of sea snails, is a bed with a small canopy. I've seen such beds in books and thought they looked like little boats.

"Look at the view." Gabito points to a window at the back.

Outside is a red rock gully. Schools of yellow fish zigzag in and out of the filtered light, flashing gold and black.

"This is our home, Tortugina," he says.

"Then let me stay," I say.

Gabito kisses my hand and sucks each of my knuckles as though they were strawberries.

"When our son is grown," he says.

"Our son? Are we having a son?"

"When he is strong enough in the world," says Gabito, "then you can stay. A man must leave his seed or else he truly dies."

"Does a daughter count?" I say.

There is a loud knocking outside the galleon.

"We will talk later," Gabito says.

He quickly swims me back to the edge and leaves me with a kiss.

Returning is never easy. My fingers are anchored in the bedsheets. I am half drowned in light quilts. Mamá's hand is under my neck and raises my head above the waves.

"Tortugina? Tortugina, please wake up."

I rub my lids clear enough to see Mamá's fat face. She sits in the wild swirl I have made of my covers. Orange lantern light flickers across her wrinkled forehead.

"Thank the dear Lord," she says. "You have come back."

She strokes my face with a damp washcloth.

"What happened?" I whisper.

"Poor little turtle," says Mamá. "You were seized with such sadness, you tried to kill yourself. But the divers saved you."

The old disappointment in Mamá's dark eyes is gone. She looks at me with a tenderness I have rarely seen before.

"My poor baby," says Mamá.

"Mamá," I say. "There is good news. Gabito is not altogether dead. He returned to me and we married!"

I hold up my hand to show her the blue wedding band. There is no band. I open my hand to show her the shell, but there is no shell.

Mamá feels my forehead.

"Tortugina, Gabito's death has driven you mad."

Mamá clasps her hands in prayer. "Why is God punishing me like this?"

Her wide back shakes with sobs.

"Tortugina, I am sorry." Mamá looks in my eyes for such a long time, I start to count her blinks. "It is beyond me how you came into the quiet blood of this family."

She wipes her eyes. The mattress rises as she stands.

"We have a guest. Dress quickly and come to the front room."

In our hallway hang pictures of dead relatives in white wedding dresses and black suits. I like to think they dance at night and trade partners between centuries when no one is watching.

Through the doorway, firelight spikes up the wall from the front room hearth. Mamá and Papá sit with the great black tent that is Mother Mary Inmaculada. They turn in their squeaking leather chairs to stare at me. Mother Mary's bird-of-prey eyes follow my progress into the room. Her wings shift under the black habit.

"Tortugina. Come in, child."

Mother Mary's voice is pitched high to catch the ear of God. So, is it the convent for Tortugina? Does Papá want to jail me in a drafty monastery that was once a barn, where I will be forced into the unnatural position of prayer for the rest of my life?

The nun's talons hold Mamá's guests-only porcelain coffee cup. The delicate cup is covered in hand-painted roses and lime-green petals with two blue-gold finches on the handle. It is the last cup of a set of expensive cups that were Mamá's mamá's mamá's on her wedding day. When I begged shamelessly, Mamá said the bird cup would be mine, when I married.

"Tortugina is a child of God," says Mother Mary Inmaculada, "and every child of God can be redeemed. Or at the very least, it is our duty to try."

Papá nods, but Mamá snorts as though Gato had brought us another dead bird.

Mamá and Mother Mary do not like each other. In school, Mother Mary was called Althea, and she had no urge for Jesus then. Her large frame was not built to duck under the doors of the nunnery but to push a plow and struggle under a giant husband. Though it is never mentioned in my presence, something happened between Mamá and Mother Mary that has a great deal to do with Papá.

"You will be a nun, Tortugina," says Mother Mary Inmaculada. "Your Papá agrees that it is the only way he will find peace. Where parents fail, the church teaches."

Mother Mary arches her pinky and sips the coffee.

Mamá's fat face seems to narrow. "Althea, you want our wild Tortugina for your little convent? This is not a marriage made in heaven."

Papá slams his heavy coffee cup on the table.

"But you agreed, Celia! She needs more discipline than we can provide."

"Hector, you are the one who agreed," says Mamá. "Do not be so eager to entomb our Tortugina."

Chapter 9

Papá and Mamá never argue in front of guests. Mamá's voice has a soft tremor that threatens tears.

"Hector, someday I want to hold Tortugina's children in my arms."

She dabs at her eyes. Mamá switches from dry to wet easily. But now she needs my help against the others.

"You will hold my child in your arms soon, Mamá. Gabito has left me a son."

Mother Mary spits coffee. The bird cup drops from her hand and shatters on the floor. Porcelain finches and painted roses roll in different directions.

"My cup!" I scream, ready to bite the nun's hand.

Papá is equally stunned. "Celia. A son?"

Mamá stands and whispers, "Just dreams. I am going to get a broom."

Papá shifts noisily in his leather chair. "Celia!"

Mamá walks past him to the kitchen. I kneel and scoop the tiny pieces of my shattered inheritance from the floor into Mamá's little saucer. The porcelain reds and blues and greens look like bits of candy.

Mother Mary glances over her shoulder at the kitchen door where Mamá disappeared. Leaning toward Papá, she speaks as though I were not there.

"Hector, your daughter's behavior is beyond anything I imagined."

Papá answers as though I were not a foot from him. "Tortugina lives in a world of her own."

I do live in a world of my own. If only I did not have to leave it so often. Mamá slams a cupboard in the kitchen.

Mother Mary rests her hand on Papá's knee.

"If she had been my daughter, Hector, it would not have come to this."

Papá lightly touches his skull in search of something to say.

"Had she been ours…" says Mother Mary Inmaculada.

I lean close to the shameless nun's beak nose.

"Mother Mary, you could not produce an heir if God himself seeded you. Your body is as infertile as your soul."

The nun's hand jumps off Papá's knee.

Papá slaps my face so hard a button pops off his sleeve.

"Apologize to Mother Mary!" says Papá.

I can smell the nun's dry breath. "You are a human drought!" I shout.

Mamá hurries in from the kitchen with her tiny hand broom.

Papá clamps his hands on the arms of his leather chair and stands.

"The discussion is over, Celia! Tortugina will be a nun!"

Mamá's face softens into a smile.

"With all due respect, my dear husband, Tortugina will not be a barren sister of God."

Papá follows Mamá's hips coming toward him that now have a rhythmic sweep.

"We will give her one last chance," says Mamá.

"What chance have we not given her?" His eyes moisten as she presses close to him. Her eyes are a wonder of seduction.

I am watching strangers who are my parents, and I no longer wonder what keeps them together.

"You cannot have my daughter, Althea," says Mamá.

Mother Mary twists the black edge of her habit.

Chapter 9

"Tortugina will choose a husband," says Mamá, "at the Promenade de los Adolescentes. What better punishment for our savage child than for her to become a wife and a parent herself?"

"I am having Gabito's baby," I say.

She shakes her head at me.

"Not a dream child, Tortugina," she says. "A real sucking, squalling, stinking little sea rat like you. Then you will grow up fast!"

Papá takes her hand.

"The Promenade, Celia? What boy would want her, this creature that God in his wisdom has given us to temper our good fortune."

Papá's words hurt, but I have learned from the results of Mamá's gentleness.

"Let me try, Papá," I say sweetly. "Sometimes there are new faces, someone who has not heard of the wicked Tortugina."

My little sarcasm, but he seems not to notice.

Mamá pouts like a schoolgirl. "One more chance, Hector."

Looking down at her solid breasts pressed against his chest, it is hard to imagine the store counter dividing them all day.

Papá chuckles, "Well, one more chance."

It is gratifying to see Mother Mary Inmaculada as close to tears as the face of a nun allows. She gathers her dignity, rises out of her seat, and keeps growing up to the wood rafters. Her shadow covers both Mamá and Papá, who cowers slightly.

"I am sorry, Althea. I should not have called you," says Papá.

His eyes cannot apologize enough to Mother Mary.

"I understand, Hector," she says. "You were desperate. Excuse me."

She sweeps past us and down the stairs. Papá follows to unbolt the front door. Mamá and I are alone at last.

"That made me very tired," says Mamá.

I am surprised by how tired I am as well, and then I remember that I am recovering from a drowning.

"May I go, Mamá?"

She wraps her wide, fleshy arms around my shoulders, and my body remembers only the good parts of her. I will take the soft heat of her kitchen smells back to bed with me.

"Make me proud at the Promenade, Tortugina."

"I promise, Mamá."

[illegible]

CHAPTER 10

THE SATURDAY NIGHT sky over the Promenade is lit by a slice of moon. Papá is dressed in his new brown suit that looks like his old brown suit. The way Mamá dresses for special occasions always embarrasses me a little. Her giant fake pearls look like carnival lights. The big imitation turquoise, silver, and gold rings and bracelets click like castanets. Huge ruby-red earrings hang like lanterns to her shoulders.

Véronica and Amanda walk ahead of us in the long white dresses of virgins on the prowl. Their black shawls are carefully draped, and their hair is sleeked into plump buns.

My shoes, nails, cheeks, and lips are all rouged, shined, and polished by Mamá. I am starched and ironed and armored in stiff white linen. My shoes pinch under the long hem that almost sweeps the ground.

"You have never looked better," Mamá says.

Chapter 10

The starched edge of the eyelet cotton collar scrapes my neck wound.

"I have never felt worse," I say.

Papá was right. Who on earth would want me? We are still the outcast family. No one looks up at us or waves a hand in greeting as we pass.

Out of their dented instruments, the band blasts mariachi too loudly. Their only official uniform is the light blue and gold military-style hats that have been passed down from generation to generation until none of the hats fit the present owners. Only death prevents the band members from playing their Saturday night calling. The worst offender of sound is twenty-year-old Sweaty Oscar, replacing his trumpet-playing grandpapá, ninety-nine-year-old Deaf Giles. Deaf Giles had been squatting to watch his deaf dog, Conga, relieve herself when a garbage wagon backed over them both.

A loud fart cuts through the slide of sour notes of "Mi Corazon."

Children laugh and surround Polo, who sells wooden ducks that make rude noises when you pull the string in their tail. His son Multo remembers to avoid my gaze, hawking his red, white, and blue balloons through the crowd. Multo's wife Estrella cooks in her small food stand, fried flour tortillas that swell crispy with the heat and are sprinkled with white powdered sugar. She turns away from my eyes only to spill sugar on the heads of little Poncho and his brother waiting with their coins.

Toothless Señora Grosera stirs hot chilies and dripping meat on her tiny flat grill but does not give me her grin.

As Papá and Mamá lead me under dark shadows cast

by the trees, Mother Mary Inmaculada wings among her flock. The nun is greeted by couples crowding the benches with more children between them than teeth. The well-behaved children lean on their parents' knees and smile at Mother Mary. The loud ones play games in the fountain, drowning paper boats with sticks.

The church bells ring eight times, vibrating through the hollow bones of deaf belfry birds and frightening them into flight. The beating of wings over the Plaza de Allende is the final signal to begin the Promenade de los Adolescentes.

The girls break from their families and gather under small white lights wound around the square-trimmed trees. Fat, skinny, tall, short virgins with breasts budding, breasts budded, hanging like breadfruit, hidden in halters. Their sleek, dark hair is curled, matted, braided, and bunned.

The girls link arms in friendships of twos and threes. At the front, Lapiza, Skinny Vicente's sister, leads with her long bean nose. Behind her is Gordo's sister with a face like an omelet. Big Luis's sister, Esmeralda, squints her weak cat eyes above a lanyard of gold beads. The band plays "Forever Promenade." On their slow journey to the wedding bed, the girls begin their clockwise circling over the stones of the plaza.

This is my first promenade without Gabito. Never again will he be among the boys gathering in small packs to circle the virgin feast. He will not join them with their big metal belt buckles that draw attention to their tight dark pants. Crisp white shirts strain tight around their chests and waists. When Gabito inhaled, I could see his nipples through the cotton. He too had heavy-heeled boots and hair so thick with grease it reflected the tree lights.

Chapter 10

The boys move counterclockwise to the girls, clowning on one boot heel then the other to catch the eye of their special love. Gordo bounces past Porca. Skinny Vicente makes a shy bow when he sees his Alta, a girl so tall there are pine needles in her hair. Tomás whispers Miquela's name. Her parents are anxious to introduce a healthy dose of Tomás's swagger into the fragile bones of Miquela's bloodline. Tomás rubs his pant leg with the edge of his palm as he passes her.

In the circling line, Véronica catches up to her only friend, a serious, dark girl with brittle hair. But the girl puts distance between them. Sweet sister Amanda watches César approach. His love for her always shows in his soft face crowned with a curly mop of brown hair. But this time, César turns away from the outcast Amanda. Poor Amanda looks back and watches him walking with his friends.

"Go join your sisters," says Papá.

"Yes," I say, "the promenade looks like such fun."

Papá never responds to my sarcasm.

"Tortugina," says Mamá. "There is Geraldo, the new boy, Señor Valencia's sister's son. Go capture his heart."

Mamá points to a boy with the dull eyes of a goat.

"Yes, Mamá," I say.

Papá gives me an encouraging push on the back. I trip through the boys' line. Their boot heels spark.

On the inside line, the girls walk with their eyes deliberately downcast. According to tradition, the girls look down at their feet as they pass the boys. It is an unshakable fact that the harder a boy works for your glance, the more value he places on your gaze. And if he values your eyes, think what high esteem he places on the rest of you.

Geraldo, the goat-eyed beast, rolls toward me counterclockwise. His face reminds me of Papá when he is preoccupied with groceries. As a husband, he would probably complain about socks and make me massage his cold vegetable garden.

I join the other girls in their downward gaze of modesty. But what good is looking down, if Geraldo does not know I am trying to avoid his eyes? In a desperate time one must be forgiven for desperate acts. I step in front of Geraldo. The force of our collision nearly knocks me over.

"I am so sorry, Señorita," he says. "Are you all right?"

He tries to move around me, but I move with him.

"Geraldo, what do you say, will you marry me?"

Geraldo looks at my eyes, my best feature, and then his glance takes in my overbite. He shoves gently past.

"Señorita, you must be mistaking me for another."

Now at least he knows that I exist and that my intentions are honorable.

When Geraldo circles toward me again, I step in front of him. I need one more small gesture to stop him, but I have no small gestures. When he starts to circle away, I arch my back so that my nipples stick out like small noses against the cloth.

"Geraldo! Life with me will not be dull," I say.

I raise the hem of the long white dress above my knees. Geraldo stops, and his face turns red. His eyes lap at my legs. I am encouraged to raise my hem higher. I look up at him like the black-and-white tease pictures in Señor Duro's back room.

"Tortugina!" yells Papá.

Other boys circle me, two and three deep, hard bodies pushing, metal buckles clashing against heavy leather belts, the friction of knife-crisp cotton. Their eyes glaze. Their pants blossom.

"Show us more!" they shout.

I am surrounded by the smoky smell of overheated boys. The Promenade de los Adolescentes now stands completely still, a line that has not stood still in three hundred and fifty years.

To capture Geraldo completely, I flip my dress up for a quick flash of underwear. The boys howl so loudly that a matador might have struck his final blow. Miquela and the girls are the last to gather. They are wide-eyed around the flames of their future husbands. They cannot believe that the outcast Tortugina is the center of the blaze.

"Tortugina!" Papá yells closer this time.

My hem drops to the cobblestones quickly to hide the show of legs. I turn slowly in place so that Geraldo sees all sides of my dancing hips and knows he is a lucky man. For a few precious moments, every boy in the village desires me.

"Tortugina!"

Papá's voice is louder than the band. The musicians in the gazebo let their instruments drop slowly from their lips. The music is replaced by loud whispers. Papá pushes through the boys' stiff bodies. Their hands jump out of their pockets. Papá grabs my arm and slaps my face. I barely feel his palm, but the sharp sound shatters something fragile between us.

"Tortugina," says Papá, "you have condemned yourself!"

Papá's fingers grip the back of my neck. He pushes me ahead of him to break through the wall of boys. Instead of moving aside, their bodies surround us. Papá wades into them, pulling me after him. The boys make way for him, but the divers ram their bodies into me. Geraldo manages a pinch on my rump, but it does not feel like a proposal.

Outside the horde of boys, Mamá grabs my arm.

"Tortugina, you promised to make me proud!"

Papá pulls me with a strong grip on my other arm. I am stretched between them like laundry on a line.

"But Mamá, Geraldo would not look at me."

Papá yanks me loose from Mamá.

"Mother Mary Inmaculada!" shouts Papá. "Please, come claim your acolyte!"

A black, flapping shadow clamps her talons on my wrist. Papá releases his hold as though to cleanse himself.

"She is yours!" he says.

Mother Mary has a jailer's glint in her eye.

"Mamá!" I yell.

Mother Mary turns her thick heels toward the convent. She splits the cool evening air with the bow of her black habit. In her wake, I am the day's catch. Had I a hook through my mouth, I could not be more miserable.

"Mamá!" I yell.

"There is nothing more I can do, Tortugina!" yells Mamá.

Mother Mary's savage pace keeps me off balance. The villagers surge in waves of orange lanterns. They turn up the wicks, and their tall shadows dwarf the buildings. Boys run wild in the street, carrying the singed smell of hot wicks and overheated metal. Girls cling to each other. There is weeping all around me as the villagers follow us to the convent. Something in the quiet weave of the village has been loosened.

"Tortugina," hisses Mother Mary Inmaculada. "You have set the devil free in El Pulpo!"

CHAPTER 11

A STAND OF distant cottonwood trees lies ahead. One small window of the convent shines kerosene yellow. The old stable looks like the nightmare tale where witches eat small children. I picture myself scrubbing dung-rotted floor planks, washing cracked plates in cold suds, with perhaps an occasional taste of fried pulpo with eggs, garlic, and cilantro to remind me of home.

Let the old nun try to tie me to a cross. I'll make her regret every moment of our lives together.

Suddenly Mother Mary halts on the convent trail and holds up her hand. The villagers stop behind us. The hiss of cicadas fills the night air as we stand silently behind the old church listening to odd snorts and the slow gait of giant hooves coming toward us. It could be the Devil, but it sounds more like a horse with a cold. If Satan has come for Tortugina, he smells of pipe tobacco.

Chapter 11

Large brown creature eyes loom out of the darkness and move into the lantern light. It looks like a long-legged cow with a sloppy face.

A man rides on top of the creature, which is piled high with provisions. The stranger's face is golden brown, and his beard is the same color as Papá's dark brown coat. The rest of him is dressed in a white shirt and white pants, soft straw sombrero, and heavy leather sandals. The open collar shows the wide, hairy chest of a man who works hard for his beans. He jerks a rope attached to his animal's head, and it stops in front of Mother Mary Inmaculada. His hands are large and stained on the tips with tobacco or the walnut finish of a wood craftsman. The man removes his straw hat in a proud gesture toward me.

"Señorita." His voice is so deep it rattles the bones in my chest. The man takes a pipe out of his beard and blows blue smoke.

"My name is Miguel Svendik from Las Mujeres, and this is my camel, Lucinda."

For the beast's long hairy legs and splayed hooves to make sense, this camel creature must have come from a place where the water is deep and muddy. And it has a name. Most of the dogs in El Pulpo have names, but not the livestock.

Mother Mary holds her lantern up to the camel's face. The creature's eyes are bordered with long lashes like a whore in Señor Duro's back-room pictures. Its rubbery upper lip is split in two. The camel snorts and covers Mother Mary's lantern with a streak of yellow snot. The nun gives a little cry, but she does not retreat.

Miguel Svendik wiggles his thick dark eyebrows at me. I wiggle my eyebrows to answer his. We are two street dogs making friendly signals. He twitches his nose. I twitch mine and he laughs.

In the boom of his laughter, I hear a flash flood roar. He is the danger of high tides. He is the threat of a monsoon. He is not the gentle underwater current of my Gabito.

Miguel Svendik kicks Lucinda's shaggy shoulders. The camel lowers itself to its knees. Had it been made of metal, there would have been a great deal of clanking.

Once the creature has squatted on the ground, the villagers surround it. Miguel dismounts by sliding off. He is shorter once his feet touch the ground, not much taller than Papá, who is only slightly taller than me, and I am not much higher than the ears of a burro.

Mother Mary steps forward to meet his gaze. "What is your business here, Señor Svendik?"

"I am searching for a wife. I want this green-eyed woman."

Mother Mary Inmaculada straightens. A proposal of marriage? These are words that are usually accompanied by months of coffee negotiations. The rogue face of this man who asks so boldly for a wife is beginning to look beautiful to me.

Mother Mary plants her heavy shoes on the trail.

"Your manners are offensive. Your beast is unwholesome. A man courts a woman in the traditional fashion or he does not court at all! And this green-eyed girl is going to be a nun."

Miguel Svendik smiles at me. "God will be disappointed today, Sister. This woman is made for a man's bed."

The villagers bleat like goats. "Did he say Be-e-e-d?"

Before Mother Mary can speak again, he steps around her and bows to me.

"What is your name, my beauty?"

No one has ever called me "beauty." This stranger's intentions are on his face for all to see. His fingers do not touch me, but they are twitching in my direction.

"Tortugina. Tortugina María Gomez."

I want to step backward until I am home. This is not a boy to play with. This is a full-grown man I cannot manage at all. I barely have the courage to look in his eyes.

"Tortugina," says Miguel Svendik.

His wide nostrils seem to inhale my name and a little part of me too. "Little turtle, have you a hard shell to hide a soft heart?"

His eyes and his question make me feel naked.

"Who is the father of Tortugina?" he says to the crowd.

To my relief, Mamá appears, dragging Papá through the crowd, and shoves him forward. Papá makes a little show of straightening his jacket and stands as tall as he can.

"I am Señor Hector Gomez," says Papá. "What do you want of my daughter?"

Everyone in the village slowly encircles Papá, Mamá, and me. This is the first time I have felt protected by these people. Though I am a stranger in my own village, I am not as much a stranger as this man.

Miguel bows and lifts his hat. "I am Miguel Svendik from the village of Las Mujeres."

He looks at Mamá. "Who is this beautiful woman by your side?"

Mamá's face turns bright red in the kerosene light.

"My wife," says Papá.

Papá moves a little closer to Mamá. Miguel speaks, and it sounds like a command.

"Señor and Señora Gomez, I would consider it an honor to marry your daughter, Tortugina."

I am sure Papá never thought he would have the opportunity to contract marriage on my behalf. Mamá moves behind me, her fingers kneading my shoulder the way she readies bread. Her prayers are answered. The problem of Tortugina evaporates with the arrival of a man on a shaggy beast.

"If you wish to marry my daughter," says Papá, "you may begin by joining us for supper tomorrow night."

Miguel Svendik folds his arms and looks as lawless as a storm.

"I do not have the luxury of tradition, Señor Gomez. I have been away from home for too long in search of a bride. I am a man on a schedule, and these are my terms. I do not require a dowry. I accept Tortugina with the dress on her back, and I want to marry her tonight. I will undertake all expenses."

Mother Mary Inmaculada stares at Miguel Svendik. "No tradition?"

The villagers turn to each other. "No tradition?"

But Papá heard the man's words in the cash register of his mind: "All expenses are mine." Mamá drops her hand behind Papá's back and pinches. Papá jumps and holds out his hand to Miguel Svendik.

"Welcome to my family, Señor Svendik."

Miguel Svendik's eyes stroke my body as though we were alone in a bed. He is the kind of someone no one is prepared for, especially not me.

Chapter 11

The heavy-chested man drops to one knee. He is a seducer from the mountains of the moon, a fire-breather from hell.

The camel is kneeling behind him on its square knees as though it too were proposing.

"Tortugina, you must answer for yourself," says Miguel Svendik. "Do you want to be my bride?"

Papá, Mamá, Amanda, Véronica, and the villagers hold their breath waiting for my answer. In this silence, I am the focus of hundreds of eyes. It is worth stretching the moment. Mother Mary Inmaculada crushes her rosary beads in her fist. I am swimming out of her reach. Mamá nods at me to accept. But I am not a fraud. First, I must tell Miguel Svendik that I am already married and pregnant. Then if he still wants me, I will go.

"Señor Svendik," I say. "Before we wed, you should know that I…"

Mamá rolls her eyes and shouts, "TAKE HER, SEÑOR!"

"Take her! Take her! Take her, please!" chant the boys, girls, daughters, sons, brothers, sisters, mothers, fathers, grandmothers, grandfathers, cousins, uncles, in-laws, and musicians of El Pulpo.

Miguel Svendik smiles and waits with patience for my acceptance of him.

I shout over my neighbors' chants.

"I will marry you, Señor Miguel Svendik, but there are things you should know."

Miguel Svendik nods. "Later, little turtle."

He bounds up off his knees to lift Papá in an embrace.

"Papá!" says Miguel.

He swings Papá in a circle, round and round, and kisses him before setting him back on the dusty trail. Papá's eyes are still spinning. "Son!" he manages to say.

Miguel kisses Mamá's hand and leaves the deep imprint of his lips on her flesh.

"You have made me so happy, Señor!" she says.

She pats Miguel Svendik's muscled arm and looks at Lucinda. "Señor Svendik, where did you get this creature?"

"The story of my camel," he says, "is one hundred years old. I will tell it to my wife one day, and she can tell it to you, if she wishes."

The faces of the villagers have changed in the last few moments. As I look around, their eyes seem to be saying, "Is there actually something of value in Tortugina that we have failed to notice all these years?"

Miguel Svendik now feels free to take me in his arms. The soft straw hat in his fist bounces against my rump. But the rest of him is not so soft. I am hugging a brick wall with a pipe-tobacco beard. Over Miguel's broad shoulder, I see something floating toward me. It looks like a mistake of nature. A dark shimmer, too fast for a storm cloud, coming straight at me. Gabito stops flying at me only when his face is inches from my face.

"Have you forgotten so soon, Tortugina," he says, "that I am your husband?"

No one seems to notice Gabito floating behind Miguel's back. The villagers buzz like hornets around us, smiling at me and yelling their congratulations. I form a silent answer to Gabito.

"Forgive me, Gabito, but to give our son a name, I need a husband who is still breathing."

These very sensible words make no impact. He wipes a silver tear from his bad eye and cocks his head. His curls shake as he sobs. He is far more sensitive as a ghost.

"Gabito," I say, "tell me what you want me to do."

Gabito flies away from me. He stops over the camel and jumps up and down on the provisions strapped to its back. The poor animal bellows and rocks on its knees. Its oriental eyes flash. Lucinda rises off the ground with a great deal of clanking. Pots and pans fall. Bags of grain spill to the ground. The villagers back away as the animal nips madly at its own back.

Gabito flies toward the cliff in a shower of sparks. A young palm bends in his wake. He drops over the edge back into the sea.

Miguel Svendik runs to soothe his camel, but Lucinda bolts down the dark, dusty trail. He runs after her calling her name. His hat bounces ridiculously. Both of them are headed in the direction of the silent convent where I was to have spent my life.

CHAPTER 12

INSIDE THE CHILLY rectory, one black shawl is not warmth enough. Any moment Mamá will bring the wedding dress. Once inside it, I am abducted for life.

Miguel Svendik scrapes a sulfur match on the rough wood of the doorway and holds it over his pipe. His white teeth turn orange in the light of the flames. Dry tobacco crackles. He inhales, quick and hollow. In the kerosene lamplight, smoke pours out of his nostrils and surrounds his head, turning the air blue. He takes the pipe out of his mouth and waves it.

"Magdalene," he says.

He's already forgotten my name.

"No," I say. "Tortugina."

His coughing laughter topples into the room. "I meant my pipe."

"You are a man who names everything," I say.

"Everything has a name. My camel is Lucinda. My pipe

is Magdalene. And there is a part of me that you will learn very well by name."

He turns his bull of a head back into the church nave and yells, "And the name of my bride is Tortugina! Tortugina is the name of my bride to be!"

His voice bounces off the walls. It doubles and triples into a choir of baritones. Villagers stop what they are doing and crane over the worn pews at Miguel's declaration. Then they go back to what is required for the fastest wedding in the history of El Pulpo. Older women flutter from wick to wick, lighting a cathedral of candles on every flat space. They place potted flowers and vases of wilted bouquets. No time to prepare for a real feast. No time to make gifts. No time to air out the cedar moth-proofing from stored dresses and suits.

Remembering Gabito's wounded face, I try once more for the truth.

"I should tell you something before we wed," I say.

He looks at me through the blue haze he has created in the doorway.

"I have no interest in women's secrets. You should keep it to yourself unless, of course," he laughs, "you are pregnant with another man's baby."

Miguel is still laughing when Mamá coughs her way through his curtain of smoke. Sweat pours down her face from the race across the plaza to our house and back again. The folds of her neck flatten as she throws back her head and gulps the icy air in the rectory.

"I had no idea I could still run that fast," says Mamá.

She holds up the long white bag and dismisses Miguel with a wave.

"Go smoke somewhere else, Señor Svendik. I will prepare our little bride."

Miguel salutes us both with a swirl of his pipe.

"It is my honor to wait for your beautiful daughter, Señora Gomez."

The door's hinges scream as Miguel closes it. Mamá lays the bag carefully on the table and collapses beside me. She wipes her face, takes a small knife from her pocket, and hands it to me.

"Tortugina, this may be the only tradition honored tonight. Each woman in our family cuts the family wedding dress free of the sheets."

I take the sharp knife and cut the tiny fishing-line stitches that burst and curl like transparent snakes around the edges of the sheet. When I pull the sheet back, a forest smell emerges, cedar chips tied in small bundles of cheesecloth.

The wedding dress is long-sleeved and completely out of style. A high collar with small buttons, unfashionable for a hundred years. The white brocade on the bodice is torn in one place. The skirt, made from yards of white silk, is yellowing at the folds. A white lace mantilla lies in a crumpled mess.

"I won't wear it, Mamá."

I have seen the dress all my life in the black-and-white photographs in our hallway. Family women who briefly sealed their bodies inside the dress and committed their lives to its meaning.

"Your wedding and the dress are a part of this family's history for five generations," says Mamá. "Undress."

Mamá turns me around and unbuttons the back of my white promenade dress.

Chapter 12

Five generations. That is about 150 years, five Mamás, with three daughters apiece. And now, I add my time to theirs. My Mamá and her Mamá and her Mamá and her Mamá, we all leave our virgin sweat in the silk.

Before I can let the starchy promenade dress fall to the ground, Mamá catches it.

"Always pull your clothes over your head." She hangs it on a wooden hook. "You'll want to keep your things clean now that you have to wash them."

"I will do exactly as I please in my own house," I say.

Mamá lowers the silk wedding dress over my head.

"I will not miss these conversations," she says.

A layered cloud of white silk covers my head with a suffocating cedar smell. If this dress fit Mamá, it will surround me like a circus tent. With a small jerk from Mamá, the dress rests on my hips. It fits me perfectly. A cedar chip is caught under the silk and cuts into my waist.

"Mamá, a chip is poking me."

"It is the first of many inconveniences you will feel as a married woman," she says.

But she reaches into the bodice and pulls it out. I expect her to start buttoning. When she does not, I turn and see she is holding the chip in her palm and drowning it in tears.

"Mamá? Is this what cedar does to you?"

She turns me gently and buttons the tiny pearls up my spine. "Twenty-five years ago, I was you."

Tears fill my eyes too when I think that in twenty-five years, I may be Mamá.

"Mamá, when you married Papá, did you know him?"

Mamá straightens my seams. "All husbands are strangers, and remain strangers until the day you die."

I want to crawl inside her dress and go home.

The wood hinges scream as Véronica opens the rectory door. She holds the bridal bouquet in a towel. She brought week-old purple dahlias dripping from the front-room vase. Véronica holds them away from her dress. She lays the dripping bouquet on the bench and sits beside them. Her frown is worse than usual. Since she has tortured me for so many years, I like to think I am the cause of her unhappiness.

"Padre Abstensia is waiting," she says in her sulkiest voice. "Everyone is waiting."

Mamá places the white lace mantilla on my head. Her bare arm brushes in front of my lips, and I absent-mindedly kiss her warm skin.

A terrible blast of organ chords shakes us through the cold rectory walls. The lip rouge drops off the table and rolls across the floorboards.

"Señora Tranquilina!" says Mamá. "She plays no better today than she did for my wedding."

The old metal organ pipes groan and echo. Señora Tranquilina bangs a horrible march that she plays faster and faster. Mamá sticks her head through the rectory door and shouts.

"You do not need to get rid of Tortugina that quickly, Señora Tranquilina!"

The music slows to the promenade tempo then slows to a dirge.

"Not that slow!" yells Mamá.

But Señora Tranquilina continues. Mamá looks at Véronica for the first time.

"The last tradition," says Mamá. "Tortugina must wear something from a married woman for luck. What should I give her, Véronica?"

Chapter 12

Véronica's cheeks suck in and out like sails. Pearl tears pour out of her eyes.

"She's wearing your wedding dress and mantilla, Mamá. That ought to bring her everything she deserves."

She squints tightly until there are only dark lashes like tiny octopus legs sticking out of her clenched eyes. Human emotions are not becoming to Véronica's face.

"Véronica," says Mamá, "tell Padre Abstensia that we are ready."

Véronica makes an animal sound like a small dog being struck and runs out of the door.

"She certainly chooses her moments," says Mamá. "You do not need to carry that rotting bouquet she brought you."

Mamá lowers the white mantilla over my face. Lamplight halos through the veil. The world turns pale and unreal.

"Remember, Tortugina," whispers Mamá. "Whatever happens on your wedding night, you are young and will recover quickly."

Mamá's arm twines in the crook of mine. It is a picnic-slow walk through the rectory door into the drafty church. Candles glow, kerosene lamps are hung on every hook. My sweat dampens the yellowed underarms, releasing the scent of former virgins. Even more, I smell the cilantro of Mamá's sweat.

Doves and swallows beat their wings against the rafters overhead. Señora Tranquilina's slow march continues its irritating drone.

At the back of the church, Papá waits. He smooths his hair, rubs his backside under the wool dress pants, and signals for us to hurry. We continue our slow pace toward Papá. He smiles at Mamá, and she smiles back at him.

"Do not expect too much of a man, Tortugina," whispers Mamá. "They can only love their dream of you. If you help him to maintain that dream, he is yours forever."

"Mamá?" I whisper. "What about my dream?"

"Two dreamers in one marriage?" She shakes her head as though I had made a joke. "We should have started this conversation years ago."

"You love Papá, don't you?" I whisper.

She drags me toward him. "More than my life."

Mamá leaves me by Papá's side and lowers herself into the pew next to Véronica and Amanda. Sweet Amanda blows me a kiss.

For the first time in my life, I slip my hand into Papá's hand, hard and stiff like his cold, vegetable toes.

Padre Abstensia nods to Señora Tranquilina, and her old fingers switch to a wedding march slow enough for a pair of cripples. At this rate, we may not reach the altar by sunrise.

Papá seems more than pleased. His graying hair shines, and his sad eyes have a freshly unburdened glow. With the arrival of a man and a camel, his world has lightened.

Papá's valued customers smile at him. They might even be smiling at me. Familiarity alone binds me to the lives that have been lived behind each of my neighbors' faces. They have watched me grow. I have watched them grow old. Age is most noticeable in their hair, which seems to have regrouped in unfortunate places. Balding Señor Aves has dark fur in his ears. Thin-haired Señora Septima has black hairs like cat whiskers on her chin. Señora Grosera's gray eyebrows are long and curly.

When Papá and I reach the altar, advancing faster than Señora Tranquilina's slow tempo, Miguel Svendik takes my hand. He wears a black jacket, short in front with long tails in back that complement his square figure. His white shirt is tucked into his white pants. A red sash circles his waist. His sandals have been replaced with a pair of shiny black shoes scuffed at the toes. He does not appear to be wearing socks. His wild, thick brown hair is brushed back and oiled down around his skull, his green eyes are as soft as cooked peas. When he smiles with the squarest teeth I have ever seen, I smile back, and for a moment, I begin to enjoy my own wedding.

Padre Abstensia rocks back and forth breathing clouds of church wine. The lilies in their white vases on the altar have wilted since last Sunday. No one has replaced the smoky candles with new white ones. But it makes no difference to me.

When the organ music ends, Miguel Svendik takes my hand as if it no longer belonged to me. We kneel in front of Padre Abstensia, his Bible in hand, as he looks over our heads at the villagers.

"My friends, we are gathered in the eyes of God to join this man and this woman in holy matrimony. Are there any who object to such a union?"

"NO!" yell the villagers.

Doves and swallows flutter in the rafters. Padre Abstensia shakes from too much wine as he looks down at us.

"It has been requested that I forego the ceremony and marry you quickly. Do you, Tortugina María Gomez, take Miguel Svendik as your husband?"

"Yes." My voice is a whisper.

With genuine concern, Padre Abstensia turns to Miguel Svendik.

"Do you, Miguel Svendik, really want this woman for your wife?"

Miguel looks through the patterned mantilla for my eyes. "I have chosen the best woman your village has to offer."

Padre Abstensia makes the sign of the cross over us. "May life not disillusion you too quickly, my son. You may exchange the rings now."

Behind us there is a shifting of bodies and whispers. Rings? In the haste of preparation, no one took the duty of the rings.

Miguel removes a small, polished wood box from his jacket. "These belonged to my parents."

There is a village of murmurs behind me.

"He is prepared!"

"Nothing left to chance!"

"A man in charge!"

Miguel opens the small box. Two gold rings. One is a thick gold band, scarred from use. The other, a smaller gold band, is worn at the edges.

Gabito's blue wedding band shimmers on my finger. It is so much a part of my skin I would not know how to remove it. Miguel's gold band is too small to slip over my knuckle. He pushes harder. The thin gold edges shave flesh.

"You're hurting me," I say through clenched teeth.

He twists the ring to loosen it, perhaps, but the sharp pain goes straight to the top of my head. Where Gabito's blue band fit so easily, my flesh plumps out on either side of this ring. Miguel's father's fat gold band slips easily over his knuckle.

"A perfect fit," says Miguel Svendik. "Like us."

Chapter 12

If only Gabito were here to jump up and down on Miguel's head.

Padre holds his palms over our heads. "By the authority of God, I pronounce you husband and wife! You may kiss the bride."

When we rise from our knees, my body is as numb as my wedding finger. Miguel lifts the veil that shielded me. His kiss tastes pipe bitter.

At the end of the kiss, the village releases a big, collective sigh. A shout erupts from Papá, followed by cries and whoops from Véronica, Amanda, César, Padre Abstensia, Señor Aves, Señora Cantata, Señor Duro. The whole village rises with a loud sense of relief. They stomp the dusty floorboards, bang their shoes on the weathered pews, and shout. Excited pigeon feathers fall from the rafters.

Women who ignored Mamá since Gabito's death kiss her cheek, grab my shoulders and kiss me on both cheeks. Their husbands who have called me names now shake my husband's hand. Even Gabito's father, Señor Emilio, offers his hand in friendship to Papá, who takes it as one would a precious gift.

Miguel gives Padre Abstensia a small handful of silver coins.

"May God have mercy on your souls," says Padre Abstensia.

"That sounds like a death sentence," I say.

There is tenderness in my new husband's eyes.

"It is a life sentence, Tortugina. From this moment on, you belong to me."

My new name. Tortugina Svendik. That will take practice. Papá climbs onto a pew and holds his hands in the air. His whistle pierces as if he were at a soccer match. The village cheers turn to silence.

"My friends," says Papá. "We had no time for preparations, yet I promise you tonight you will drink my best aguardiente in honor of my daughter Tortugina's wedding!"

I cannot believe my ears. Papá's precious aguardiente that he sells at a good price? My eyes fill with tears.

The divers lift Papá onto their shoulders. The mariachi band plays the wedding march and leads the village out of the church.

The aisle is empty except for the stranger by my side and dark little Señor Deguerra with his big black photography camera that he props up in the aisle. His assistant holds up the flash powder.

"Say 'queso,' " he says.

"Queso," Miguel and I repeat with a show of teeth. "Cheese." And the flash blinds us.

While Mamá carts off the stained silk relic to store for her next daughter's wedding, I change quickly back into the real world of everyday cotton.

CHAPTER 13

ACROSS THE Plaza de Allende, the mariachi notes of Sweaty Oscar's trumpet blast a path to Señor Ignacio's taverna. Music leaves an easy trail to follow. Our bodies move as one shadow down the stone steps of the church into the midnight celebration. My new husband's hand completely covers mine, but it does not shut out thoughts of Gabito. When wedding night consummation comes, I wonder if Gabito will jump up and down on my new husband's back with his fiery sandals.

Miguel Svendik slips his hand under the wool shawl and caresses the back of my new white blouse. It surprises me, his gentle touch as he slips his fingers down to the creases of the blue skirt and feels my bottom. My thoughts of Gabito are stronger than ever.

Miguel Svendik and I pass through the plaza, the fountains with children's stick boats, the flaking bandstand, the stones where the feet of Gabito and Tortugina wore their mark, my dark bedroom window above Papá's store. Even the air smells different, as though I am walking through a dusty memory.

My fingers are caged in Miguel Svendik's hold. I pull away and lick my ring, turn the tight band to allow the flow of blood.

"Will we be happy?" I say.

Miguel's face is shadowed under his soft sombrero. "That is up to you," he says.

He takes my hand again and does not let go.

In front of Señor Ignacio's taverna, familiar silhouettes glide to Sweaty Oscar's mariachi music. Some of the women lay out platters of refried beans and yesterday's chicken rescued from their kitchens. People will eat it only when they are too drunk to care what they put in their mouths.

Miguel pours me wine as we sit. I do not feel as married as Mamá and Papá, as the people who sit in front of fireplaces dozing.

The old madame, Señora Estonia, with a freshly painted face, totters to our table and leans over Miguel.

"Miguel Svendik and his accidental bride," Señora Estonia says. "I have lived too long when whores like you find husbands."

"You have indeed lived too long, Señora Estonia," I say. "You will never feel a man's caress again."

Señora Estonia trumpets a laugh through her elephant-ivory teeth.

"I have felt the caress of many married men," she says. "Your husband's hands will soon be on some whore's ass, Tortugina. I only wish it were mine."

Her knobbed fingers tweak Miguel's cheek. He gently pats her sagging bottom.

"I love crazy old women," says Miguel. "I hope you are like her when you're old."

"Diseased and despised?" I say.

Miguel laughs and jumps up to help Papá settle a box of aguardiente bottles on our table.

"My friends!" yells Papá. "On this night I lose my youngest. This special aguardiente is a tribute to my beautiful daughter."

I cannot hide my tears at Papá's declaration. Miguel puts his arms around me.

"Why are you crying?" he says.

"Papá called me beautiful," I whisper.

Papá stands back and allows the villagers to circle the boxes and pull out the beautifully labeled bottles. His precious aguardiente has made this night an event in the history of village weddings.

The bottles are unsealed and the aguardiente poured into shot glasses. The villagers raise their glasses to toast Papá and wish happiness to our family. They throw the drinks back in one gulp and fill their glasses again. They toast me with far too much joy.

Papá sits down across the table and presents a dark, dust-streaked bottle to my husband.

"Señor Svendik, I bottled this one the day before Tortugina's birth," says Papá. "The taste is wild and strong. I thought she was going to be a boy."

Papá fills a shot glass of my aguardiente for himself and one for Miguel.

They clink and throw the liquid down their throats.

"May I have a taste of my birth aguardiente, Papá?" I say.

Chapter 13

Miguel Svendik winks at Papá. "We know what burning water does to a woman."

They both laugh the way men do at jokes about women, usually behind their backs. Papá pours another drink and toasts me.

"To a decent night's sleep," he says. "Thank you, Tortugina!"

Miguel allows me a sip from his glass. The aguardiente's strong anise flavor is so sweet it curls my teeth. But I cannot resist more. When Miguel is distracted with Papá, I drink the whole shot glass in one gulp. Fermented molasses, 60-proof, my throat is on fire. My eyes water, lungs hurt, head turning somersaults, but then I have never had liquor. I don't know if it is strong and wild like a boy. I have never tasted a boy either except for Gabito, and he is all blood and salt. There was the fat boy who tasted like chocolate. I think I must be drunk. It is not a bad feeling, though Miguel keeps sliding in and out of focus.

"It is time for us to go," says Miguel Svendik.

His eyes have taken on a dark glow as he looks at my breasts. I am glad to have numbed myself with Papá's fire water.

"Men and woman of El Pulpo!" Miguel Svendik shouts.

The villagers turn toward him as a silent herd of grazing cows might shift toward a dinner bell.

"I thank you for my bride," he says, "and for your hospitality. My wife and I are leaving."

A sudden breeze from the sea sends a chilly farewell. He climbs aboard the patient Lucinda, who stands like a statue among the dancers.

"Are you ready, Tortugina?" says Miguel.

How could I ever be ready? To leave Mamá? Mamá picks up a bundle from the bench and puts it into my arms. Inside is new underwear, a change of clothes, a beautiful cotton nightgown, and most precious of all, the pink-striped swimsuit for the dive I have yet to make. These clothes are dowry enough for the crowded back of a camel.

Mamá's arms pull me tight. "Tortugina," she whispers, "my little dreamer."

"Señora Tortugina María Gomez Svendik." She sings my new name like an old song. "Go with God and be good to your husband."

My husband had better be good to me, I think to myself, but I decide to let Mamá have the last parting word. As soon as I turn away from her, Amanda embraces me and wets my face with her tears.

"I will miss you," says Amanda.

"You will be the only one," I say.

"I know," says Amanda. "Véronica, say good-bye to our Tortugina."

Véronica barely nods her head in my direction.

Miguel Svendik leans down, grabs my wrist, and pulls me onto the camel's burdened back. The animal groans under the added weight.

"Easy, Lucinda," says Miguel.

I wedge into the soft mattress of supplies strapped to the camel's back. It is cooler above the ground, above the music, the dancers, and the family tears.

The villagers are anxious to return to Papá's aguardiente. It is good to know the celebration will continue long after I am gone. The moon lights Mamá's damp face. She is smiling, but I know her sad smiles too well. I blow a kiss and she blows one back.

Miguel flicks his stick against Lucinda's neck.

"Hut, hut!" he says.

Lucinda shakes and snorts. The villagers step away, fanning their faces from Lucinda's loud fart.

"Hut, hut, hut," says Miguel.

Lucinda launches us up the cobblestone street. I look back from my new height. The shadows of the dancers and the drinkers grow smaller. The camel carries us up Calle de Serpiente toward the main road that runs north and south along the sea.

Soon the sound of camel hooves is the only music. Lucinda's long-legged stride rocks me front to side to back to side to front. The lights of the wedding-cake village with a hundred black doors are behind us. Miguel Svendik and I ride away from El Pulpo as close to the stars as the hump of a camel allows.

CHAPTER 14

THE STARS ARE so close, my nipples would graze them if I took a deep breath. A sea breeze salts my face. Blossoms pungent as night cling crab-tight to the shingled trunks of palms.

Ahead of me, Miguel Svendik stares out at the sea road and nudges his heel into the camel's neck. Her hooves kick up dust under us. The back of Miguel Svendik's white shirt is solid as moonlight. His hips sway one way then the other. He is a slow dancer, back and forth, side to side, broad shoulders, thick head of hair unstirred by the breeze.

My thoughts rock back and forth with the rhythm of Miguel's hips. Back down the road toward El Pulpo, Mamá, Papá, all of them will be sleeping. Papá's good aguardiente will be pissed into the earth by morning. The bruises I left on Mamá's days will heal now. I wonder if she will forget me.

Chapter 14

The future is the clean white slate of my husband's back. He knows nothing of what I carry into his village. In my new home, I will bury my disgraces from the past deep inside and create anew who I am. Until I am discovered, I will be Señora Perfección.

"Hut, hut," says Miguel.

Lucinda picks up her pace through swaying palms on either side of the road. To the left, the beach is bright and blinding. The sand is a chalk-white pasture of moon and damp smells from a silver estuary.

Miguel Svendik glances back at me, dark eyes, under dark brows, under bright moonlight. Securing Lucinda's reins to the supplies, he turns his legs and his thick body around to face me, knees to knees. He pulls his white shirt over his head and unties the front of his pants as easily as if he had disrobed on a camel every day of his life.

I have never seen a man this naked before, and the shock does not let me think beyond the parts of him. I try not to stare at the dark triangle of hair in his lap. His snake lies somewhere in the shadows. Moon lights his hairy, oxen shoulders.

"You look like livestock," I say.

He laughs. "My little virgin."

He reaches for my legs, pulls me toward him, and slides off my underwear. I am barely balanced. He allows my legs to return to either side of the camel and arranges my underpants on his head like a white cap.

His hairy fingers spider under my dress. There is no possibility of rescue. No Gabito in sight. Ahead are pale dunes, cold and hard as plaster.

I shut my eyes and try not to mind the slow approach of

his walking fingers toward my woman's mound.

I hear a familiar cough. When I open my eyes, Gabito is floating behind Miguel's shoulders. Even the good side of Gabito's face turns ugly as he surveys Miguel's nakedness and my underwear on his head.

"Tortugina, you're killing me all over again," says Gabito.

I look over Miguel's shoulder at Gabito and say aloud, "You must know in my heart I will always be yours no matter what the rest of me must do."

I pucker an air kiss to Gabito, who breaks into open sobs.

"My eager bride," says Miguel.

Miguel shifts forward, so close I can smell his long journey to find a wife, his smoky nights roasting small animals under the stars.

His fingers shake with the one button of my blue cotton skirt. We both watch it fall open around my hips. He pulls my blouse over my head. The damp night chills my nipples.

I cannot shut out Gabito's sobbing. I feel ugly, having him see me sitting naked before a strange man. My arms seem monkey-long.

"Do not be afraid of me, Tortugina," says Miguel. "I am only in a hurry."

Miguel reaches down the side of Lucinda and gathers a leather water bag. He wets a rough cloth and washes his face, his underarms.

"I clean myself for my bride," says Miguel. "A man must be clean before he comes to a woman for sex. Even if she is his wife."

Miguel holds the wet cloth to me.

"Tortugina," he says. "Would you like to wash the part of me that will enter you?"

Chapter 14

Gabito's voice fills my head with a high whine.

"Tortugina," says Gabito, "it is a man's job to wash his own burro!"

"Gabito, go away!" I say only to him.

He disappears suddenly. Lucinda's hooves clack loudly against dead palm branches scattered on the road. Gabito's slender shadow is no longer floating beside the camel or flapping over the white sand.

"What are you looking for?" says Miguel. "We are alone, Tortugina. No one is on the road this late. Would you like me to wash you?"

On the road just ahead of us, small waves break and streak up a stretch of wet sand. Gabito stands shirtless with a rage so blistering his face illuminates a small stand of palms. As we reach him, he scoops into the ragged gash of his chest and pulls out his beating heart. He holds it up into the moonlight for me to see.

"NO!" I yell and startle Miguel.

Gabito throws his severed heart on the dusty road in front of Lucinda as we pass. The camel hoof crushes into the bloody heart, making a moist butcher sound.

Miguel's fingers squeeze my knees.

"Tortugina, what is wrong?" says Miguel. "You are so pale."

I look back down the road for the flattened heart, but I see only dunes turning a dull gray as a thin cloud covers the moon.

Miguel smiles and reaches for my hand.

"Tortugina," he says, "let me introduce you to Angelicus Maximus."

He slips my hand into the untied front of his pants and wraps my fingers around the dark snake between his legs. It is soft and damp.

I am backstage, and this is the puppet I have never seen—this secret thing that bulges and deflates with regularity behind the curtain of men's pants. It is not raised by levers or lowered on ropes. Awakened from its slumber, Angelicus Maximus grows hard and silky and salutes a woman's touch. My fingers barely wrap around the hardness bloated on blood. How big can it get? It does not seem a lot different from a burro's, though a burro's is black and reaches nearly to the ground. It is larger and darker than a pig's or a monkey's or a dog's. And there is a distinct pulsing. I have never been so close, and my curiosity wants to cut the thing apart to see if it has its own small heart.

Miguel moves my hand to his balls.

They are not perfectly round as I had pictured balls. They are soft furry sacks, one side larger than the other, more pear than apple shaped. It is a soft undercarriage, like fruit pods with soft seeds.

Miguel sighs as I run my fingers over the bumpy silkiness of Angelicus Maximus. If he is happy with this, perhaps I can avoid consummation on a camel. Though Gabito has fled, I feel as though the eyes of the universe still hover in the blinking of the stars overhead.

Miguel leans forward with a kiss that is more of a caress. I taste our short life together on his tongue, the tobacco from his pipe, the cold beans and rice from our wedding feast, the wine, and the anise flavor of Papá's aguardiente.

Miguel wraps his hands under my buttocks as though I were two halves of a morning grapefruit. He raises me up over his lap, legs cold and dangling on either side of his heavy thighs. As he lowers me, the blunt head of Angelicus Maximus pokes at my tender valley.

"No," I say.

Suspended above Angelicus Maximus, I push my feet into the blanket and straighten my legs. Miguel balances me, fingernails in my bottom. What happens when this bull of a man finds I am not a virgin?

"Ah, my little virgin," he says. "Relax your legs. I promise that you will enjoy this."

My legs tighten like steel.

"The delicate operation of deflowering," I say, "must be on a white bed with white sheets. Everyone knows that!"

Miguel is not listening. His fingers pull me down. My dampness closes over the head of Angelicus Maximus. I feel the shock of a sharp pain.

"No!" I scream.

I am broken into liquid. The membrane of childhood was there after all. What did I do with Gabito? Was his Angelicus only air?

Miguel Svendik's eyebrows rise with a sweet moan. We stare into each other's eyes, too close to focus, but I smell his pipe breath.

"Ahhh," says Miguel.

Angelicus Maximus does not stop after his dramatic entrance. He noses through my curtains of flesh, and I slowly discover the pleasure of his friction that differs from Gabito's friction, though I am not sure how. Clamped in warm folds, Angelicus Maximus rolls inside me with the motion of Lucinda, our four-legged wedding bed.

Being touched from the inside reaches a long way. My heart softens under the hard strokes of Angelicus.

Miguel breathes louder, closes his eyes, and throws his head back. I am looking into the purple roof of his open mouth, his pink tongue, crooked bottom teeth. Agony. If I were cutting off his legs, his face would look the same. He turns wild under me, twisting. I try to slow him down with my legs, but his hips keep me wide.

And then I feel a separate heat inside my body. It rushes up through my legs, into my groin. The virgin pain disappears. Our hearts gallop into each other's chest. Blood jammed. I need to scream. His arms squeeze me too hard. I can't breathe. Inside me, a spasm clamps from side to side, looking for a way out.

"God!" yells Miguel.

His shoulders drop with a rough gasp. He is breathing hard, slack-jawed. He stares at me as though his brain had been removed.

Miguel lifts me off his lap and puts me back on the blanket. Angelicus Maximus, that fierce, red animal, has shriveled into hibernation within its own skin.

I am still blood-bloated. I press as hard as I can, knead my palms into my cramped groin. I cannot make the muscles release. The pain is worse than the deflowering. This did not happen with Gabito.

Lucinda continues the sway of sex. There is dark blood on the blanket under me.

"Tortugina," says Miguel, "I love you."

He dresses slowly with a smile into his white clothes. I dress too and wrap a blanket around my shoulders. My husband makes a gentle caress over my belly. I wish he could feel the cramps that he made in me. They are receding too slowly.

"Tonight," whispers Miguel, "I have given you a son. I will call him José after my favorite uncle, Mattea after my mother, Sergio for my father, María for my grandmother, Miguel because he is my son, Tortuga because he is your son."

José Mattea Sergio María Miguel Tortuga Svendik.

"And I will teach him to spell it."

Men and their sons. I want a daughter.

Something wet drips on my face. Gabito hovers above me. The hole in his chest where his heart still beats wildly is leaking.

"He is my son, Tortugina!" says Gabito. "The seed was planted the day of our wedding! I will call him José after my father, Francesca after my mother, Roberto after my grandfather, Emilia after my grandmother, Torta because he is yours, Gabito because he is mine! Mine!"

José Francesca Roberto Emilia Torta Gabito Ramirez.

"And I will teach him to spell it," I sigh only to Gabito.

Tonight, under the stars by the chill of the sea, there are too many men for one wedding night. A bit of meat floating inside my womb looks up without eyes or nose or lips.

"Mamá?" says José.

CHAPTER 15

IN THE MORNING light, long-legged Lucinda quickens her weary stride for home.

"We are nearly to Las Mujeres, Tortugina," says Miguel Svendik. "Do something with your hair."

The jungle is so green and thick on both sides of the trail that I cannot see through it to the sea. I rub my eyes to clear the dreams of last night, but I have wakened into a dream of colors I have never seen before. Blue flowers the size of Mamá's ceramic serving dish. White silken lilies that would sew into an excellent gown. Bees buzz around stamens of pink succulents splayed in the curves of black branches.

Miguel unstraps a wine bag, aims a long arcing line of wine between his teeth, swishes, and spits it out. With his purple teeth, even he is a new color.

I pull my loose hair back into a bun and inhale the fluid fragrances. Little José stirs deep in my belly. All I hear of him is the soft snoring of liquids in and out, like a tiny tide.

Chapter 15

"Las Mujeres," says Miguel, pronouncing it like a schoolteacher.

"Las Mujerrres," I say. "Las Mujerrrrres, Las Mujerrrrrrrrres."

My R's do not roll as well as his. My efforts are distracted by the sound of a mariachi band blaring in the distance. Branches of wet leaves slap my arms as Lucinda trots faster toward the music.

"I'd forgotten," says Miguel, and a deep gloom settles on his face. "It is La Dia del Circo. You will meet the village at its loudest."

"I love a circus," I say.

As Lucinda plods between giant anthills, I picture the circus of my childhood. The caravan camped in the plaza of El Pulpo. The striped canvas tent smelling of hay, a two-headed donkey, and clowns dressed in layers and layers of torn rags to resemble colorful, shaggy beasts.

Ahead a purple and yellow sign hangs between two palm trees: "Bienvenido a Las Mujeres."

We pass under the sign, and the damp trail ends. Lucinda's hooves pummel cobblestones and houses appear, surrounded by the ample arms of flowering trees.

What makes my breath weak is that none of the homes of Las Mujeres are the solid white of El Pulpo. These are each painted with two brilliant colors. We ride past one house painted sunrise yellow on the bottom half and turquoise blue on top. The next one is a two-story house colored bright orange with a lower half of strong purple. The best, the home that almost makes me faint, is a light green and red house. It is covered in pink bougainvillea with star orchids hanging like a fringed evening shawl off the iron balcony.

"In El Pulpo," I say, "one color was good enough for everyone."

"In Las Mujeres, it is the rule of two," says Miguel. "For balance, the viejas say."

A life balanced with colors! Perhaps I can balance the colors in myself. My shocking reds that hurt Mamá, my dark purples and painful blues balanced with the gentle sunrise yellow of the walls. If Las Mujeres were a beautiful woman, I would kiss her hem.

Lucinda trots us into a large square paved with black cobblestones. A mosaic fountain sprays upward among a small grove of palms. Lining the square are the municipal buildings, a taverna, a dry goods store, and an ice cream shop. Only the church is a solid color, pink, built like a child's vision of a sand castle with towers, turrets, and saints pointing from its parapets.

Miguel kicks Lucinda as though he intends to ride quickly through the square. But when the villagers see us, we are surrounded like an island. They point at me, but I cannot hear what they are saying. A marching mariachi band is so loud Miguel has to shout.

"This is the main square, named after a strong leader, Don Pedro the Cruel and the Just," says Miguel. "I will get us home quickly!"

"But I want to stay," I say.

Children dressed as camels, birds, and dogs throw wild chamomile and dill under the feet of the camel. The subtle fragrance of the herbs rises and distills the sweet candy and heavy fried odors from the stalls.

No one will allow Lucinda enough room to pass.

Midget flamenco dancers throw lit firecrackers that

spook the camel. She sidesteps into a group of giant white-faced clowns on stilts that bob around us with red smiles. Huge fat men, dressed in striped suits, clap to the music. A band of young women dressed in tight red dresses have pasted fur on their faces and arms. Handsome young boys in blond wigs, costumed in pink shirts and silver tights, turn somersaults on a tightrope, high above us.

I start to tell Miguel that this is the best day of my life, but a drunken giant of a woman in a light blue dress slaps his leg.

"Miguel Svendik," shouts the giant. "How far did you have to go to find a woman who would marry you?"

"My bride, Tortugina Gomez," shouts Miguel. "This is Sheriff Nina Fumar."

Miguel kicks Lucinda's neck and tries to hurry us past.

A woman sheriff? I did not know such things were possible, though she is larger than any man I have seen. Her hair is wound in a bun the size of a small dog. The muscles in her neck and arms flex as she grabs Lucinda's rope and pulls us in the direction of the stage.

"You cannot leave us on such an important day, Tortugina," says Sheriff Nina Fumar.

Pacing the stage, a beautiful midget woman holds her hands out for silence.

"Welcome to Dia del Circo," she says. "Welcome to Miguel's new bride and future voter, Tortugina Gomez. I am Mayor Perfecciona Alban, named by my parents because I am perfect in every way."

A woman mayor? Such things are possible! Las Mujeres was well named, the village of women.

Miguel kicks Lucinda, but Sheriff Nina Fumar has the rope in her hand.

"Now, my friends, hear why," says the small mayor, "we are, as a village, superior in every way. Mothers, bring your babies closer to hear our story for the first time. Children, make way for your grandparents who have heard it all their lives."

The crowd is packed around us and pushes Lucinda closer to the stage. The mayor leans over and speaks to us as though we were all her children sitting in front of an evening fire.

"One hundred years ago, Las Mujeres was a dull place with dull people."

The crowd sighs in unison. "We were."

"One hundred years ago to the day, the wicked Señor Tattoo, Maestro de Ceremonias of El Circo del Tattoo, arrived with his circus."

The people boo loudly as a wiry little man in a blue suit struts onstage, his face and hands covered in painted blue tattoos.

"Here is our wicked Señor Tattoo, my friends! He abandons his circus and the poor players in our village."

The crowd throws water balloons at him, and the painted tattoos on his skin run together.

"But," says the mayor, "we are grateful to Señor Tattoo who brought us our glorious ancestor, Casimir the giant clown from Bohemia! Casimir's direct descendents please step forward!"

Led by the enormous sheriff, big villagers dance onto the groaning stage.

Although everyone else is having fun, Miguel looks desperate enough to hack his way through the crowd with a machete. With the sheriff gone, Miguel pulls on Lucinda's rope and kicks her neck until she finds a small gap in the crowd. We inch away from the stage.

The mayor waves for silence.

"Señor Tattoo also brought us the original Señor and Señora Enano, the tango midgets from Venezuela. I am that couple's direct descendent! Come! Come! Here are my brother and sister!"

A man and woman midget, dressed in flamenco costumes, stomp loudly on the hollow stage. The audience applauds as the two midgets dance heel-pounding steps with the mayor.

"Now welcome the hairy women," says the mayor, winded from dancing.

Young girls with hair pasted on their faces dance onstage.

"The original, glorious Señora Peludo was from the highlands of Peru," says the mayor. "Her great-great-granddaughter has managed to retain her furry inheritance and her beauty. Welcome, Señora Nauseobondo!"

We have traveled a few feet away from the stage when the villagers, especially the men and boys, yell loudly and throw bouquets at a slender, beautiful woman in a tight red dress and high heels. Light cinnamon-colored fur covers her face, arms, and legs.

"A kiss, Señora!" yell the young boys.

She is escorted onto the stage by a man in a dark tailored suit who looks four hundred pounds heavy.

"And the weightiest man in the village," says the mayor, "descendent from the pulpy loins of the original circus fat man from Brazil, the great Señor Flacido."

Explosive yells erupt as four more fat people are pushed up the steps and onto the sagging stage. The modern incarnations, the great-great-grandchildren of the circus, dip their heads at us slightly, like royalty.

"Miguel," I say. "Stop. I want to see this."

"And the camels from Egypt who pulled Señor Tattoo's circus wagons," says the little mayor. "Esposa and Esposo. We celebrate our beasts of burden."

Children dressed as camels jump onstage, beating white drums.

Miguel frantically kicks poor Lucinda, but the animal cannot move more than a few feet.

"But the finest performer was Miguel Svendik's great-great-grandfather," the mayor says, sweeping her short arm toward Miguel. "Thor Svendik, the triple-jointed Norwegian acrobat who wore a pink shirt and silver tights."

All eyes sweep toward Miguel, who is kicking Lucinda. He stops and cringes as boys with dyed blond wigs do wild flips onto the stage.

"Calm yourself, Miguel!" says the sheriff. "No one can escape their ancestors. Especially the cursed house of Svendik."

"The cursed house of Svendik?" I say.

There is silence, with all eyes turned on me until the mayor shouts from the edge of the stage.

"Miguel," says the little mayor, "you have not told your bride?"

"Yes!" snaps Miguel. "No!"

Dark anger creeps up the back of Miguel's bull neck. He violently whips Lucinda's neck. The packed villagers let us inch past the gauntlet of their solemn eyes.

The mariachi music begins with a heavy strum, and Mayor Perfecciona finishes her speech, loud enough for everyone in the square to hear.

"One hundred years ago," she says, "on this very day in

the Square of Don Pedro the Cruel and the Just, Señor Tattoo stole away with the circus money, after the performance. He was later killed in a fight over a crimson woman in the North. The circus people were abandoned in Las Mujeres, for which the village gives eternal thanks."

I turn at the loud roar of voices. Someone tosses a piñata shaped like a circus wagon into the air. Children grab sticks, shatter the papier-mâché wagon as it lands, and attack the candy like devouring crabs. There are many sides to paradise in Las Mujeres.

As the crowd breaks up into smaller celebrations, Miguel kicks Lucinda into a trot, past a blue and white taverna on the corner with a big sign, Señora Peludo's Taverna.

The hairy woman, in her tight red dress, who was dancing onstage, shouts at me.

"Hello, Tortugina. I am Señora Nauseobondo, the owner of Señora Peludo's Taverna. Come by for a welcome drink!"

I wave back, but before I can say anything, we are out of the square trotting down a small street. Lucinda knows the way past orange trees in full bloom. Under a green awning, there is a big shop with a large, open front door. Inside, a shiny tortilla machine chugs, with the squeak of pulleys. It sounds the same as Señora Porción's El Fuerte, but not as noisy. Tortillas ride the rollers out of the machine and fall into a large basket. Miguel reins Lucinda next to the door, where the old proprietress props her burning cigarette on her lower lip.

"Give me a high stack, Señora Flora." He tosses the coin into her hands.

The old woman rolls the steaming tortillas into brown paper and folds the edges tightly. Miguel reaches for the tortillas, but her blue-veined fingers hold the steaming pack up to me.

"Welcome, Señora Svendik."

Her white sleeves are so wide that when I look down from the camel's back, I see her pale armpits.

"You must be strong," says Señora Flora, "or the curse will affect the son in your belly."

I slide my hand over my belly. "What curse?"

Her milky eyes widen. "Did he not tell you?"

The old woman steps back and shakes her head.

Miguel nudges Lucinda down the winding road. His shoulders are at sharp angles as though he is hiding behind a rocky shelter, but he cannot escape the question between us.

On either side of the street, the houses get smaller the farther we ride from the center of the village. The roads become more twisted as they slope to the sea cliffs.

My husband's back is no longer a clean white slate.

"What curse, Miguel?" I say.

Lucinda snorts and pulls, anxious to get home. Miguel nudges her neck to pick up the pace and points toward the cliff.

"There is your home, Tortugina," he says. "Does it look cursed to you?"

Actually, it does. There are two identical houses perched on the edge of a cliff overlooking the sea, with a small path between them leading down to the sand. Both houses are painted a cold, pale purple on top and a horrible gray-blue on the bottom. They look like a pair of bruised breasts. All the other homes in Las Mujeres are tints of harmony. These colors strain the air, especially the lime-green doors and shutters.

Chapter 15

"Cousin Fecunda chose the colors," says Miguel, "and paid for half, so that I would paint her house too. Ours is on the right."

Miguel guides his camel down the dirt path between the unhappy glare of the two homes. The buildings are so close that we can look into each other's windows. The cousin's lime-green door opens. A dark, handsome man, dressed in canvas pants and a coarse white shirt, steps out onto the porch. He carries an empty box and closes the door gently, as though there were sleeping children on the other side. His muscles look strong under the rough cloth. He is the perfectly proportioned man that Gabito would have become.

"Ah," says the dark man. "Your green-eyed bride."

Miguel straightens his back. "Domingo, this is Tortugina Gomez. Señor Domingo Peres is the husband of Cousin Fecunda."

As Domingo Peres lifts his straw hat, the shadows of his face disappear. My heart believes immediately in the honor of him. His skin is deep with sun lines. His lips have been sculpted by the wind. His black eyes say welcome as no one has ever said it before.

"You have chosen well, Miguel," says Domingo. "Señora Svendik, it is my great honor."

Domingo hoists the box to his shoulder and walks down the sloping sea-path lined with tall pepper trees and palms. My lips want to wing like a silent bird to his dark neck and leave a kiss.

Domingo turns his head briefly, as though he felt it.

Again the cousin's lime-green door opens. The biggest woman I have ever seen fills the frame. Her naked children hold onto her shoulders, cling to her legs, and gnaw at her barnyard thighs. Her dress is too tight to hide the rolling bulk of her jelly parts. But her sandaled feet are delicate. Had a bull mated with a ballet dancer, this woman would be the result.

"There you are, Cousin Miguelito!" Her voice is a broken shovel through gravel.

Miguel's face opens to her like the legs of a woman in love. This is not the face he has shown me.

"Fecunda," he says, "have you had your child yet?"

Fecunda's laughter drowns the sea. She rocks on her feet. "You, of all people, cannot tell that I have dropped my new little fish in the pond of life?"

Miguel laughs as though she had kissed him. She holds up an albino infant with pink eyes. His laughter stops. Fecunda slaps her belly.

"I have many stories to tell you. Come have coffee and tell me about your adventures."

Miguel's voice changes.

"Cousin Fecunda," he mumbles. "This is my wife, Tortugina Gomez."

Fecunda's pale gray eyes move up and down my body as though she were rubbing out a spot.

"Is this as good as you could get, Miguel?"

I sit up straight on the supplies.

"I am the best my village has to offer."

Her eyes snap. "It must be a poor village."

Miguel presses my foot hard in a warning squeeze.

"Tortugina, Fecunda likes to tease. I know because we grew up together. She is a distant cousin."

Fecunda shifts two or three children, so that she can flex her hip toward me.

"Distant enough to marry," says Fecunda. "How is that for a tease?"

Her gray eyes are not teasing.

"He is married to me," I say.

I bare my teeth in a smile that makes the children cry.

Miguel quickly slides off the camel, pulls me into his arms, and escapes to our lime-green door.

"I will show you your new home, Tortugina."

Fecunda's shout stops him in his tracks.

"Come, Miguel. Have one cup of coffee, and leave the bride home."

He turns us around to face her. "Tomorrow, Fecunda. We must unpack."

Fecunda plucks at her children.

"Tortugina, if he will not come, then you come. I have stories about Miguel that you should know. Did he tell you about the curse?"

I look up into Miguel's angry face.

"I have heard, but I do not know what it is," I say.

"You did not tell her?" Fecunda laughs. "What a devil you are."

Miguel hugs me tightly to his chest. "It is just a silly story. There is no curse, Tortugina."

"One cup, Miguelito," says Fecunda, "if you know what's good for you."

Miguel makes the same sigh Lucinda makes at the end of a long day. He lifts his thick eyebrows with apology.

"One cup," he says. "I will be back."

Miguel puts me down gently and bounds across the dusty path to Fecunda's house.

I am left standing with my heart in my hand, like Gabito

by the side of the road. I do not know whether to be grateful or not at the sound of footsteps in the path. Someone will see my humiliation.

Señor Domingo returns carrying a box filled with flopping fish. He puts his burden on his stairs and cleans the smell of fish from his hands in a bucket of sudsy water.

"Pardon me, Señora," says Señor Domingo. "Would you like some help?"

I nod.

He makes Lucinda kneel with gentle strokes, and we begin to unpack the cargo. I can still smell the fish on his hands. We both stop on the stairs with packages in our arms when laughter spills out of Fecunda's kitchen. I do not like Miguel's loud laugh. Fecunda's rough bray tightens my stomach.

Señor Domingo looks at his occupied house with eyes that are infinitely sad.

CHAPTER 16

MAMÁ'S KITCHEN WAS her refuge. She was happy alone with her thick iron pans and fresh produce. I am merely alone on my first morning in Miguel's kitchen with its light-blue ceiling. I do not know where to begin to make it my own.

Domingo and I left Miguel's cargo by the wall, along with a few souvenirs. I am one souvenir of Miguel's trip, having unpacked myself, shed my shawl, and placed myself on one of his chairs.

I sip Miguel's bitter coffee and remember the well-ordered shelves of Papá's store. This kitchen is a woman's arrangement: the spacing of rice, flour, sugar jars, garlic, and herb clusters hanging on the wall, the stacks of pots on the stove. I think it must be Fecunda who oversees. I move the salt and pepper bowls from the side of the table to the center. Everything that was in some kind of order, I re-order, until I feel some of my disorder in the room.

Chapter 16

I cannot stop thinking of Señor Domingo's kind eyes. We have a sadness in common. If he came through my door again, with his dark calm, I would go to his boat and live with him on white fish and wine.

Miguel opens the back door with the late morning light behind him. I pick my steaming cup off the table and inhale the heat.

"Did you enjoy your cousin's coffee?"

He hangs his head and looks at the stacked packages piled along the wall.

"I stayed too long," says Miguel. "I did not mean for you to do this by yourself."

"Señor Domingo helped me."

That shames him. I get up and cut a slice of cheese and tomato for him, with hot chilies, and fold it into one of the old woman's cold tortillas.

He sits and I drop the plate on the table in front of him. He folds the sparse meal into his mouth until his cheeks are tight and churning. His eyes start to water.

It is the red peppers. Revenge is simple in the kitchen. He pushes the plate away and drinks a bottle of beer in one gulp.

"A good first meal," he chokes.

Wiping his hands on the tablecloth, he stands up and wraps his arms around me. My nose is crushed in the trail dust of his shirt.

"Have you seen the house yet?" he says.

I shake my head. He walks me into the next room that is so dark no shadows dwell there.

"This is where I come to be alone," he says.

Miguel opens the shutters. Afternoon light spreads across a dark wood floor. A heavy, hand-carved bench sits in front of a stone fireplace. The bench looks like Miguel, with its massive, carved back, thick curled arms, and powerful legs. A dark wood hutch suffocates one entire wall. Painted tin trays fill the shelves. On one side of the room is a dining table as big as a coffin, surrounded by high-backed chairs. People are irrelevant when it comes to this kind of furniture.

Miguel Svendik runs his hand over the table's stained finish. "This is my work."

He wants me to like it. But my eyes are drawn to a chair by the fireplace that is delicate of limb.

"That chair is my father's work," he says.

Geese flock in an intricate pattern on the back of the chair. A soft pillow on the seat is hollowed from use. I recognize the shape of the bottom. It is Miguel Svendik's nest for his silent moments.

Over the fireplace hangs a small painting of a foreign landscape with tall pointed trees, a beautiful yellow-ochre villa, a fountain, and a soft blue sky. It matches the light sky-blue of the ceiling.

"Why are the edges of the painting burned?" I say.

Miguel's eyes are suddenly on a journey past the fountain to the yellow villa. When his eyes return to me, they are wet with tears.

"My father burned all of my mother's things after she left us, but I saved the painting from the ashes."

Miguel lowers his thick body into his father's delicate chair. I imagine the fireplace filled with his mother's things: a smoking painting, melting gold, fine-fringed shawls turned to cinders.

Miguel sits forward in the chair.

Chapter 16

"My father wanted a wife more than he wanted to breathe. But he could not find a woman who wanted to marry him."

His voice sounds smoky, inhaling the singed memories of his mother. I stare at the painting.

"Was that because of the curse?" I say.

"Tortugina! That is a fairy tale! Some people are stupid enough to believe it, but I have proven it wrong, with you!"

"Will you tell me how?" I say.

"Later." He grabs a knife and a piece of half-carved wood from a small table next to the chair and begins to whittle furiously.

"Has this anything to do with your mother?"

"No! The story of my mother began when a white-haired professor came to dig at the ancient Indian ruins outside the village," says Miguel. "He was Italian. His young wife was called Celestina. It was said by everyone who saw her beauty that she was an angel."

Miguel's hard strokes carve the rough shape of a woman.

"My father was sent to repair the closet door in the professor's room. That is how they met."

He brushes the wood chips off his knee.

"One day the professor died in the ruins. Celestina buried the old man with the last of the grant money. On the way back from the funeral, Celestina sat down to weep in a grove of brilliant flame trees. My father came to comfort her tears. That is all he hoped for. But Celestina was a woman who had to love someone at every moment of her life. For the first time, my father felt a woman's touch, and then could not live without her.

There is a roughness in Miguel's voice.

"My father never understood why my educated Italian mother married him, a simple carpenter. I remember Papá was the happiest man alive, while she was with us. They did not speak much. Papá said later, copulation was their common language."

Miguel cuts the wooden figure into a slender body.

"My father built her this home and painted it red and purple, for the colors of his heart. After some time, Celestina began receiving letters from a man in her village. She left for Italy when I was four and sent us a piece of paper that erased our family. Father burned the annulment in the fireplace, with all that she left behind, except for me and the bottles of vintage wine. The painting is her family's home. She is buried there."

Miguel throws his crude carving of a woman into the fireplace.

"She is buried here too." He rubs his chest, as though his heart were tearing in two.

For the first time, I feel tenderness toward the man I married. He pulls me into his lap and presses his wet cheeks into my blouse. This dampness opens my heart in a way Angelicus Maximus never could. I rub the sun lines along the back of his neck.

"Tortugina," he says, "promise you will never leave. I will not have my sons suffer as I did."

"Sons?" I say.

"Promise," he says.

I let the moment carry me into a promise. "I promise," I say, though I have never been good at promises.

"Good," he says. "I want to show you something that I think you will like."

He lifts me off his lap and leads me to a beautifully carved door on the other side of the room. It is oiled but unstained, so the natural design of the wood has guided the carving of small angels. I do not need to ask.

"My father's work," Miguel says.

He opens the door. "This room has been waiting for you for a long time, Tortugina."

I step inside a large rectangular room painted dark blue. Lining the walls, I count twelve child-sized beds with thick, lovingly carved headboards. At the end of each bed is a child-sized set of hand-made carpenter's tools in an open wood box.

"You and I will fill this room with our sons," he says.

I place my palms over my belly. "Twelve sons can kill a woman."

"The boys will always have each other," says Miguel, "just as Fecunda's children have each other."

He picks me up in his arms as though I were a baby. "I have one last room to show you."

The bedroom, of course. It is crowded with more of Miguel's heavy furniture. Things he probably could not sell. A bureau, a desk, a chair, and a giant armoire with carved leaves. The headboard is covered in bloated cherubs. Covering the bed is a large quilt that droops onto goatskin rugs.

This room's ceiling is painted the same sky blue as the kitchen, the front room, the children's room, and the hallway.

"Why are all your ceilings blue?" I say.

He puts me down on a goatskin rug. "All ceilings in Las Mujeres are painted blue so the spiders will think it is the sky and not build their complicated webs over our lives."

"In El Pulpo, we knock them down with a broom," I say.

A musky smell is suspended in the room, as though the sex had started without us.

"Here, we will make my sons," he says and sniffs us both. "I think we could use a bath."

He opens a heavy door to the outside. The door is so poorly matched, it shrieks against the frame.

"I am better at furniture," he says.

A wide veranda overlooks a garden and the sea in the far distance. Purple bougainvillea twists up columns to the red tile roof. The warm afternoon air is filled with the scent of honeysuckle burning like incense in the sun. A stone-rimmed fishpond is filled with green lily pads.

"I have made you this beautiful garden," he says.

His green eyes gather in the colors of his work. One side of the garden is overcrowded with vegetables and dangling crab-sized flowers. There is a large patch of corn, ripe tomatoes, squash, melons, and grapes.

I work my finger through the hole in my pocket. What is left for me here or in the house? Everything smells of his hands.

"Maybe you should make your own children too," I say.

Miguel laughs. "Tortugina. We will have a hot shower and you will feel better."

He reaches above my head and unscrews a cap on a metal pipe that is sticking through the roof. Sun-warmed water soaks our hair, clothes, and skin. He undresses himself and me, then caps the pipe. With a wet sea-sponge, he soaps us both, and the soap falls onto the clothes under our feet. He stamps and twists his feet on his white soapy clothes.

"I wash my clothes in the bachelor way," he says. "You can do the same."

Chapter 16

I stamp and twist on my soapy clothes while we take turns sudsing each other's dusty parts. When the water falls on us again, it washes away the fragrance of the road. Miguel shakes his wet hair like a dog. I shake my hair too, since there are no towels here. We leave our wet footprints across the veranda tiles, over the goat rugs to the bed. I am almost too tired to sleep. We hold each other under the quilt and trap dampness between our skins. Breasts to nipples, we are the rule of two finding a balance. He rolls me stomach down, face on the sheet. His knees separate my legs. He pulls me backward, so that I am up on my knees. This is the mounting position for street dogs that I watched in the Plaza de Allende. Never again will I wonder how it feels for them. Angelicus Maximus pumps into my dampness. The explosion comes fast for him, but not for me. He is released into sleep. I am wide awake with the same unbearable ache in my woman's mound that he gave me on the camel. He rolls over on his stomach and spreads out like an octopus, until there is no place left for me to rest. I listen as his whistling snores use up what little air is left in the room. His furniture hoards the rest.

The cramping will not let me sleep, but I am learning to make it disappear faster than before. Miguel's wetness dries on my thighs as I slide over the sheets out of bed and into the afternoon warmth of the garden. The warm sunshine is a balm on my sore, naked, camel-bounced body. In case there are giants or midgets or furry neighbors lurking, I kneel behind the leafy vegetables and crawl down a furrow. The air is plant heated. My knees and palms plod the warm earth, over ripe melons. A tomato plant droops from too much ripeness. A rasping sheath of corn scratches my ribs.

At the end of the garden, I find one small patch of dusty red earth that Miguel Svendik has not yet covered.

I squat and relieve my bladder in the middle of the dust. This tiny piece of earth is mine. The loin cramp from Miguel's quick sex is gone now. I curl around the wet spot, nesting in the warm dusty earth, blanketed by the sun, and fall asleep.

CHAPTER 17

ACROSS THE PATH, Señor Domingo opens his lime-green door. He has come to know me as his early morning companion. A great wad of folded fishnet rests on his shoulder. He comes to stand beneath my window.

"Good morning, Señora Tortugina," he whispers. "I hope your day is good."

I give him a warm corn roll packaged in a palm leaf. He stuffs it in his woven lunch sack.

"You are very kind, Señora," he says and lifts his hat.

Below Señor Domingo's everyday words are deep tremors. Though he is so ordinary, when he speaks, it feels as though great plains shift below the surface of my life.

"You are a good friend, Señor Domingo," I say.

Whatever I say seems to please him.

From the veranda, I watch Señor Domingo's small figure walk to his boat with the net on his shoulder. My hot corn roll bumps in the lunch bag on his hip. He and another man, one of the giant Casimir clown clan, push their boat into the sea and jump aboard. My great longing to set sail with him has not diminished.

"Tortugina!"

Fecunda walks toward me wearing a long yellow smock that makes her look like a human sunrise. She carries her kitchen fork, and when she is close, she touches my chest with it.

"Keep your eyes on your own husband," she says.

She presses the prongs harder then raises the fork to her mouth, pretending to eat my heart.

"You came over for this?" I say.

She smacks her lips.

"Miguel wants you to work," she says, "to pay him the dowry you never had. He wants me to invite you to join our Women Divers' Cooperative."

I choke on my coffee. "Divers?"

"I hope that is of no interest to you," says Fecunda.

"When?"

"Now."

I have been waiting all my life for this moment. I throw the coffee cup into the garden and run to the bedroom. Miguel is awake and dressed.

"I cannot fix breakfast today," I say.

I slip on my pink swimsuit underneath my clothes. Since Mamá made it so long ago, it is a little tight. Today it will feel water for the first time. In the kitchen I throw a towel around my neck, grab a few tortillas, a bucket, and fly out the door.

Fecunda and children are waiting in the path with baskets balanced on their heads. Fecunda's iron hair is caked to her head with the grease of sleep.

"So, turtle-girl is going to join us," says Fecunda.

Miguel opens our front door. Tucked under his arm is his carving, the half-finished head of the Virgin.

Fecunda blocks him at the door with her hands on her hips.

"Miguelito," says Fecunda. "This is a trial. If there ends up being less money for me, she is fired!"

Miguel laughs.

"Cousin," says Miguel, "you call yourself a business-woman? With two more hands you will have more to sell."

Miguel feints to the right and then, when Fecunda moves, runs left around her big hips. He blows me a good-bye kiss with his chisel hand.

"Work hard, Tortugina, and do not disgrace the house of Svendik."

The "cursed" house of Svendik I want to remind him. My disgrace is always assumed.

Fecunda stamps her foot then turns on me. "Why are you standing there like an idiot?"

Fecunda's feet splay outward in a duck waddle. Her older children follow in a line, carrying the smaller ones on their hips. They look like a long, basket-headed animal. I follow them along the landscape of Las Mujeres that slides easily from land to sand, from sand to sea.

Red-eyed and looking straight ahead, Fecunda has more on her mind than the tiny albino clinging to her breast. Over the steady rush of waves, she shouts, "Cousin, I will watch you closely. One mistake, you are out."

I tighten the hold on my basket, reviewing what I learned from watching Gabito.

"Fecunda, if you are an example of the village divers, I am already better than any of you. You are lucky to have me."

Chapter 17

Fecunda grabs my shoulder with the hand that does not hold the albino. The smell of her sweat is harsh, garlic blended with baby vomit. The children scuttle away from us and disappear around an outcrop of stone.

"You are nothing more than a cursed Svendik bride! You have married into the house of Svendik because no woman in her right mind would have Miguel for a husband…including me!"

Fecunda's eyes are as wild as whitecaps.

"What is this terrible curse?" I say.

"If Miguelito does not tell you, I will not!"

Fecunda's great yellow bulk rolls like a keel-less tug over the sand. Her thighs rub together with a chafing sound. That woman cannot move without causing friction.

Far up the beach, a large cove with clear blue water covers miles of shallow reef. Huge whitecaps break at the edge of the reef and unruffle into smooth swells a few feet above the coral.

On the beach, three pregnant women sit and smoke pipes under a palm tree. They look older than me by a few years, but much younger than Fecunda. When they see Fecunda's children running toward them, they help each other up. I can only wonder about a village that sends its pregnant women to dive.

Fecunda pulls a pipe from her cleavage as the pregnant women stoop to hug the children.

"Rosa, Mimosa, and Auntie Patina," says Fecunda, "this is Tortugina Svendik. She thinks she is better than us."

"Not in all ways," I say, "but I can hold my breath to the count of four hundred."

Fecunda blows blue tobacco smoke. "You see what I mean?"

Instead of being impressed, the women look confused. The giraffe-necked woman in a blue smock slaps me on the back like a man.

"I am Auntie Patina. I saw you at Dia del Circo yesterday."

Her chin is even with the top of my head. Her skin is stained like a quilt with different shades of brown and pink. The patches of color seem to change as if she were moving through pockets of dappled light.

She frowns at me. "I have to say that we are not happy to share our earnings. In fact, there is little advantage for us."

I slap her on the back harder than she slapped me.

"I promise to out-catch all of you."

A squat woman with a bun of coppery hair and bright red lip rouge takes my hand. "I am Rosa. You are welcome, if we profit." She presses my palm to the red smock covering her stomach.

"It is kicking!" she says.

Her baby knocks itself against my hand. None of these women look like they can walk long distances, much less dive. Perhaps they hold rocks and sink to the bottom for their catch.

A shy, black-haired woman with long dark lashes and a pale smock holds her hand out. "I am Mimosa."

"Mimosa," says Auntie Patina, "you will teach Tortugina."

Mimosa's lips part in a big smile. The gaps between her teeth would leave a strange pattern on her husband's shoulder.

"Hello, Tortugina," Mimosa says sweetly. "Would you like to know what we do?"

Chapter 17

"There is only one question on my mind," I say. "Does anyone have enough good manners to tell me the secret of my husband's curse?"

Auntie Patina shakes her head.

"It is not manners we lack, Tortugina. We in the Divers' Co-op are businesswomen. Fair trade. Tell us a secret first."

That seems fair. I have many secrets that I do not want and so I will give them to the divers.

"I am married to another man," I say, "who I truly love. His child is inside me. I married Miguel Svendik because my husband is dead. But not really dead."

The women whoop, laugh, and slap each other on their backs.

"That," says Fecunda, "is the Svendik curse. Tortugina, you are the true destiny of Miguelito."

"I will tell her," says Auntie Patina.

The women take the opportunity to pull their pipes out of their smocks and light them.

"You know from the circus pageant about the young acrobat, Thor," says Auntie Patina.

"In the silver tights and pink blouse," says Rosa.

"He is Miguel's great-great-grandfather," I say.

Auntie Patina nods. "When the circus was abandoned here, he was kept by the ancient Señora Sepulchura and became her boy-whore. Even when her granddaughter married Thor, the old woman insisted on his favors. She became pregnant with Thor's child. It died inside her and could not be gotten out. She blamed Thor for her agony. Before she died she left this curse on her family."

The women in unison chant the curse: "May the house of Svendik suffer the curse of knowing only the pain of love without the pleasure."

"She cursed her own descendents," I say. "Could there be a more stupid revenge?"

"Welcome to the family," says Fecunda.

Fecunda gives her children a last hug. "Stay out of the water. Gather only fallen coconuts and do not die."

The children leave their baskets to be filled by the women, and run up the beach.

Fecunda and Rosa, Mimosa, and Auntie Patina unsnap big safety pins from their chests and spread their legs apart in the sand. They bend over their smock stomachs and stretch their hands through their legs. Pulling the back of their smocks up front, through their crotches, they pin the material on their waists to make short pants.

"How can you dive dressed like that?" I say.

The women smile and wade into the ankle-deep water. Their sandals crunch the reef skeletons. I pull my skirt and blouse off, ready for the dive in my pink-striped swimsuit. When I pick up my bucket and wade into the shallow water, the four women turn to stare and laugh.

"Where I come from," I say, "the divers wear swimsuits. They leap off cliffs fifty feet high and hold their breath."

Fecunda empties her pipe against her palm and sticks the stem deep in her cleavage.

"Tortugina," says Fecunda, "we can hold our breath too. Shall we show her how good we are, ladies?"

The women inhale in unison. With small knives, the women bend, twist, and cut black mussels off the rocks, tossing them into the baskets floating next to their knees. They stand and release their breath.

Chapter 17

Fecunda spreads her arms. "You see how professional we are, Tortugina. Now let us see you fill your whole bucket without taking a breath."

Fecunda's laugh starts them all laughing again. The heat rising in my face only makes the women laugh more. Rosa caws like a crow. Auntie Patina is louder than a mule. Mimosa's fingers cover the smiling gaps in her teeth.

"You call yourselves divers?" I yell. "You are a joke!"

Mimosa nods her dark braided head. "We are a joke, Tortugina. Fecunda named us the Deep Diving Cooperative thinking we might charge more if it sounded dangerous. But everyone knows we stand in a few feet of water and there are few difficulties in what we do."

My stomach feels like Lucinda kicked me. All those years of training, holding my breath, for nothing.

Mimosa wades over to me. "Tortugina, just do the mussels. The little red crabs are hard to keep in the basket. The gray and white patches in the shallows are oysters, but they are hard to cut loose."

Fecunda calls back over her shoulder.

"The most prized is the tiny green snail, 'carmelo verde,' because it is like a sweet green candy. We are lucky if we find a handful a week, and the villagers pay dearly for each one. Try to find those and impress me!"

Impress Fecunda? She'll be lucky if I do not strangle her. Mimosa pulls a delicate silver chain from her deep bosom. A tiny emerald shell hangs from it. She sucks the shell and holds it into the sun. It glows like a jewel with the moisture from her mouth.

"I wear one for luck," she says.

Fecunda, Rosa, and Auntie Patina lift their feet gently,

walking in different directions across the reef. Mimosa steps into the shallows. "Tortugina, stay away from the edge of the reef. A strong current can pull you out to sea."

The tide drifts out past my calves in foaming tails. Beneath the water are white and gray oyster shells, bunched close together. I grab, twist, pull, and toss them into the bucket until my knuckles are bloody.

I picture Señor Domingo with his white sail wide open speeding to my rescue. "Come with me, Tortugina, and we will never return to land!"

Spray soaks my back and interrupts my daydreaming. I turn and find myself closer to the edge of the reef than I meant to be. Danger has a current all its own, and I am made for it. Unless I dive, I will never know if I am a diver like Gabito. I let the deepening tide shift me closer to the edge. The water is up to my breast. A basket of shells rattles behind me.

"Tortugina!" shouts Fecunda. "Come back! Miguel will kill me if you drown!"

A giant wave breaks at the reef's edge and curls above my head. I inhale air as the water covers me. Doubled undertows drag me over the edge, shredding my swimsuit. A snaking current wraps around my waist and pulls me from warm surface water down into a cold blue valley. No bottom to the sea, no white sand to reflect the sun.

Swimming toward me out of the dark blue is a familiar face. Gabito takes me in his arms and cradles me out of the cold current upward toward the sun.

"Tortugina," says Gabito, "how I have missed your wild, sweet body."

His restored heart pumps under the membrane of his chest, and his bubbles are in my hair. Gabito covers my face with sweet kisses. I smooth his hair over the crack in his head and wrap my legs around his hips.

"Tortugina," he says. "It is impossible to gather enough of you in my arms."

His captain's suit floats off with my shredded swimsuit and we are naked. Gabito is inside me. He is perfect inside me, pushing gently, so that little José does not flinch in my womb. We move together, the same rhythm, the same time, we are the same. Gabito pumps so far inside me there is no more Tortugina. Then, a sudden sweet release of every muscle that has been clenched since Miguel left me aching on the side of the bed. Inside my flesh, I am as warm and loose as syrup, soothed in Gabito's sugar-brown arms. The burden of curses drifts away.

"Gabito, we must stay like this forever."

We are both so far inside each other's pleasure we can barely hold on.

"It is not your time, Tortugina. You must go home for our baby."

"I know." I wrap my arms tighter around his neck. "But no one here likes me. I am an outcast because of Miguel."

He strokes my face with his long fingers. "If I make the village love you, will you be content for now?"

"Can you?" I say.

Gabito gives me one long kiss, and I taste good-bye. Then he swims in a circle around my body faster and faster counterclockwise. The sea begins to swirl, with me in the center. Like a cork from a bottle, Gabito shoots me through the top of the waves into the air.

My reflection darkens the waves under me for an instant then shatters as my sandals splash safely onto the reef.

Rosa, Mimosa, Auntie Patina, and Fecunda are watery figures up to their crotches.

"Tortugina!" shouts Fecunda.

She churns toward me. The women follow her, a herd of heavy thighs and bouncing stomachs, plowing through the waves with panic on their faces. I think I recognize a chance for friendship in their eyes.

Mimosa is the first to reach me. She throws her long headscarf over my nakedness and takes my bucket. I did not realize I had it in hand or how heavy it was.

Mimosa looks down and screams. "My God in heaven!"

Rosa splashes close and looks inside. "Look!"

Auntie Patina sticks her giraffe-neck over. "Oh, bless you, Tortugina!"

I do not know what I have done until Fecunda reaches into my bucket and pulls out a fistful of emerald shells. She puts one between her teeth, sucks, chews, and swallows. A smile fills her face. Each woman pops a green snail, sucks, chews, and ends with a stupid grin.

Gabito's promise is fulfilled, but the change is so sudden, it feels like a nosebleed.

Fecunda puts a shell in my mouth. She is feeding me her gratitude. "Suck and chew."

My mouth fills with the saltiness of brined olives and the cool richness of fresh raw oysters. There is also something sweet and remote. No wonder they are a delicacy.

Fecunda, Rosa, Mimosa, and Auntie Patina cocoon me inside their arms and help me to the sand. The mixed scent of them is like home. Fecunda's garlic skin, Auntie Patina's wine breath, Mimosa's chopped mushroom earth scent, and Rosa's flower perfume. I let them drape their arms around me and dry me with their towels.

Tears would escape me if I had not had such practice holding them in. Approval, like sex, even with Gabito, is not entirely pleasant when experienced for the first time.

I am caught in the spider web of their friendship. Their appetite frightens me, but I am more afraid that they will not like the taste of me. This must be what it is like not to be Tortugina. A normal person, with friends, must live continually inside this confusing euphoria.

"Thanks to Tortugina," says Fecunda, "who is bound to me by the unshakable contract of marriage, we are all going to be very rich."

CHAPTER 18

MOTHERS AND DAUGHTERS crowd the long rows of market stalls filling their baskets with fresh produce. Bolts of colored cloth form hammocks between the roofs, filtering afternoon sun.

Señor Domingo guts perch in his fish stall, removing the gills, the head, then slicing fillets.

"Fresh fish!" he sings in a dark baritone.

Señora Acola sits on a small stool across from him, dividing her birds-of-paradise into bouquets. She sells plumeria, pink hibiscus, purple jacaranda, and Arabian jasmine fitted in large rusted cans.

"My plumeria brings luck in love!" she chants.

Across from our stall, the vegetable vendor shakes a dry gourd to the beat of his sale song. "Cactus makes your children strong! Avocados make them smart! Green beans for the blood. Peppers for their hearts!"

"Meat's a treat! Get your pigs' feet!" yells the butcher.

Chapter 18

In our divers' stall, I spread a thick layer of ice on the plank counter. Auntie Patina wedges oysters around the rim. Rosa packs mussels, like tiny headstones, into the ice. For decoration, Mimosa lays slivers of green palm next to the shells. In the corner of the ice, she places her blue ceramic bowl full of lemon-tree thorns for those delicate eaters who prefer pricking the green snails free of their shells.

As I work, I realize that this collective effort feels like purpose. That is what Mamá wanted me to know about Papá's store. It is not too late to learn. But it is having friends that changed my world, and the world has changed according to my new senses.

"My friends, soon you will be counting your money," says Fecunda.

She picks up a bell marked "For Emergencies Only." It looks small, but the loud clang breaks the song of the vendors. Villagers halt in mid-purchase, turning their heads as if all their bodies moved on one crank. Fecunda raises a tight-woven basket filled with my green snails above her head. Her great lungs reach to the far end of the market stalls.

"Neighbors, my cousin, our newest diver, Tortugina Svendik, has bravely gathered a full basket of green snails by making the dangerous dive off the end of the reef. Come and buy these treasures, while they last!"

Villagers abandon Señor Domingo's perch, Señora Acola's flowers, and the vegetable vendor's produce poetry. They speed toward our stall like a tsunami curls toward a beach.

Fecunda protects the basket by settling it right in front of her. Bodies crush through the narrow rows of stalls to our booth. With all the arms in the air, fists full of coins, it is like being eye level with the tails of a hundred wagging dogs.

A pregnant woman grabs my hand and will not let go.

"Tortugina," she says, "a handful, please. I must make a boy this time!"

"My father is sick," yells a young man. "One scoop for soup."

"Let me cure my life!" begs a ravaged man. "Three handfuls will do."

"Tortugina! Tortugina, Tortugina!" they shout.

Just as Fecunda predicted, we are surrounded by money. Selling as fast as we can, one scoop there, three scoops here, handfuls of snails into the palm leaf that Auntie Patina holds. She folds the green sides perfectly so that only the salty ice water drips out.

If the shells cure everything, why not a marriage? I slip a handful into my pocket.

Tiny Mayor Perfecciona wiggles through the bodies to the front. "Tortugina! Remember me? Give me two handfuls!"

I can barely see the top of her head over the counter.

"Twenty pesos, please," says Fecunda over the roar of her customers.

The mayor raises a small hand above the counter of ice and throws her coins in our tin box.

Señora Nauseobondo is right behind the mayor. "I must have those snails for my dandruff. Two handfuls." She drops the coins in the box. "If you bring a scoop of snails when you come to my taverna, you and Miguelito can drink as much as you like."

Chapter 18

She leaves with her package, and the villagers climb on top of each other to fill the gap left by the Señora's perfect hips.

"Tortugina! Take my order! Tortugina! Take my money!"

Two old women pull at my fingers as though they were milking them. To get rid of them, I shove a scoop into their hands without the palm leaf.

Fecunda grabs the coins that drop into the ice, but shakes her head. "Tortugina, we have standards. Please package the sales."

Suddenly Fecunda has professional pride. But the villagers have no pride at all. Old push young, women push men, mothers push fathers, daughters push sons.

"Getting rich is exhausting," I say.

Rosa and Mimosa cut more palm leaves, breathing as if they were plowing a field. "Tortugina, slow down."

Fecunda leans over, her lips touch my ear. "Tortugina, smaller handfuls. We will run out too soon."

Though Fecunda watches over my shoulder, I continue to give each person a true handful. They receive their snails like a benediction.

I work fast until there is only one handful of snails left in the basket. The villagers push, and under the pressure of their bodies, our bamboo stall begins to splinter.

A gray-haired woman grabs my freezing hand.

"Please, Tortugina. Let me have the last ones. My husband will die without them."

"He will die with or without the snails, Aurelia," says Fecunda. "Go home."

The gray-haired woman's eyes do not move from my face. I scoop the last handful for her. Fecunda catches my wrist and squeezes until the shells drop into the melted ice. She shouts over the noisy crowd.

"An auction for the last handful!"

Her answer comes with the force of their bodies crushing and splintering our stall. The ice tips, and the last handful of green snails scatter in the dust.

Villagers drop to their knees, picking up one or two muddy snails from the market filth. They stick the snails down their dresses or in their pockets or even in their mouths. One old woman lowers her wrinkled lips to the empty basket on the ground and drinks what is left of the snail water.

Rosa, Mimosa, Auntie Patina, and Fecunda are down on their knees picking up coins fallen from the tin box. All I can see are the shifting backs of shirts and crawling shawls.

Señor Domingo helps me up out of the debris, before stooping to help Fecunda find her coins.

Aurelia, the woman with the dying husband, covers her face and cries. I reach into my pocket and give her the few snails I had stored for my own use. She hugs me to her breasts. The feel of her reminds me of Mamá's warm embrace. She pulls out a coin.

"Bless you, Tortugina. Bless you."

I take her coin because I have professional standards too.

My throat is dry from the dust kicked up by the scrambling villagers. I lean over a water bucket and scoop a drink. There, in the dark liquid of the bucket, is my beloved Gabito, grinning his lopsided smile.

"Are you happy now?"

"Gabito. I feel as if I am standing too close to a bonfire."

"Happiness is always a mixed blessing," says Gabito. "Now you must give me something to relieve my suffering."

"Anything," I say.

"You must promise never to sleep with your pig of a husband again."

Is he crazy?

"Pushing Miguel out of my bed would be as difficult as rolling a whale off the reef," I say.

"Or," says Gabito, "the snails disappear."

That is the problem with favors. They can be taken back, and then you are twice empty.

"I promise," I say. "I promise I will find a way."

He knows I am no good with promises, but we both want it to be true enough. I hate him a little when he sinks back into the uncomplicated water bucket of his life.

CHAPTER 19

PAST THE SILENT pews, Fecunda lights our way through the church with a shimmering lantern. Her bulky silhouette is my guide.

"Fecunda, why are we here?" I say.

"For your own good," she says.

She turns down a short hallway, and we pass an elaborately carved altar. I have never noticed before, but now, in the lantern light, I am startled to see a large portrait over the altar. It is a woman, the most repulsive excuse for an old woman I have ever seen.

"Who is that?" I ask.

Fecunda holds her lantern up. Flames make romance of anyone's face, but not this creature. There are so many wrinkles, it is hard to distinguish the lips or nose. Only her unnatural eyes are rat-sharp.

"Señora Sepulchura," she says, "Miguel's great-grandmother. She is the woman who made the terrible curse on your family. She cheated the artist out of his pay, so he came back one night and made her even more hideous than she was." Fecunda laughs. "A good thing she was too blind to see it, but everyone else could."

She waddles to the end of the corridor with her lantern and pushes open a well-worn door. Inside is a plain room with a stone altar piled high with dry oat flakes and hundreds of melted white prayer candles.

"This is your salvation," says Fecunda.

On the wall over the altar hangs a portrait. This woman is even more peculiar than the hideous Señora Sepulchura. Her middle-aged face is strong, with intelligent blue eyes, and her hair is pulled back in a black bun. A black beard covers the bottom half of her face.

"Who is she?" I say. "The bearded lady from the circus? A relative of Señora Nauseobondo?"

"Show respect to Blessed Saint Uncumber," says Fecunda. "She has helped many women who do not want to sleep with their husbands."

"How?"

"By making them unattractive to their spouses. Now, put these oats on the altar and pray for help."

Fecunda sweeps the old oats off the altar. Now that I am snail-rich, she cannot do enough for me. I dump my fresh offering in a pile.

"Will this work?" I say.

"Tortugina, you wanted my help. I am helping you, but hurry. It is not good to be seen near the chamber of Saint Uncumber. Every husband knows why their wives come here."

"Dearest Saint Uncumber," I say, "I have made a promise to my dead husband, Gabito, not to sleep with my living husband, Miguel. I want to keep my promise. Please make me unattractive to Miguel. I pray not to wake up with a beard like you, dear Saint Uncumber, but let him find me repulsive in some way. Amen."

"I have another old wives' trick," Fecunda says, "in case Saint Uncumber fails you."

It is early evening outside before we return to my house. Fecunda pours the pig's blood, cold from her root cellar, into a small, thin bladder made of pig intestine. She shows me how to push it up between my legs. The chill of it sends shivers through my body. Even José shudders in my womb.

I stroke my belly to calm José. "Has this really worked?"

"Husbands see the blood and think they are harming the child growing inside you. Then he will leave you alone. If Saint Uncumber is not quick enough with her repulsion miracle, this is your insurance."

She helps me tie a rag between my legs to catch the blood.

"I will see you tomorrow, my little diver," says Fecunda, "for more snails."

She gives me a little hug and a small envelope of palm leaf.

"Put this powder in his bath," she says. "It is a relaxing herb and will slow him down. And remember, a good marriage is like everything in life, an arrangement of bribes, if not outright deceit. Men will do without sex if you frighten them or give them too much to eat or drink. I see you have set your table with that in mind."

The yellow tablecloth is spread under the flowered plates. A vase of daylilies sits in the center with a bottle of wine. Soup is hot on the stove. Dinner waits warm in the covered pan: a large beefsteak, rice, fresh carrots, and on the counter, a chocolate cake big enough for five men.

"Good luck tonight, little turtle," says Fecunda.

She pats my shoulder and swings the back door shut.

I am glad for a few moments alone, to ready myself for Miguel. The blood pouch inside me begins to warm, but there are still bloodstains on my hands. I wash quickly and change to an old robe that hides my figure. My hair slicks back into a greasy bun. Perhaps now there is less chance that my beauty will entrance him.

The big pot, boiling with bath water, is steaming up the kitchen. I empty the hot water and Fecunda's herbal potion into the huge tin tub beside the stove, adding enough cold water for a comfortable bath.

Outside, the clumsy clash of wood and metal of Miguel's toolbox serves as my warning. The door flies open. His body fills the frame.

"Tortugina," sighs Miguel, "you look beautiful." He sniffs. "Mmm, beefsteak."

In the doorway he shakes the chips and sawdust from his hair, strips off his filthy work pants and shirt, and drops them on the floor.

Standing naked, he steps over his clothes into the room and offers me a beautiful blue orchid, the gesture of a fully dressed suitor. The scent of a bean and garlic burrito from lunch still lingers on his beard. By the look of him, it must have been a good day for sanding. There is sawdust in his pores.

"Tortugina," he says, "last night I dreamt I was a boy again, sitting alone. No girl wanted me. Then you touched me and we danced all night. At work today, I painted the Virgin's lips to look like your lips."

His dry lips kiss mine.

"But I have an overbite," I say.

Angelicus Maximus presses against my belly.

"Please, Tortugina," says Miguel. "I have been dreaming all day of your cool fingers on me."

Fecunda says the first line of defense with men is hygiene. I wrinkle my nose.

"You need a bath," I say.

Angelicus bows his head. Miguel sighs and steps into the tub. As he sinks beneath the hot water, it spills over the side. His scarred knees are islands above the surface. He dunks his head under the hot water, blows bubbles, and sits up. Steam ribbons off the top of his thick hair.

He hunches forward, and I scrub his back with the sea sponge. When I finish, he relaxes back into the curve of the metal tub with a deep sigh. One-eyed Angelicus, distorted and soft, watches me from below the suds. This is the time I like Miguel best. Cradled in steam with arms curled between his slick legs, confined.

Very slowly, he stands up in the tub to be rinsed. Twice he nearly topples.

"I am feeling a little..." He grabs onto my shoulder to steady himself. "Carving this Virgin is killing me."

"You work too hard," I say.

A naked Miguel always reminds me of a grown bull trained to stand on its two back legs. I pour warm water over his shoulders and wash away the soap. Wherever my fingers touch, his flesh trembles. This is not the sign of a man who would embrace abstinence.

I help him out of the tub and drape a towel over his wide shoulders. It hangs open like a cape. He looks down at

Angelicus, and Angelicus looks up at him.

"There is an old saying, Tortugina," says Miguel. "But I am too full of steam to remember. Come here."

Miguel puts his wet hands on my shoulders and pushes me until I am trapped against the wall. The hot soapy scent of him is suffocating.

"Look," I say.

I reach down and pull my bloody rag into the lamplight and wait for his eyes to understand. Instead, they fill with tears. The tight rings of his wet hair shake with sobs.

"What is wrong?" I say.

"If there is blood," he says, "then our little baby is dead." There is such deep sadness in his voice that for a moment I believe him.

"Mamá?" says José.

"José, everything is fine." I speak silently to my son. "This is just strategy."

"José is not dead," I say. "Fecunda says this happens to pregnant women when the men are big as you are."

Fecunda also says, "Flattery is the second line of defense with husbands."

Miguel wipes his eyes. "One of the few things I remember my mother saying is that blood from a pregnant woman means the death of the baby. Who are you to argue with my mother?"

It is true, a wife does not argue with the mother-in-law. Now I am caught between logics: mine, his, and his mother's.

But I am also thinking of Gabito's angry face and the snails.

If I can keep Miguel off me with the excuse of pig's blood, then he will see my belly grow. He will be so grateful for a son, I can make him leave me alone until José is born. Perhaps by then I will have grown a beard or found a new excuse for celibacy.

"Let our arms console each other," he says. "Our son is dead."

I relax against the strong thump of his heart through damp muscles, still heated from the bath. He smells of rose soap and cedar. For the first time our bodies touch without sex binding us, just a pleasant congealing.

"Mamá?"

"Hush, José," I say silently. "Never spoil a good moment between parents."

I feel the full safety of the fortress that is my husband Miguel, his body offering nothing but comfort. His bearded lips brush my forehead.

"I know you are as sad as I am, Tortugina." His voice seeks to console me. "But we can make another son. We must make sure we have one in your baking oven at all times. I will be gentle. I promise."

My body turns as cold as Fecunda's root cellar. The drug in the bath has barely slowed him. The excuse of blood is not working. Saint Uncumber, where are you?

Beyond the horizon of his naked shoulder, on the surface of the steaming bath water, I see the green-snail friendship of Fecunda, Rosa, Mimosa, Auntie Patina, sinking below the surface and disappearing.

Miguel's body flattens my back against the spiny stucco.

"No!" I shout. "Not until the blood has all come out! It might poison your seed!"

Fighting for a lie takes the same effort as fighting for a truth.

Chapter 19

His fingers cuff my wrists to the wall. "My seed will plant itself in your blood and live!" Miguel's eyes are stone. "Tortugina! I want a son!"

He lifts my bottom until my toes dangle above the ground. Miguel grinds his weight against me, knifes upward, hammers against the bone. Even drugged, he is strong as a beast.

"Mamá!" shouts José.

I picture José charging out of my womb to kill Miguel Svendik.

With Miguel, it is always over fast, with one loud release of hot air in my face. He pushes off the wall. With his support gone, my body collapses to the floor. Angelicus Maximus settles back to innocent proportions.

Stooping over the tin tub of water, Miguel washes Angelicus again. The drying hair on his body forms spikes in the kerosene light. He inhales deeply and sniffs toward the stove like a dog sniffs a tree.

"Ah, beefsteak," he says. "Clean yourself and put my dinner on the table."

Wrapped in the towel, he leaves wet tracks across the floor.

Gabito's head floats up out of the tub. His eyes hold even more pain than Miguel's.

"I fought him, Gabito. I drugged him! I tricked him. I even prayed to a bearded saint. Please do not take away the snails!"

Gabito's head lashes out of the water.

"Why not kill him!" yells Gabito. "You killed me!"

I slap his cold face, and he shatters into a million drops.

My legs tremble so badly that I collapse next to the tin

tub. Inside me, José is breathless. He taps on the side of my womb.

"Is it over, Mamá?" says José.

I run my hand over my belly to soothe José.

"Yes, José. It's all over."

CHAPTER 20

MIGUEL STEERS MY pregnant stomach, swollen as wet wood, to his carved doors at the entrance to the church. His critical eyes appraise his version of Heaven carved on the left, his Hell on the right. Heaven is in perfect symmetry, with bearded saints in square robes. Their hands are folded, their eyes cast heavenward, faces rigid with redemption. But I am drawn to Hell. It is more like my life: fluid with tortured figures, edged with the unredeemed, a rough-hewn monument to the cursed.

I have always hated Miguel's Church of the Virgin. Gold-leafed and filigreed, wall to ceiling: altars, pews, alcoves. I prefer the simplicity of my old white church in El Pulpo, with one silver cross on a pale altar, a vase of flowers. At least there, if I had a problem to discuss, God could find me.

Miguel and I walk down the aisle of resentful stares, boos, and hisses from the villagers in their pews. Miguel is used to the status of outcast and oblivious to everything but my stomach. After nine months, I should be used to both. I did my best, diving again and again, trying to find snails. But without the help of Gabito, it was hopeless.

Rosa pretends that covering her new daughter, Rosita, with her shawl takes all the concentration in the world. She cannot spare a moment to greet me. Next to her, Auntie Patina bounces her freshly christened baby, the gray-eyed Gloria. Fecunda is too busy suckling her latest, Pilar, a stiff baby named after salt. Señor Domingo holds Albino and looks up at me with a patient smile. Mimosa entertains her clubfoot infant, Poncho, with her emerald snail necklace.

From these people I have learned the equation of life in Las Mujeres: no snails = no wealth = no friendship.

Little José splashes inside my belly, stirring a monsoon of gas. I am so tired of being ignored that I want to fart out loud. Passing Mayor Perfecciona, I let one loose, loud and sharp. The sound spurts into the farthest shadows in the church. Miguel's face turns the red of a bishop's robe, but Mayor Perfecciona still does not turn in my direction.

"Was that you, Señora Perfecciona?" I say.

Miguel muscles me into our pew in the first row where the cursed are closer to God. We sit alone except for Olivita, the cloth-wrapped leper, at the end. The barrel of my body lowers onto a fat yellow pillow that Miguel had the seamstress sew for me. My bottom spreads on the embroidered flowers with the delicate pink slogan, "Trasero de mi esposa, For My Wife's Ass."

On the main altar are inlaid red letters, a smug thought floating above the Virgin that Miguel carved: "PERME REGES REGNANT, Through Me Kings Reign." The

Virgin's fingers are raised as though all suffering were eased by a small gesture. The Virgin's calm blue eyes seem barely aware of the spikes through her son's crusted palms. He hangs in the alcove to the left, the crown of thorns clinging to his brow. The broken bones of his feet are nailed under him. If she could not help her own son, what can she do for me?

Behind us, Señor Domingo leans forward in his pew.

"How are you feeling today, Señora Svendik?" says Señor Domingo.

Fecunda kicks him. Miguel puts his arm around my shoulder and turns proudly.

"The Hermit rolled the bones and said my son will be here within the week."

"Congratulations," says Señor Domingo.

When he sits back, Fecunda hisses furiously at him.

I press the discontent of my back into the pew. My belly is so big, I cannot see my toenails. There is no maternal bliss in being bloated. José strains and turns like a trapped fish in the gauzy liquid of my stomach.

Padre Monástico flips through his Bible, and the villagers shift into quiet. I let my eyelids drop to nap position for the sermon. Instead of veins floating in darkness, I see José's face, red and water-wrinkled from my fluids. He touches the wall of my belly.

"Is it time, Mamá?"

His fingers feel the curve of my belly.

"It is never a good time to be born," I say silently to José. "This would be a particularly bad time. Why do you ask?"

José's hands clutch the edge of the prenatal abyss.

"Mamá, something is changing in here!"

Chapter 20

Sweat soaks my white maternity dress to transparency.

"Not now, José! I am in church!" I say.

Miguel lifts his hand from my steaming shoulder and wipes it on his pant leg.

"Tortugina, what is it?"

Without warning or pain, a pale waterfall pours out from between my legs. I clamp my thighs shut, but the liquid soaks the down pillow and drips from the pew onto the floor.

"Lord, we thank you," reads Padre Monástico, "for the blessings of the stars and the sea…"

"Help!" I yell. "My water broke!"

Padre Monástico looks up from the dry pages of the Bible.

"Holy Mother of God!" says Padre Monástico.

I cover my crotch with my hands. The trembling Padre crosses himself.

"Padre Monástico, my wife needs the doctor!" shouts Miguel.

Unaccustomed to staring between a woman's legs, Padre Monástico grabs the shoulders of a choirboy. "Where is the doctor?"

"He is delivering a calf for the cripple's wife," says the choirboy.

There is a terrible cramping in my belly, worse than food poisoning. A jagged shard of pain cuts across my back. Miguel Svendik kneels beside me and lowers my rigid back to the dry planks of the floor. He carefully places the Wife's Ass pillow of soaked goose-down under my head.

Below the Virgin's gaze, we are a wet nativity, not unlike her own emergency in the manger. More comfort should be coming from her painted eyes. I double up and roll the pain from side to side. Fecunda is suddenly there with her hands on my knees.

"Ah, cousin," she whispers. "Lie still. With a birth in the church, all betrayals are forgiven."

She raises her head and shouts to the back of the church.

"Señora Comadrona! Get your old bones up here. My cousin is having a baby!"

The floor creaks as the villagers rise and chant, "Señora Comadrona!" Their voices urge the old woman up.

Her stork-thin legs flap around the corner of our pew. Her leather pockets are full of small stones, one for each child she delivered in the last fifty years. As she lowers herself between my legs, Señora Comadrona's knees pop like firecrackers. She clucks to herself, "A new one. A new one!"

She spreads her shawl over my bent legs and removes my wet underwear.

"Bring water and wine!" yells Señora Comadrona. "Water and wine!"

Behind the Señora's stooped shoulders, Fecunda whispers to Rosa, Mimosa, and Auntie Patina. The altar boys, drunk on the blood of Christ, do not move. But Rosa, Mimosa, and Auntie Patina know where to go.

Another painful cramp, worse, tears through me. José's tiny fingers feel their way along the jellied lining.

"Ow!Ow!Ow! Mamá," says José. "I'm afraid!"

"Get out here, you little coward. You're killing me!"

Waves of cramping sweep the pain in like a storm. Above me Miguel chews on his stained handkerchief. Suddenly, the pain washes back, a receding tide. All the muscles slacken, off duty for a few minutes.

Chapter 20

My head rolls, my cheek rests against the cold floor.

A yellow cat pads under the dusty pew, followed by three orange kittens. Their fur is stained red from the colored glass of the window. The last kitten shrieks as a child steps on its tail.

Mimosa lowers a large bowl of water next to Señora Comadrona. The old woman takes the bottle of wine from Rosa and drinks a long drink. The rest she pours on my woman's mound. My stomach and back muscles are strained down to the bone. José must be as big as a calf. If only the small slit between my legs were a door with a simple latch.

Señora Comadrona kneads my belly with her palms.

"Push!"

José moves to escape, a fish paddling madly upstream. My ears are full of his pounding blood. I tighten every muscle to push him out into the world.

"You are no longer a welcome guest, José!" I say. "Out! Out!"

"Push!" says Señora Comadrona.

"I am pushing!" I yell.

José's head slips forward in my womb. The old woman's dry fingers stretch me.

"Mamá!" says José. "Make her leave me alone!"

"Oh, he is coming fast," says Señora Comadrona. "I have never seen a child come so fast. Your next child will be like spitting."

I would die now if I believed there was more of this to come.

"A few more pushes and he will be here. Push!"

There are no more muscles left to tighten. I bare my teeth at her to show I am working.

"Push harder, you lazy girl!"

If I were giving birth out of my nose, it could not be more painful.

"He is almost here!" she says. "Give me a rag to catch him!"

Miguel takes off his white embroidered shirt and drops it in the Señora's lap.

"Mamá," says José, "what do I do now?"

"Follow the water, José!" I yell. "Follow the water!"

"My head is in a vice!" says José.

"Get out here now or I will make you wish you were never born!"

"Push!" yells the old Señora.

"Shut up, you old witch!"

"PUSH!"

My muscles squeeze the soft bones of José's skull. His slick head slowly slides outward against tearing flesh. We are hurting each other for the first time.

The pain makes breathing impossible. His head rips through. Shoulders, stomach, ass, rubber legs. The last things to swim through are his tiny toes that feel like a trickle. Señora Comadrona cradles José in Miguel's white shirt, like one of her precious river stones.

Olivita the leper stares over her collapsed nose at my perfectly formed baby. Fecunda, Rosa, Mimosa, and Auntie Patina pass the bottle of wine with happy tears.

Old Señora licks José's eyes clean and puts one finger in his mouth to clear out any evil he sucked from me. There should be a lot.

"Mamá!" José screams as Señora makes a knot and cuts his umbilical cord with her old fisherman's knife.

Chapter 20

Blood sprays over her old face and Miguel Svendik's chest. José waves his tiny fists in the air.

"Mamá!" yells José. "The old woman cut off my penis!"

I am too exhausted to explain.

"You have another," I whisper.

"Tortugina, he is beautiful!" says Gabito.

Gabito, with golden epaulettes, hovers next to me and kisses my cheek. I burst into tears.

"Gabito, bastardo," I say silently to him. "Not a word for almost nine months?"

Dark hair is combed, he looks rested and almost normal.

"Forgive me," says Gabito. "I am sorry it has taken me so long to forgive. Let José's birth be a new birth for us, too."

I am too tired for a fight. His invisible voice is soft, tear-broken with longing.

Miguel reaches through Gabito and picks up José, wrapped in the bloody shirt.

"What lungs!" says Miguel. "Listen to my son! Listen to my son, everyone!"

"My son!" says Gabito.

"Our son!" I say aloud to whoever is listening.

Miguel lifts José into the air. The villagers can see my son's perfect body, the promise of his manhood, the flaccid, blood-streaked umbilical cord dribbling pink liquids on Miguel Svendik's bare chest.

"This is the happiest day of my life, Tortugina," whispers Gabito, and his breath touches my ear.

"This is the happiest day of my life!" shouts Miguel. "Let this birth remind you to temper your anger at my snail-less wife. Come to the taverna, and I will buy everyone a drink!"

The village cheers happily for the new baby and louder for the wine.

Padre Monástico waits until José is lowered then makes the sign of the cross over the tiny limbs. "This boy is a child born in church on the day of the Virgin. No child can be more blessed."

José reaches up and grabs the old Padre's finger. The Padre and José both gurgle.

Señora Comadrona pushes once more on my belly. Out slides a translucent red and brown mass with slippery sides. She drops it into the bowl of clear water.

"The placenta will tell us the boy's fortune," she says. "Then you must bury it under a tree and watch how the plant grows."

Padre Monástico looks down at the floating mass and claps his hands. "It looks like a church! The boy will enter the priesthood."

Miguel's tired smile turns to a frown. "That is a chisel if I ever saw a chisel. My son will be a carpenter like me."

Señora Comadrona shakes her head. "It looks like the head of a goat. He will be a shepherd."

She tips the bowl toward me, and I lift my head.

"It is a star," I say.

"A star," sighs José.

Señora Camadrona whispers a prayer and pats my face with her bloody hand. I feel her sticky print on my cheek. Rosa, Mimosa, and Auntie Patina help the old woman to stand, unbending her popping knees. The baby stones shift in her pockets.

"Pay me now," she says. "I must go to the river to find a special stone for José."

Miguel Svendik slips several coins into her stained hand. Then he kneels beside me and lowers José onto my wet breast. My little boy's bird-heart beats outside of me. His skin is softer than warm air. I cannot feel it with my fingertips. My little son, what is he but a piece of meat hugging a soul?

"You see," says Miguel Svendik. "Making love every night did no harm. We made a perfect boy. Look at the size of his balls."

"Hold on to our precious son," says Miguel. "I am taking you home."

I wrap my arms around José as Miguel lifts us both to his bare chest and carries us down the aisle.

I am sleepy with José's soft snore. His tiny fingers curl and uncurl on my chest. I am his blue sky. He is my little spider building his unbreakable, silken web over my heart.

CHAPTER 21

JOSÉ'S SCREAM WAKES me.

Miguel draws back a soft layer of mosquito netting around the four-poster bed. Señora Comadrona is behind him holding the lungs that woke me.

"Tortugina," says Miguel, "your son needs you."

José's musical voice that has been floating silently from my womb for nine months now sounds like a wounded crow.

"Feed me! Feed me!"

It is well known that new infants do not need to eat. New mothers are given a day of respite before they are sucked dry for the rest of their lives.

Señora Comadrona's stork face pokes through the mosquito netting. Her smile has almost no upper teeth and even fewer on the bottom rung. She unravels José from her bloody shawl and puts the screamer on my breast.

"José, don't be such a baby," I say.

Chapter 21

"Feedme, feedme, feedme!" José screams.

"What happened to your vocabulary?" I say.

"Cousin," shouts Fecunda. "Stick your nipple in his mouth."

Rosa, Mimosa, and Auntie Patina giggle and drink wine as they nurse their own infants. I had not even noticed them sitting with me like good friends.

"Thank you, cousins, for coming," I say.

I push José's tiny face into the dark brown nipple of my breast. Though it is not bloated with milk like my cousins' breasts, he fills his mouth with me. The slippery start and pull of his soft gums tugs softly into the rhythm of a heartbeat.

José chokes on his saliva and spits me out. Drool turns his tiny chest slick. His impossibly small razor-sharp fingernails squeeze my breast.

"MILK! MILK! MILK!"

Miguel plugs his ears, but there is no barrier against the lungs of a hungry baby.

"Do something!" shouts Miguel.

"José," I say. "If you suck, it will come."

José tries again. The suction of his mouth could carry a heavy chair across the room. I clutch handfuls of sheets from the pain. He spits me out again.

"MILK!"

Señora Comadrona lays one cool hand on my breast and elbows little José off to the side. José is outraged.

"MINE!"

The old woman's thin fingers squeeze my nipple so hard the pain sickens me. But still there is not even a drip of white liquid. The top of her old head leans over, her coarse gray hair rubs my chin. The almost toothless Señora sucks me so hard my toes curl.

"Help!" I yell.

"Dry chichis," she says, licking her lips. "I will go to the Hermit."

The old Señora winds a damp lock of my hair around her finger and cuts a curl. It disappears into her beaded pouch. She sticks her palm under Miguel's face.

"I must pay the Hermit for his remedy," she says.

"You cannot even breastfeed without costing me money, Tortugina." He flips the Señora a silver coin.

Señora Comadrona's stork legs carry her out the door, where she will tell everyone about my dry chichis.

"MILK! MILK! MILK!" screams José.

Miguel rips the mosquito netting open. He sticks his calloused finger in José's mouth to shut him up. I grab the sleeve of his shirt.

"Chichis are like people," I say. "They get frightened. Give them more time."

"His crying makes me crazy," says Miguel. "If you cannot provide for my son, Fecunda will."

"Milk is not the measure of a mother, Tortugina," comforts Gabito, as he settles next to me.

"How long have you been here?" I say.

"I never left your side," he says.

Fecunda undrapes her bright shawl with tiny silver bells on the fringe to reveal little Pilar feeding on one enormous breast. Fecunda has two huge troughs on her chest with enough milk to feed all the children, a herd of calves, and most of the dogs in Las Mujeres.

"Holy Mother of God, look at those," says José.

Chapter 21

He holds up his little arms to Fecunda's great dripping breasts. "Take me!" he screams. His fingers unclench toward her breasts.

"This is too much noise," says Miguel. "Teach this woman of mine how to be a mother, Fecunda. I will be in the backyard planting José's placenta under the banyan tree."

Fecunda gloats as she sits down on the bed with Pilar sucking gently on one breast. Fecunda's light-skinned newborn has a body as rigid as an ironing board. Pilar releases a man-sized belch.

Fecunda nestles José into position against her unused breast. José grabs her, sucks and roots.

"Gently, José," I say. "You are only a guest!"

José cries tears of relief with the abundant warm milk that spills into his mouth. Pilar takes delicate mouthfuls. José's cheeks bulge like coconuts as he gulps. As she looks down at José consuming her in great draughts, Fecunda shakes her head.

"Your boy is a greedy little feeder," she says.

José drains her limp while Pilar is still sucking delicately on the other half-full breast.

"Tortugina," says Gabito, "look what our son did!"

"Are they not supposed to do that?" I ask.

Fecunda picks up her empty breast and waves it like a slice of ham.

"After eight children," she says, "I have never seen such an appetite."

"MORE MILK!" cries José.

He plants his tiny feet against Fecunda's fat and lunges at Pilar on the other breast. Pilar spits milk at him to defend her territory.

Fecunda lifts José and drops him on my chest wet and wheezing from the short flight. His mouth opens and closes, reminding me of Señor Domingo's perch deprived of the sea.

"That beggar needs another breast," says Fecunda, "and it is not going to be mine."

The bed rises a few inches as Fecunda stands.

"Here we are!" say Rosa, Mimosa, and Auntie Patina, herding themselves over to the bed with their new babies. Infants are crushed between rolls of cousin fat as the women exchange places.

Rosa puts little Rosita down on the bed. She opens her blouse and draws out one enviable breast. She has small purple nipples shaped like lily pads. Her cheeks, covered in peddler-cart rouge, curl into a wide grin as José reaches for her.

"It usually takes one lullaby per breast to put Rosita to sleep," she says.

She begins a lullaby, but José drains Rosa flat so fast there is no song left in her eyes. Rosa's painted green lids drop tears on José's head.

"Look how ugly the little beast has made me," says Rosa.

"With this kind of appetite," says Fecunda, "he will be so fat in a week, you will have to diaper him with a tablecloth."

The women all laugh. Mimosa with her clubfoot infant, Poncho, takes a turn and is sucked limp as a wet sock. With Auntie Patina's contribution from her multicolored breast, José's tummy finally reaches maximum bulge. He settles into sleep with white bubbles drying on his open mouth, snoring like an old dog.

The women pass the bottle of wine to replenish themselves. Rosa is drunker than the rest and bangs the bottle down on the nightstand.

Chapter 21

"Shall we see what this little beast has to recommend him?" says Rosa.

She unpins José's diaper. As she pulls back the flaps, the cousins whistle.

"Oh, he will be popular with the women," says Rosa, licking her wine lips.

"Balls like a ripe peach," says Mimosa.

Fecunda pulls José's penis, stretching it as far as it will go. José awakens with a contented gurgling smile and returns to his slumber.

Gabito, who has been silent through all this, winces.

"Tortugina, it is not a toy! Give my son's penis some respect!"

I push Fecunda's hand away from José.

"What are you doing to my son?" I say.

"A man needs all the help he can get," says Fecunda. "You must do this for him. It is our gift to the daughters of Las Mujeres."

José's little member is straight up like a vote.

"When the boys get older," says Mimosa, "they tie on stones to lengthen themselves for marriage."

"I have never done such a thing!" says Gabito.

In his sleep, José pees against Fecunda's chins. The women laugh as she wipes herself with a clean diaper. They bundle their infants quietly so as not to wake José and his appetites. Fecunda with Pilar, Rosa and fat Rosita, Mimosa with club-footed Poncho, Auntie Patina and Gloria of the gray eyes disappear out the door.

A scent rises off José, as though he had been stored separately in soft cheese. His little lips against my breast stir such quiet pleasure that I never want to move from the warmth of this position. Is it possible that I, Tortugina, can be distracted from my dream of being a diver by this wondrous delivery? Gabito wraps his arms around us as we nestle into the sheets, and it seems almost possible.

A breeze from the garden's tangled scent floats through the window. I kiss the top of José's head, lightly layered in golden-brown hair. My mouth fits over his tiny fist. I count his fingers with my tongue. He gurgles and smiles with a little sigh.

"Oooh, Mamá," says José. "So far, I am very pleased with life."

José is happy.

I am exhausted.

"What do you know of life, José?" I say. "Feeding at the breast of women, the feel of sex."

José burps. "There's more?"

As long as my little José lies in the arms of a woman, he will be content.

I close my eyes and I am inside his baby dream. He floats in a woman's arms. Her vast face that is mine looks down at him, and he looks up at me and sees a human landscape. Clouds of black hair over soft dune shoulders, my smile, longer than a coastline. I have cliff-white teeth, and my nostrils are sea caves. He opens a hinged door in my womb and climbs in.

Someday José will have his own moustache, and what will be my compensation, my prize, for bearing the tyranny that loving him will have over my life?

Part Two

As the world grows older and no wiser,
High-stepping to the same ruined tune,
What can we do but dance together
And retreat to the insanity of love?

CHAPTER 22

ABOVE ME THE dark pouches of Miguel's face quiver with almost sixteen years of disappointment. His matted loins pump up and down between my legs in the morning's ritual thrust for sons.

"Give me sons, give me sons," chants Miguel.

Trembling hair halos his head. He drops enough tears on the furrows of my flannel nightgown to sprout all those unborn carpenters. Finally, with a sigh and a dribble, Angelicus Maximus once again releases his little fish inside me. Miguel rolls off my body praying still louder.

"Give me sons. Give me sons."

His rage for heirs is worn in our sheets. He sits up and spits away evil spirits around the bed that he is certain are making me barren.

"This time I have gotten you pregnant! I know it!"

He wipes his eyes with a balled fist and blows his nose on the sheet.

Chapter 22

"At least we have José," I say.

Miguel drops back into the sheets and closes his eyes. He drools now when he sleeps. His lips move in his dreams that never bring peace in sixteen years of such effort. Only when he eases into the darkest slumber do the woodcut lines of anger disappear.

I slide to the edge of the bed. My naked thighs are wet with the unborn. I plug my feet into worn sandals that take me to my own morning ritual.

The only thing beautiful left in me after all these years is my black hair, which swings in a long braid. My overbite has gathered wrinkles. My laugh lines are frowns. But I still have my sweet dreams of Gabito, and when Gabito is angry with me, I dream of Señor Domingo Peres and his dark Indian face full of our unlived love.

Squatting on the damp tiles of the veranda, I loosen a brick in the wall and pull out a bottle of vinegar and a small sea sponge wrapped in a bag. I soak the sponge with vinegar, hold my breath, and shove it inside me.

"Do not give me sons. Do not give me sons."

At the first rush of vinegar, Miguel's small army of carpenters drop their tools and die. It is easier to think of them as faceless battalions rather than potential sons. If it were not for Fecunda's vinegar remedy, eleven sons would have buried me by now. The lining of my woman's mound is sore, raw, and burnt from the years of genocide. A smear of aloe spreads enough cool jelly to lighten the pain.

Under the shower pipe on the veranda, sun-warmed water dilutes my acrid scent. I blot myself dry and watch the fishermen's white-winged boats sail onto the sand with their catch.

Señor Domingo is always the first to leap off his boat. I will buy one of his fresh fish and cook it for José's birthday.

Quietly, so as not to wake Miguel, I dress in what has become my uniform: white blouse, blue skirt. My sandals are better trained than puppies. They know the way to José's room.

José does not like me watching him sleep. But today he is sixteen, and this is the only time to count the years on his face.

The light in his room filters through a small window above the bed. On the sill is his first Madonna carving that showed his promise. The face belongs to the skinny neighbor girl, Pilar. No one in the village is quite as plain or mean as Pilar, and yet José has loved her since they shared Fecunda's breasts as infants.

Hooks on the wall hold his few clothes. There are no pictures, only a small black-and-white poster of a traveling show. José's carpenter tools lie in a box at the foot of his bed. Over his bed is his carved pine plaque with block letters in the old style: "To touch heaven with my work."

It is a well-kept room, for a boy. The eleven smaller beds of unborn sons are stacked to the ceiling in one corner. My husband keeps his dream in an inconvenient pile. José lies on his side. Curly black hair spreads across his pillow. He is hugging his own honey-brown shoulder.

I kneel by his bed to worship my son's adolescent face. Under long dark lashes, José's eyes rush back and forth following a dream. He smiles, moans, presses his hands down below the sheets. This is the time I should leave, but I do not.

I enter his dream just in time to see Pilar, who has taken on the proportions of a voluptuary, lower her soft green robe below a rosy bottom. Her dark eyes look at José. Together, she and he breathe in a duet of flushed skin. I leave his dream as quickly as I enter and pull the sheets up over his shoulders. The church bells ring loudly enough to open José's eyes.

"Happy birthday, José," I whisper. "Do I need to remind you that Pilar was born a nun? It is not coquetry that she ignores you. It is blind indifference to anyone but Jesus."

José squints sleepy eyes at me.

"Please stay out of my dreams, Mamá."

I kiss the swell of his brown cheek.

"Sleep as late as you wish. Your father will not make you work today."

In my kitchen the day begins, as it does every day in this bruise-colored house. Roosters crow up and down the winding streets, answered by the street-sweeper's song and the steady foot-patter of children running for morning tortillas.

Little Salvador tosses me a paper-wrapped package of hot tortillas through the kitchen window. I lean out and drop coins into his hands. He gives me a quick smile because I always add an extra coin.

Five tortillas for Miguel, five for José, three for me, flat in the hot pan with a layer of sliced tomatoes, melted chunks of soft cheese on top, cilantro and peppers, and a big cup of coffee with sugar.

José's appetites are free to roam today. He will not return home with wood chips in his hair. Even when I give him enough coins for the whore Esmeralda who lives at the edge of the village, he'll spend his day spying on Pilar. My poor son will die a virgin if he saves himself for that pure vessel.

Gabito leaps from the water bucket like an acrobat and smooths his navy uniform. Unlike the rest of us, nothing changes with Gabito. He is always the same half-beautiful man. I no longer see his fault lines.

"Ready for José's sixteenth birthday?" I say.

Gabito's eyes overflow with excitement. We have become such good friends that we tolerate each other's nonsense. He ignores my marriage to Miguel, though true to his word, he will not give me the snails back. Since there is time enough in my dull life, I can comply with the demands of a second husband. It is a small consolation for Gabito that there is no pleasure for me in Miguel's pumping ritual. Gabito can see from my face that I barely tolerate my wifely duties.

"Today our son is sixteen," says Gabito.

I promised him that on José's sixteenth birthday, we would tell him Gabito is his father, but I am afraid of what will happen.

"Do you still want to appear to José and tell him who you are?" I say.

Gabito adjusts his damp wool jacket and turns so that I can see only his bad side.

"Look at me, Tortugina," says Gabito. "I am in shreds. The boy not only has a dead man for a father, but there are no fathers uglier than me. Think how disappointed he will be when my..."

Gabito replaces his weeping eye in his socket. It has been a long time since I noticed Gabito's leaking face, the thin membrane that protects his heart, his lips that curve in an unnatural smile.

"You see, I cannot control anything. He will hate me. I just cannot do it."

What he really means is he has not finished mourning his perfect beauty. But I am so deeply relieved that I speak out loud to Gabito as though we were husband and wife in the real world.

"Then we won't tell him," I say. "It will be for the best. José might tell Miguel. And this is what will happen to me if Miguel Svendik finds out José is not his son."

I slap the table as though killing a bug. Gabito jumps and we laugh.

"You see," I say. "He even frightens you."

Pipe smoke from Magdalene drifts into the kitchen. I turn quickly to see Miguel's bull shoulders filling the doorway. He is barefoot, and smoke pours out of his nostrils.

"José is not my son! Is that what you said?"

The only time I spoke out loud to Gabito in my house, and Miguel was there to hear me. My fingers tighten on the cup.

"What is wrong with you?" I say. "Of course he is your son. I was joking with God. We are like that together."

Billows of Magdalene fill the room. Miguel seems to be on fire. "Tell me the truth!"

"Tell him the truth, Tortugina," Gabito says to me.

I try to drink my coffee, but Miguel knocks the cup out of my hand.

"Tell me!" he yells.

"You know you were first," I say. "You saw my virgin blood."

Miguel's lips turn white. "There are women's tricks!"

All our years of no babies are rushing toward me.

"José looks nothing like me," says Miguel.

It is true. Thank God. José looks exactly like Gabito, except for the destruction. Gabito snorts from his superior position on the ceiling. I hear my voice losing conviction.

"He has your skill with wood," I say.

A weak, embarrassing lie. José is far better than Miguel. I move so the table is between us. Miguel trembles like an earthquake, and our wall of illusions crumbles. For once we look into the deceit that is our lives.

With a brutal cry, he lifts the table up over his head, the legs pointing at the ceiling. He straightens his arms, and the table legs plow four holes into the sky-blue stucco that falls around us in pieces.

Miguel throws the table at the window, and the glass shatters.

"Who is José's father?" yells Miguel. "Tell me the truth!"

His brows are thick as thorns.

"You, you are his father!"

Miguel grabs my braid and jerks me off my feet. He twists the braid around his hand. My roots are screaming. He drags me over the wood floor, over the threshold, into the backyard. The red dust billows up my skirt. At the woodpile he grabs the newly sharpened hatchet. My heart is a wild caged thing. I kick at him and scream, "Help!"

He pushes my head down on the wood block. The grooves gouge my cheek.

"Tell me who the father is!" he shouts.

The heel of his hand, the full weight of him is on the side of my head. My eyes are watering. He raises the hatchet. I want to tell him the truth, though the words cling to the back of my throat.

"Tell the bastard, Tortugina!" yells Gabito.

Chapter 22

"José was fathered by a ghost. Gabito. I killed him by mistake. It is you, Miguel. You are the only father he knows!"

Miguel's hand pushes harder on the side of my head. If I were a melon I would have burst by now.

"José is not my son," he says. "No son of my loins walks this earth!"

He raises the hatchet over his head. "What have you done to me, you whore!"

The hatchet blade slices toward my neck. I twist away and feel hands grab my hips and jerk me back from the chopping block. Not fast enough. The blade slices through my braid and the skin on the back of my head. Warm blood flows down my neck, over my shoulders. The wound is a dull ache, a terrifying run of liquid. I am shaking too badly to run, but I crawl behind Gabito.

Miguel kicks my bloodied braid off the chopping block and wedges the blade out of the wood. Raising the hatchet again, Miguel steps straight through Gabito to me.

"Whore!" yells Miguel.

José runs into the yard toward me with a bath towel around his waist.

"Papá!" screams José. "What are you doing?"

José kneels beside me, strips the towel off his body, and holds the cloth against the back of my head. Poor José has known Miguel's temper all his life, but this is the worst he has ever seen.

Miguel stands over us breathing hard. He spits at us, turns, and throws his blade into the trunk of the banyan tree. I feel the force in my skull.

"Papá, my tree!" yells José.

At the base of this tree, sixteen years ago, Miguel planted José's placenta. "Tortugina! You see what you made me do!" screams Miguel.

He stumbles across the yard toward Fecunda's house.

"Help!" screams José. "Someone help!"

CHAPTER 23

BEHIND OUR CLOSED shutters, Señor Domingo uses black fisherman's thread to stitch the cut on the back of my head. The smell of fish on his bloody hands turns my stomach.

José's job is to blot the trickle of blood and lay slices of aloe on the wound.

My job is to drink myself painless. We are all drinking, a very good bottle of old red wine that Miguel left behind, saved from his mother's time. After all, we are celebrating José's sixteenth birthday. It is a special wine, a special day, and a special bloodletting. So far, neither has asked what the fight was about.

"José," I say, "I am sorry this has turned out to be such a bad day for your birthday."

Gabito rages and, pacing the kitchen, swings his short naval sword in the air.

"Bastard!" he says.

Chapter 23

José pours us all another glass of red wine in my mismatched glasses.

"Ah, well, Mamá," he sighs. "You are alive, at least. And sixteen is such a sad year, anyway."

Domingo ties the bandage around my head just tight enough.

"Why do you say that it is sad, José?" asks Señor Domingo.

José drinks half his glass before he answers.

"I am at the age to marry. I want to marry Pilar, but she ignores me. She will not come to my house, and not once has she thanked me for my gifts."

"I thought everyone knew she intends to be a nun," says Señor Domingo. "With her limited nature, she is well suited."

"You will find another girl," I say.

"NEVER!" says José.

José finishes his glass. This is a strange day, without solutions.

Miguel's voice and the smell of his pipe float across the path from Fecunda's. Señor Domingo's sad eyes are weighted as a hound's. He is having as hard a time as I am trying to ignore them. Even if I close the shutters tight, there is always enough space between the slats to hear their laughter.

José hands me a yellow scarf, and I cover my bandage. The balm of superior wine does not erase the pain completely. José fills our glasses again and we raise them.

"Happy birthday, José," I say. "We still have our tradition. Open my present."

He opens the soft brown tissue tied with dried grasses. It is the same every year. I have no imagination for such things. I left a little sentiment under the grass bow. José slides it out and reads aloud.

"Tonight is the sixteenth year you have been my son. I have loved you all your life with all my heart. Love, Mamá."

José unwraps the shirt I sewed so carefully. It is soft white with glowing silver threads of embroidered turtles. He takes off his old shirt and stretches into the new one. The white against his golden skin stops my breath. I made this shirt, this beauty, and this boy. He kisses my cheek. There is the soft start of a moustache above his thick red lips.

"Another shirt. Thank you, Mamá," he says.

"It is beautiful workmanship," says Señor Domingo.

José brings me a long, newspaper-wrapped object. It was his idea to give me a gift on each of his birthdays.

"I made this for you," he says. "Sorry, Señor Domingo, I did not know you would be sharing my birthday, so I have no gift for you."

Señor Domingo nods. "I am honored that you allow me to join you."

José has carved me another Virgin. Virgins line my shelves. His first baby-made statue was a block of soft balsa with grooves and bumps that matched the ups and downs of my life. As he grew, his Virgins assumed my face, chiseled with my hollowed overbite and sad edges. He became skilled under Miguel's careful teaching, and his Virgins grew thinner as I grew thinner, with arms open to encompass small hopes. That is when I began to look as I do now. Even in soft candlelight, this Madonna looks like a woman who has given up on prayers. Her face is true to my darkest moments. His Virgins are my mirror. But there is only so much reflected truth one can take at this stage of life.

"Do I really look that bad, José?" I say.

Chapter 23

My fingers move lightly over the statue's face.

"Bad? No, Mamá. Just you. Should I have lied with my art?"

I pat his cheek. "Yes."

"I will make her younger," he says.

"Next year," I say.

Señor Domingo turns the statue in his strong hands.

"José, you are a finer carver than your father. I would like to hire you to make me a figurehead for my boat. That is your birthday present."

I have never seen José so dazzled since he reached puberty.

"Señor Domingo, this is the best gift you could give me. I have always wanted to carve bigger. Thank you. You will have a figurehead that will be talked about in every village!"

Gabito has sheathed his sword, and his transparent fingers stroke the fine folds of the Madonna's robe.

"Our son made this beautiful thing, Tortugina," he says.

He stands behind José proudly. Their brown eyes are so alike, each pulling at my heart from his own world.

A quiet knock on the kitchen door interrupts us.

"Papá?" whispers José.

We do not know anyone with such a courteous knock.

"Who is it?" I say.

José's chair squeaks as he gets up and walks through Gabito to the door. Gabito touches himself where his son passed through him, tears welling in his eyes. He floats to the kitchen counter and sits, bewildered by the two sides of himself, love of his son, fear that José will hate him.

José takes a stumbling step backward from the open door. He is having trouble breathing.

Pilar stands in the doorway with the morning sun behind her. A white collar surrounds her bony face.

"Pilar," whispers José.

Pilar's flat black eyes peek around the room and settle on Señor Domingo. She steps inside and delivers her commandment.

"Father, Mother said to come home." Her razor voice could geld a ram.

Señor Domingo is no longer smiling. "My daughter, Pilar. She herds our family like sheep."

José puts his trembling hands in his pockets. "Pilar, what an honor. Please sit. It is my birthday."

Pilar's eyes are fixed on her father and her mission. "Father, come home."

"Pilar," says Señor Domingo, "where are your manners? Sit down and wait until I have finished my business in this house."

Pilar's eyes kick from side to side like flames caught in a breeze. Her black nun shoes do not move.

Poor José's legs are trembling beneath his pants.

"Please sit just for a moment, Pilar," says José. "It would honor me."

Pilar may as well be watching José from behind thick cloistered walls. As he moves, his foot catches on the chair leg and he trips. He catches himself and pretends he meant to pull the chair out for her. His eyes draw upon what little beauty she has to nourish him.

"I am going to tell Mother you refuse to come." Pilar turns to the door.

"No, wait, Pilar!" says José. "Wait! Talk to me!"

Pilar disappears out the door into the morning breeze, and José runs after her.

"I love you. I have always loved you!" he yells.

Chapter 23

Gabito dives through the door after José. I am left sitting beside Señor Domingo. We watch the late morning haze outside my kitchen door.

"I apologize for my daughter," he says. "Perhaps I should go."

Because we are alone, I look at Señor Domingo in a new way.

"Stay," I say. "You have saved us from a very sad day."

"It is you who saved me, but then, all my days are sad."

These words from a man who never complains. It must be the Italian wine, so full of sentiment. I know why he is sad, but I pretend I do not know.

"Why are you sad? You are the finest fisherman in the village, and all your children are healthy."

"Those are my blessings," says Domingo. "But I am weak. I allow Miguel to come every night to my house and drink with my wife because it pleases her. He pretends my children are his. Today I was going to kill Miguel. It was José's cry for help that saved me from a murder."

I tug at my scarf.

"Then my mutilation has worked well for everyone."

He sees the humor in my eyes. I want to put my hand on his lined face, to feel the skin of this man, but I do not.

"You are a man of great patience and restraint, Señor Domingo."

Señor Domingo's eyes are tender.

"Please, after so many years," he says, "call me Domingo."

He bends forward slightly to encourage me. I whisper the sweet informality.

"Domingo," I say.

When I inhale, I do not breathe air. I breathe him. His smell of fresh fish is growing more like sex. I whisper again.

"Domingo."

His fingers brush my hand. It is a relief to be touched by a man who is not my husband.

"Since the first day Miguel brought you home on the camel," says Domingo, "I have always wanted to tell you, we share so much more than our mutual suffering."

It is almost painful to move my hand away from him.

"I am sorry, Domingo," I say. "My concern is for my son."

"Mamá?"

José is framed in the door like a carving from the Hell side of the church door. His face is red. His eye is swollen shut. His hair looks like someone tried to pull it out by the roots.

"It did not go well with Pilar?" I say.

"It is a beginning," he says, looking back and forth between Domingo and me.

"Is Señor Domingo my father?" says José.

I cough up my wine. Domingo laughs.

Gabito floats through the door and stands shoulder to shoulder with his son. Both have one good eye now, and their good eyes are raging at me.

"Tortugina," says Gabito, "my son thinks this man is his father!"

I can only ignore Gabito when he is like this.

"You know who your father is," I say. "Why do you ask, José?"

Señor Domingo smiles. "If you were my son, José, I would be proud to tell you."

"Señor Domingo," says José, "you look at Mamá the way a man looks at his beloved."

"I do care for your mother," says Señor Domingo.

Gabito bellows like a bull stuck by the picadors, one sharp wound to ignite his temper.

"And I do not look like Papá," says José.

"I hate to disappoint you on your birthday, José," I say. "But there is no man alive who is more your father than Miguel."

The candles flicker as Gabito bats himself angrily around the room.

"What do you want me to say, Gabito!" I say only to him.

José smiles. "Then Pilar is not my sister?"

Señor Domingo laughs again and shakes his head. "No, José."

José picks up a half-bottle of wine.

"My birthday wish has come true. Pilar came to my house. I am going to my room to drink and dream of our wedding."

Gabito spins in his own confusion until even the hanging garlic begins to move in the breeze. "Tortugina! I want to tell José he is mine! I have to tell him! I do not know what to do!"

Gabito's grief is too big for my kitchen. He flies out the open door with the most terrifying scream I have ever heard.

I am afraid he will return. I am afraid he may never return.

Domingo and I part chaste. He and Miguel Svendik pass each other at my door, each man seeking the bed of his wife to snore off the liquor.

CHAPTER 24

A HORIZONTAL RAIN floods the veranda. One moment it is silent, the next, a storm out of nowhere. Wild gusts uproot my tomatoes, peas, and squash, sending the plants sprawling root over root against the fence. Church bells ring an alarm, but I do not know the crisis.

I step out onto the veranda and pull my shawl over my head at the sound of a terrible crash. A dead seagull slides off the roof in a waterfall of broken tiles.

The once dusty lane between my house and Fecunda's is now a brown stream of rushing water. Sheriff Nina Fumar's giant body shuffles down the watery path headed for the sea. She carries little Mayor Perfecciona on her shoulders.

"Follow me! Watch your feet! Bring rope!" shouts the little mayor. "Domingo and the fishermen are caught in the storm."

Domingo! He knows the sea better than he knows his own wife. I run into the house and bang on the doors of José and Miguel.

Chapter 24

"Wake up! Emergency!"

Without waiting for them, I leave the safety of the veranda with a rope slung over my shoulder. Wind and rain tear at the yellow bandana, drenching my head bandage.

Señora Nauseobondo splashes down the path in a man's big boots and canvas pants, carrying a brandy bottle. Farmers, storekeepers, municipals, bartenders, drunks, and Padre Monástico, all hastily dressed from their early awakenings, carry ropes and blankets toward the beach.

Fecunda's door flies open. The warm rectangle of light breaks to pieces in the wind. Fecunda, a force of nature herself, plows into the dark storm, her eyes stretched with fear. Behind her, the children carry hooks and ropes and a wool blanket. Fecunda is not thinking as she tries to run, steps too fast, slips, and belly-plunges forward into the stream.

She shakes her head and wipes her eyes with one hand. She is shaking too badly to rise. She howls into the storm, "Domingo!"

I step into the flow of brown water and rush to her side. "Fecunda! Get up!"

Fecunda pushes herself up into a kneeling position. We balance each other as she rises. Roots, stones, and bits of wood bump our legs as we are swept down the flooded path.

Fecunda and I, the children, Miguel and José splash out of the wild, unbounded torrent that trenches down to the sea. We are the last of the villagers to reach the beach.

With strong ropes and the strong backs of the villagers, Aurelio's bucking blue boat is hauled beyond the grasp of the sea and left tilting on the sand. Rafael's boat, Salvador's boat, Nicola's boat. They are pulled one by one from the sea. The boats are safe, and the fishermen are safe, swarmed by their families, swathed in blankets, and drinking Señora Nauseobondo's brandy. Only Domingo's yellow boat is still tossing high in the waves, too far away for the rope to reach.

By the sea's edge, Fecunda beats her head in a helpless dance. No part of her is strong or long enough to save her husband. In the blinding wind, it is impossible to see if Domingo is still on the boat.

Fecunda screams, "Domingo!"

"Papá!" scream his children.

Sheriff Nina Fumar's massive bulk wades into the waves with an anchor hook tied to a long rope. She herself is tied to a long rope held by a line of men. Sheriff Nina spins the hook in a wider and wider circle above her head and finally throws it with all her force at Domingo's boat.

The hook falls short.

A towering wave sucks Domingo's boat into the curl and pushes it toward shore. Sheriff Nina throws again, and this time the barbs catch on the inside of the hull.

With a roar heard over the storm, the villagers run to help the line of men haul the boat ashore. Fecunda, the children, José and I, even Miguel with a bleary hangover, all pull on the rope that will save Domingo.

The storm tries to take the boat out again, but as one village, we pull Domingo's boat toward the beach. If we had hooked a whale, it could not be a worse fight.

I look up into the sky and silently beg Gabito. "Gabito, help him! I will never forgive you if he dies!"

As the boat is drawn closer through the savage waves, we can see that Domingo has tied himself to the short, broken mast. He waves to us, unties the ropes around his waist, and grabs an oar.

Long legs of lightning run stilted across the sky. Suddenly a flash, then a jagged streak pierces the clouds and strikes Domingo. For a split second his wet body is frozen in the light. And then he is gone.

"Domingo!" Fecunda is not alone in the wail that rises into the wind from the hearts of all the villagers.

We pull and pull, but the boat grows heavier as the cracked hull takes on water. At last Domingo's boat rests on shore, a black burn mark near the mast, through the hull, but no Domingo.

"Damn you, Gabito!" I yell silently at him. "You could have saved him!"

Fecunda's face is pale with disbelief.

"How can this happen to a man who calls the sea his mother?" she wails into the storm.

I stop breathing to stop time. If this moment passes to the next, it will begin the time in which Domingo is dead.

The children stand silently, as we all do, hoping the sea will give us back the body of this beloved man to bury among his family.

Sheriff Nina Fumar's giant body waits with patience in the freezing surf. Finally she shouts over the roar of the ocean, "There he is!"

Moments later, a black, loose-limbed form is thrown ashore. The sheriff races to pick up Domingo before the sea sucks him back. She lays him on the beach.

Fecunda and the children run toward him. The wind makes no dent in her now.

Villagers gather around the family in a protective circle. Domingo lies in the center, his blackened skin welded drum-tight across his bones. His eyes and mouth are drawn shut. His teeth are set to greet death.

"Domingo!" wails Fecunda.

Two of the sons wrap their father in the wool blanket.

Padre Monástico's wet white hair blows in the wind, and he makes the sign of the cross over Domingo's burnt body.

I leave the circle and lean on Domingo's boat for support, the part of his boat that carries the name "Precioso, Beloved." I will always remember that he was the best of men. José comes to stand beside me. Perhaps he is thinking of the beautiful figurehead he was going to carve for Domingo's boat.

Domingo's sons pick up his wrapped body and put him on their shoulders. He must weigh almost nothing with all the meat of his muscles charred to a crisp.

The dark gray clouds and wild wind are gradually draining back to the sea, leaving the sands washed clean.

Miguel supports Fecunda as we all follow them up the dune and through the brown stream. José trails a few feet behind Pilar. I am last in the procession, hugging the small comfort of perhaps having known Domingo's last loving words.

The lime-green door opens, and Fecunda's house fills with wet people and death. Domingo will need to be washed, the family consoled, a meal cooked.

I walk to my side of the path through layers of silt and wood. The backyard is filled with broken limbs and split tiles. There is cold comfort in the lighter rain. I let it wash over me, let it feel like tears because I cannot cry yet.

Chapter 24

The fishpond overflows. Carp flip in mud puddles. I scoop their orange bodies back into the water. Sitting on the stone, I watch them send ripples from below. A death howl rises up inside me, but before the tears begin, a pair of dark eyes float from under a damaged lily pad.

Gabito rises out of the water. Raindrops run off his skin like oil as he climbs out of the pond. His boots are topped with waterweeds.

"Tortugina," he says. "So many tears for another woman's husband?"

He props himself up on the stone next to me. I shiver as he leans closer. His smile looks blood-stained.

"He was my friend, Gabito. He was the only one who was kind to me. Why did you not help him?"

Gabito scoops up a tiny orange carp and gently places him back in the water.

"There was nothing I could do. I do not have such powers."

He watches two carp below the surface swimming together. There is bitterness in his voice.

"Last night, I knew I could never tell José I was his father. Then I thought I had lost you too, to Señor Domingo."

I move away from the touch of his wool jacket. Gabito holds more darkness in his heart than I ever knew.

"Señor Domingo was killed for a smile?" I say.

"I did not kill him!"

He says it with such force that I want to believe him.

"Perhaps that is true," I say, "or you would have killed Miguel Svendik by now."

He drags me up and over to the corner of my house and points to Fecunda's kitchen window.

"Look, Tortugina," he says. "Miguel Svendik is dead to you already."

Inside Fecunda's kitchen, with Domingo lying burnt on the long breakfast table, Miguel holds Fecunda tenderly in his arms. He enfolds her, a gentle expression on his face. I have never really seen them together, not like this. His embrace is sweeter than all the sex in the world. I can see it is a good love.

Now the tears begin, and I am certain they will never stop. Gabito wraps me in his arms as though I were very small. He still smells like home, El Pulpo, and the green smell of the sea. I am as beloved to Gabito as Fecunda is to my husband. Whatever Gabito has done, he is my only love. He holds me tight.

"Ah, Tortugina," sighs Gabito. "Things will be so much simpler for us when you are dead."

CHAPTER 25

THE CEMETERY IS overgrown with untended flowers trumpeting up the walls of the yellow limestone church. On the shale roof, an old cast-iron weather vane points to the cove where Domingo died. Gray clouds spin apart in the cold sea air.

I hold José's hand for warmth. Loose candy wrappers whip against our polished shoes as we walk toward the edge of the crowd. The lunch I cooked smells good on José, fried potatoes and onions.

In the freezing gusts, crowds of mourners gather around the closed coffin of Domingo. Black hats, black dresses, black shawls and jackets dark as crows. It is strange in Las Mujeres to see everyone in one color.

José leans gently against my shoulder, holding a small replica of Domingo's boat, "Precioso," to leave at the gravesite. He looks at the closed coffin.

Chapter 25

"Mamá, what do the dead look like, when they are not burned up?"

"The same as in life, José, only more formal."

Domingo, Domingo, I will only remember you as you were. You are loved for so many reasons. You will always be recalled with the taste of fresh fish in our mouths.

Padre Monástico licks his lips and prays in silence as the last of the villagers take their places around the upturned earth. At the head of the closed coffin, Fecunda and her children stand so close to each other in their mourning clothes that they could have been cut from one piece of cloth.

Above the wind-shaken pages, the Padre raises his hand in a gesture that includes us all.

"Let us sing the fisherman's lament, to lighten our sorrow that is as heavy as one of Domingo's halibuts on a bed of rice and greens with a side of cloved prunes."

Fecunda looks up at him, but she says nothing. Padre sings with the voice of a castrato. His mouth is surprisingly large for such a little-boy voice.

Take our brother, oh Lord.
He swims with the fish,
The fish he once caught.
The fish we once ate.
A good man swims
With the fish. AMEN.

It is much easier to picture Domingo swimming with the fish than lying in the cold earth. We all want Domingo to swim from the sea with his net, ready to feed us again.

The chorus is broken by Fecunda's hawk screech. Her body lurches onto the creaking support planks that hold Domingo's wood coffin above a six-foot hole. Her gloved hands lift the heavy, carved lid and push it off. In the dark-stained rectangle, Domingo's charred Indian face seems to float above the whiteness of the sheet.

"Domingo!" she wails.

Fecunda lowers her body into the coffin, covering poor Domingo. I expect his legs and arms to flail, but all I see is Fecunda's rump. Support planks crack under her weight.

The giant arms of Sheriff Nina Fumar drag Fecunda off the coffin just as the planks give way. The coffin tips. Domingo's head hits the top. His black shoes bounce once above the wood rim as the coffin drops through the broken planks into the grave. Fecunda wails into the wind, and even the cormorants are thrown off course.

Mayor Perfecciona pats Fecunda's thigh. "Fecunda, you are behaving like a jackass," she says. "Drop the lid gently on the coffin, gentlemen, and let us continue with the dignity this man deserves."

Miguel Svendik moves slowly to Fecunda's side. His footing is certain as he stands beside her. Whenever Miguel is this close to me, I have a terrible itch on my head. The scab on my scalp remembers the raised ax, the missed weight of my braid.

He looks up at me as I scratch my black scarf. Fecunda must feel the heat of his gaze leave her. Her thick elbow jabs his ribs. He is caught breathless by the blow. She points at me through her tears.

"Tortugina, you dare come to my husband's funeral, you whore. You seduced my Domingo in your kitchen last night!"

Chapter 25

Mayor Perfecciona snaps her fingers at Fecunda.

"Fecunda, enough! There's a time and a place for slander!"

The villagers' eyes widen with interest. "This is the time and place! Let her speak."

"Very well, what is your retort, Tortugina?" says the mayor.

They turn to me as though they were all attached to the same weather vane.

"Señor Domingo was kind enough to come for José's birthday," I say. "I invited him because Miguel has abandoned us for Fecunda's kitchen. Miguel and Fecunda drank together almost all night. Señor Domingo kept us company until Miguel came home."

Fecunda leans her widow's bulk against Miguel. The weight would crush lesser men, but her touch makes him younger. He has a glow that only comes with the kind of love I have seen in Gabito's eyes and recognize immediately.

"Fecunda and I were together," says Miguel, "but not alone. We were with the children having dinner. Is that right, Pilar?"

Pilar's head nods up and down like a long-beaked heron spearing minnows.

"Domingo and I were with José!" I say.

Miguel's face streams with tears. "I do not care, Tortugina! I have lived too long under the unhappy curse!" Miguel speaks in a voice that comes from a heart I did not know he had.

"I want happiness! So, with all my heart, I, Miguel Svendik of the cursed house of Svendik, declare my undying love for my cousin Fecunda Peres and her children."

A cold wind blows under my scarf. The villagers speak in outraged whispers.

"This is bad luck!"

"Domingo is not even buried yet."

"Perhaps he can hear them."

Fecunda speaks to the crowd with no shame in her voice.

"I declare my love for Miguel Svendik. I will live with him, as his wife, but there will be no marriage because of the Svendik curse, and because of Tortugina. If you remain my friends or not, it makes no difference to me. You still have to buy my shellfish."

Wives cling tightly to their husbands. It was easy to ignore Miguel and Fecunda's love for each other as long as it was hidden. But to witness it in the daylight, to confront such passion in the cemetery, they must all face the fragile nature of their own unions.

Fecunda leans close to Miguel and kisses him on the mouth. If a face could shatter from joy, it would be his.

"Shame, Fecunda!" shout the villagers. "Shame, Miguel!"

For one fleeting moment, I am no longer an outcast. I am on the same side as the villagers.

"Shame on you!" I shout.

José, anger flushing his face crimson, looks up at Miguel.

Miguel is not finished. He waves his hands for attention and speaks in a voice as flat as Pilar's eyes. "You, José, are not my son. You and your mother, I disavow!"

José's beautiful frescoed face crumbles with confusion.

"But I am your son!"

"Ask your mother," growls Miguel.

"Papá, how can you call me a bastard in front of the whole village?"

José throws his small carving of Domingo's boat at Miguel, runs through the crowd and out the iron gates.

"Tortugina," says Miguel. "Look what misery you have made."

"Miguel," I say. "Look what misery you have made!"

I pull the black scarf and the bloodied bandage off my head and turn to show the villagers my wound, a huge scab with black stitches. A cold breeze makes the wound hurt like teeth on ice.

"This is what happened when Miguel tried to cut my head off," I say.

His deed registers in the long memories of the villagers and in the eyes of Fecunda.

I step closer to the mud-slick gravesite so that Fecunda and Miguel can have a good look.

"You see, Fecunda," I say. "You see how Miguel Svendik serves love? And you, Miguel, you have tethered yourself to a fat sea cow for the rest of your life! Who am I to not wish you well?"

I throw the blood-dried bandages at Fecunda, a rosy gift for the pretend bride. The back of my head is a silent accusation as I walk slowly away, letting my footsteps retreat along the same path José has taken.

CHAPTER 26

THE VILLAGE CHILDREN sing outside Fecunda's window:

Señor Domingo is hardly dead.
Fecunda takes Miguel to bed.

Fecunda's gray breakfast smoke soots my windowsill. Her house still hogs the sunrise. Through the closed shutters I watch Miguel step out onto the top step of Fecunda's house, yawning and stretching as though he owned it.

Fecunda's life has changed so little. One morning her tent dresses hang in the closet next to Domingo's cotton shirts, the next day it is my husband's coarse pants that are draped in the dark beside her shapeless wardrobe. With Domingo gone, I am more widowed than Fecunda.

"Tortugina?" Gabito rises from the sink, glorious in his pressed naval jacket, bright red cummerbund, tight white pants, and boots he has polished to a wet shine. He wears the silly captain's hat that sits on his head like a giant snail.

Chapter 26

"What are you dressed up for?" I say.

Gabito adjusts his blue jacket and white tights.

"I have decided to tell José," says Gabito. "Should I appear to him all at once or gradually?"

I am tired of tragic men.

"Do it this time, Gabito," I say. "He has lost one father. What could be better for José than to know he has another father who loves him?"

Gabito clicks his black leather heels together, smooths his hair, and stands up straight. He was never this nervous on the cliffs. Now that Gabito is finally ready, his nerves spread to me. This could end so badly.

"He will not talk to me, Gabito," I say. "This is his first day as a declared bastard, and that is very different from yesterday."

"Take my hand, Tortugina," says Gabito.

I feel the coolness of his damp skin. So much hope in his eyes, it may blind him to good sense.

"Be very gentle with how you do this, Gabito," I say.

I lead the way to José's door. There is no answer to my knock.

"José, I am coming in."

His door is the only one in the house that opens without a creak. José is still dressed in his funeral suit and sits on ink-stained sheets. Wads of paper litter the floor. He writes with the same intense gaze he has when he carves, his tongue making his mouth into a Q.

"José," I say. "Please forgive me. I am sorry I lied to you. Your real father is Gabito Ramirez. He was the most handsome and best octopus diver in all of El Pulpo."

He looks up for only an instant before turning his eyes back to his writing.

"So, I am still a bastard," he says.

"Your father was killed by the sea," I say.

"Be honest with him, Tortugina," says Gabito.

"It was my fault that he was killed by the sea," I say. "An accident."

"Then my father is dead?" says José.

"Not truly dead," I say. "He loved me so much that he came back to me as a ghost. We married and you were conceived. I married Miguel Svendik to give you the name of a living father."

José looks at me as though I have eaten an infant.

"Gabito, he thinks I am crazy. Show yourself!"

Gabito holds his head in his hands, beats his damaged brow with both fists.

"What a wonderful birthday," says José. "I find I am a bastard, and the son of a ghost and a madwoman. Thank you, Mamá. Thank you, Papá."

"José," I say, "this is not a joke."

I gesture toward Gabito, who stands inside the door, shaking as blood and sweat pour off him.

"He is right in front of you, José."

José stares through Gabito at the door, waiting for an entrance.

"Gabito!" I yell. "Do not do this to me!"

Gabito rubs his damp hands on his pants. He kneels in front of José and touches the boy's face with his transparent fingers.

"José," whispers Gabito, "I am so sorry. I thought I could do it."

Gabito closes his eyes, not willing to witness his own disaster.

José folds the paper with the blue ink into his jacket pocket.

"Well, Mamá?" says José.

There is no pity in his eyes.

"I have written to Pilar asking her to marry me. We will live far away from you and your madness. You will not tell me who my real father is because you are ashamed of him."

"No, José," I say. "I am not ashamed of him, or you!"

Never before has José left me without a kiss.

He walks right through Gabito, and my poor idiot ghost of a husband dissolves with a cry.

CHAPTER 27

"TORTUGINA!"

It is the bullroar of Miguel. He kicks the back door open as though it were still his to destroy.

Miguel's wide body in my doorway blocks the soft light behind him.

"José pasted this poem on Fecunda's house," says Miguel. "It is an obscenity."

He throws the wadded paper at my chest. José's wrinkled, looping scrawl charges across the page with passionate swirls:

FOR PILAR
Little Pilar, your beauty all the world can see.
I declare my love for you in this decree.
I know you love Jesus and not me.
But the son of God cannot give you a baby.
Say you will be mine and marry me!
All my heart,
JOSÉ

I am glad he chose carpentry as a profession.

Miguel shifts just enough in the doorway that the sun streaks into my eyes.

"Tell José," he says, "that he can never court Pilar."

For once we agree. "Yes, as a wife she would be useless."

"Not that," he says. "It is because she is my daughter, and I will not allow your bastard near my daughter!"

He swings his carpenter kit away from me and turns to his day of grain, stain, and wood, chiseling old deities with new faces. With his broad back as my target, I throw a barb.

"Pilar is no more your daughter than José is your son," I say.

His shoulders rise as though I had actually stabbed him. He drops his wood kit and turns on me.

"You need a lesson!" he says.

I know those eyes. I know what they can do. My head wound feels hot.

"Not again!" I say.

I grab an iron poker with both hands. There is madness in my eyes. Miguel retreats backward out of the doorway, ready to defend himself. Swinging the poker in front of me, I follow him to the gate. He hurries into the path, never taking his gaze off me, and disappears behind Fecunda's lime-green door.

The morning clop of Lucinda's splayed hooves rouses me out of my anger. The camel gallops up the path at a heroic pace. Lucinda's sloppy face is breathing hard. On her hump are tied bushels of bright flowers. And riding on top of the bundle is my disheveled son.

"José!" I shout.

José speeds the camel by me. Spittle hangs in necklace loops from Lucinda's lips. Her small furry ears rotate as she sees me.

"José!"

"Stay away from me!" shouts José.

Following the compass of love, José steers Lucinda to the lime-green door. Crushed, heavy-scented blossoms release clouds of perfume against the camel's heat.

José's slips his fingers around a musky pile of succulents and throws them at Fecunda's door. They hit with force and scatter on the porch.

"Pilar!" shouts José. "You smell better than all the flowers in the world!"

The odor of Fecunda's frying dinner fish in heavy garlic is no match for the perfume of love. Fecunda leans out the kitchen window, shaking a small floured fish.

"Stay away from my daughter, you muttonhead. You are as crazy as your mother!"

José's arm is cocked with another fistful of flowers. "For Pilar!"

He throws, and the flowers land on the shelf of Fecunda's large bosom. Fecunda drops the fish, backs into the kitchen, and slams the shutters shut.

"José, you idiot child, you must win the mother to win the daughter!" I yell.

With a strong yank on the ropes, José loosens a bale of flowers.

"These flowers are for Señora Fecunda," he says, "and her beautiful daughter, Pilar!"

Bale after bale of sweet-smelling flowers drop from the camel onto Fecunda's doorstep. Frangipani, star orchids in jeweled strings, and long-stemmed tiger lilies. The pile is so high that the lime door is only an ugly memory.

There is a slow squeak of wood against wood as the front door opens. In a breath, the tower of bloom collapses into Fecunda's kitchen. But Pilar is not among those struggling in the mound of the perfumed petals.

José stands up on the camel's bare hump, spreads his arms, throws back his head, and yells, "Pilar! I love you. I love you! I love you!"

"José," I say. "Get down before you fall."

He is transfixed, staring upward into the sky. In a whisper of disbelief, he says, "Pilar?"

Pilar thrusts her small face over the edge of Fecunda's roof garden. She is pale between two large adobe pots filled with trembling pink bleeding hearts.

José stretches his arms to her, as close to his love as the hump of the camel allows. He presents the gift of himself to his beloved.

"Oh, Pilar," shouts José.

His body stretches upward. Looking down at him is the celibate constellation of Pilar's face: flat black eyes, the tight line of her lips, and her thin black eyebrows.

"Pilar," says José. "Did you receive my gift of the Madonna?"

Pilar holds a beautiful statue over the edge of the roof. José inhales deeply. Even at this distance in the purple light of late morning, I see that the beauty of this statue far surpasses anything José has done before. This Madonna is a full woman beneath her delicate rose-colored robe. One hand is forward as though touching a tender child. Her face is heart-shaped, and the tilt of her head has a celestial sweetness. This creation of José's is the closest an artist gets to God.

For the first time, I am grateful for Pilar just as she is. José has found a glass full of inspiration in her dry well. He spreads his arms wider, as though she might jump into them fully transformed by his love.

"Pilar," says José, "you are more beautiful than the Madonna."

"Blasphemer!" She opens her white fingers and drops the Madonna.

"No!" yells José.

The Madonna strikes him on the forehead, and he falls backward off the camel. The Madonna lands on the ground beside him. Her heart-shaped head breaks at the neck next to Lucinda's hoof. José reaches for the headless body. He sits up and holds the Madonna to his heart, as though that might make her whole again.

"José," I whisper.

He looks up at the roof.

"Pi-lar!" screams José.

But Pilar is gone. Bleeding hearts tremble in her wake. José's slender neck is as bent as his wilted flowers.

I check the small gash on his forehead as he cradles his creation. For a moment he fits them together.

"José," I say, "if you come home I will fix you a chocolate cake."

"You want me to eat?" he says.

"I want to offer you a solution, but cake is all I know to say," I say.

He places the Madonna's damaged body and head in my hands. The dullness in Pilar's eyes is now in his.

Chapter 27

"I have to eat," says José. "My mother wants me to eat."

He staggers across the path to the old oleander bush, plucks flowers, and folds the poisonous blossoms into his mouth.

"José," I say, "no one is worth dying for!"

I try to stick my fingers into his mouth, but he pushes me away. He gags, chews, and starts down the path to the beach with handfuls of oleander. His feet crush the runner of petals that fell from the camel.

"At least come home to die!" I yell.

I run to catch up with him, raising the Madonna's body above his head. I slam the hard wood across the back of José's skull with more force than I intended. His body falls onto the piles of forgotten flowers. My fingers probe the poison petals out of his mouth. Gabito must act the father now and tell me what to do with our poor suffering son.

Why is it so hard to keep everyone alive?

CHAPTER 28

THIS FAR UNDER the sea I never expect to see light. Currents pull me away from my pillow to liquid sands where Gabito does God-knows-what in his tilted Spanish galleon. I am still angry with him for making me look like a fool in front of poor José. We have driven the boy half crazy with the truth.

"Gabito," I yell at the unlit hull. "Are you there? I need your help!"

The sunken galleon looks like an ancient church behind layers of translucent mold. On the slippery green wood, small crabs wrestle with their dinner. A school of tiny yellow fish swim under my nightgown. I should have dressed, but who thinks of these things in dreaming?

"Gabito," I yell, "I'm coming in!"

Gabito's head rises out of the hatch, and his black hair unfurls in the lemonade light.

"It is about your son," I say.

Chapter 28

Gabito nods. His gold epaulettes are dull on his shoulders.

"I am so sorry, Tortugina. I am such a coward."

He disappears back down the hatch, and I swim after him. His boots kick ahead of me through the long, narrow passage of doors.

Schools of gray fish scatter ahead of us in the corridor filled with seaweed. His white-costumed legs disappear through the captain's doorway, the only door that is clear of seaweed.

"You see, Tortugina," he says. "I have spent my time away from you well. I have prepared your home."

The teak walls and thick-planked floor are polished. Brass instruments radiate a pale gleam. Yellow and blue fantails, bunched like floating bouquets, circle the hanging lamp. The one window in the rear of the cabin is open and fills the room with streaked light. On the captain's canopy bed is a hand-loomed bedspread. Not a trace of moss or dead snails remains anywhere. He deserves more time for praise, but my thoughts are filled with José.

"Gabito," I say, "I am angry at you."

He sits at the teak table and presses his hands together as though he were a captain solving a nautical problem.

"What can I do to help," says Gabito, "that does not involve materializing in front of José?"

I sit down on the polished chair.

"The only thing that will save him is Pilar's love," I say. "Our son has impossible dreams."

"What is wrong with impossible dreams?" he asks.

He sees that is not the answer I wanted.

"Dreams can kill you," I say. "José just tried to poison himself because the nun will not marry him. I stopped him, but he will try again and again. We both know what a perfectionist he is."

Gabito sighs. He takes my hand, and we float to the bed. I curl beside him like the old married couple that we are, my head near his good cheek. Before I killed him, his lips were so full and red, the top wider and more pronounced, a slight echo of my overbite.

"My poor son," says Gabito.

I brush hair off his bad eye and gently guide it back into the socket.

"At least we have never hurt each other as much as Pilar hurts him," I say.

Gabito's split lips turn up into his unnatural smile.

"Tortugina, every path you have taken is covered in my blood."

"Please be serious, Gabito," I say. "The only crack in Pilar's stone heart is God, and what can we do with that?"

Gabito cups his hands behind his head and blows bubbles from his mouth up to the ceiling. If he were not frowning, I would think he had lost interest in our conversation.

"I would like José to marry soon," says Gabito. "You have sat on the boy's heart long enough. The weight is not healthy for a young man. I think I have a plan to help José win his heart's desire."

We are a wounded troupe that stands before Fecunda's large lime door. José with a white bandaged head where I hit him, skin flushed from the last of the oleander's poison flowers, and me with my scarf-covered swath. José rests the heavy bucket on the doorstep. He looks too much like a grown man in the dark formal suit from Miguel's trunk, stored from his father's father's time. José cocks his head away from me, consumed with Pilar.

Dressed in an itchy weave worthy of a wedding, I carry an old bottle of good wine from Miguel's mother's Italy, much too fine for Fecunda's peasant taste or mine.

Gabito floats just behind me, so handsome, his shoulders thrown back with the pride of his plan. His gold epaulettes shine in the early evening light. For the occasion, his red cummerbund is now draped across his chest and pinned with a gold medal. The captain's blue wool jacket has crisp edges in the sleeves. If only he would let José see him.

Gabito leaves a damp kiss on my ear. I touch my earring and rub off his lips' blood between my fingers. His large hands circle my waist, and he squeezes gently.

"It is never too late to be a good father, Tortugina."

Gabito and José are all the armor I need to face Fecunda and her willing slave, Miguel.

José's right hand is in the air, unable to complete the knock. He turns. "How do I look, Mamá?"

His face is glossed in sweat. He is so tense that his right shoulder is stuck higher than his left, as though he were a coat hanging wrong in a closet.

"Irresistible," I say. "Now knock."

Drops of sweat break from the roots of his dark hair and run down his cheeks.

"José," I ask, "what is the worst that could happen?"

He gives me a look.

"I mean besides your suicide."

He closes his eyes and knocks hard with the heel of his hand. The door opens almost at once. Pink-eyed Albino, small for his seventeen years, pulls it wide. But it is Fecunda's striped dress that fills the gap with the barricade of her stomach.

"Are you dressed for your own funeral?" she says. "Albino, throw these beggars out!"

José holds up the bucket. "Look!"

"What is this?" exclaims Fecunda. "I do not need more fish!"

She looks down into the bucket and scoops up a handful of tiny emerald shells. She holds them to her nose and inhales so deeply that one of the shells is sucked into her nostril. She sticks her finger up her nose, rakes it out, pops it in her mouth, and crushes the salty sweetness with her eyes closed.

"Mmmm. You little cheat, Tortugina," says Fecunda as she swallows. "I knew you could find them if you wanted to."

She pulls the bucket out of José's arms as though she expects him to resist. Albino reaches for the snails at once, but his mother slaps his hand away.

"There's a fortune here, you little insect! Get away! Why are you standing there? Welcome our guests!"

Fecunda's eyes narrow as she slowly backs into her kitchen, one thigh chafing against the other. She sits like a royal queen at the head of the table with the bucket in front of her. Small citronella candles on the windowsill do not cover the strong smell of drying fish. Albino, the last of the unmarried children besides Pilar, brushes crumbs from the long breakfast table where his father's burned body lay only days ago. Then he serves us coffee with his soft white hands.

Gabito floats around the room poking into corners, drifting over Miguel Svendik's mighty chairs that have taken over Fecunda's kitchen. The carved cupboard covers one whole wall and is stuffed with her cracked crockery.

To her credit, it is an organized kitchen with cloves of garlic, onions, and herbs hung by the sink from a hook next to a basket of vegetables. Above the basket, inevitable fruit flies circle in a gray haze. The kitchen has the unusual feature of a two-story-high ceiling for hanging, salting, and drying large fish. Gabito plops himself on top of a tread-pedal sewing machine piled high with neatly stacked clothes.

My eyes are drawn to Domingo's trophies, a valuable narwhal tusk and a single whale vertebra. They hang on the wall next to a shark jaw that frames a black-and-white family portrait. The young Domingo stands beside a much thinner Fecunda, holding three of their eight smiling children.

I step onto a light brown mat. It cries out, rises from the floor on two pairs of furry feet, and sticks its wet nose in my crotch.

"Zapata!" says Fecunda.

The dog flops back onto the floor in exactly the same position, with a tiny knot of wagging tail.

"Tortugina," says Fecunda, "tell me about these snails. And speak quietly. Miguel is asleep." Her slow smile stops a gloat. "I tire him out, you know."

"Of course," I say. "Miguel's exhaustion has nothing to do with working as a carpenter and a fisherman."

She leans over the bucket in front of her and inhales the sweet, salty smell.

"Tell me what I have to do to get more of these snails."

"Do not rush me, you old tenderloin," I say to Fecunda.

Gabito floats over to sit beside me and puts his feet up on the table, his hands resting comfortably behind his head. Just as he predicted, Fecunda has pounced on the green snail bait. Now we must allow her to swallow the sharp hook.

"We brought you Miguel's finest wine to celebrate," I say.

"Celebrate? Celebrate what?" Fecunda snorts impatiently at Albino. "Bring us some glasses!"

José picks up the dusty wine bottle and uncorks the heavy odor of the wine's past romance. I smell an ancient vineyard, hunched hand-tilling peasants, and the scent of Miguel Svendik's Italian mother in the fruit. The bouquet fills Fecunda's bleached kitchen with the smell of a sweeter landscape.

Fecunda leans forward, but she is stopped by her stomach against the edge of the table.

"You will drink first so that I am sure you are not poisoning me," she says.

José pours the heavy red liquid into each glass. The little Latin I remember rises to the occasion.

"Et cum spiritu tvo," I say. "To lift the spirits."

"Drink!" says Fecunda. "Then tell me what you want!"

I feel her foot tapping on the floorboards.

José drinks quickly, also suffering from impatience. The thick, earthy syrup spreads across my tongue. Drop by drop, I swallow it and feel the warmth of the earth in my shoulders.

Seeing it is not poison, Fecunda gulps as though the nectar were merely local wine. She waves the empty glass, drinks another, licks the wine off her lips with a slow tongue, and looks softened.

Chapter 28

"Fecunda," I say, "my son has something to ask you."

Before he speaks, José clears his throat. He cannot keep his eyes off the glass-beaded door that leads to the bedrooms.

"Señora Fecunda," says José, "I have come to ask for Pilar's hand in marriage."

Fecunda whoops like the cranes on her roof. Albino laughs too, though she drowns him out.

"That skinny little nun?" says Fecunda.

José turns a furious shade of red. "You are never to speak about Pilar like that!"

That stops Fecunda. She sees he is serious and gives him the answer he deserves.

"She is a pain, little woodworker. No one but you and God would have her. How are you going to win her? And what do I get out of it?"

She runs her hand through the bucket of snails and throws several in her mouth.

José's trembling fingers lift the contract out of his pocket and lay it in front of Fecunda. She sits back in her chair and folds her arms.

"I cannot read," she says.

José, as the gentle son-in-law to be, reads it to her. "I, Fecunda María Pyhria Peres, give my daughter Pilar Conchita Peres to José Svendik in marriage. The bride price will be a bucket of green snails once a week. This is promised by Tortugina Svendik, the mother of José Svendik."

José seems to be holding his breath. He pulls a small bottle of ink and a thin wood pen out of his jacket. He opens the bottle, dips the metal pen tip in the ink, and holds the pen toward her.

Fecunda wipes her left hand on her dress. Her wide fingers are used to the broader strokes of the kitchen. It takes all her concentration to make her mark. But it is not an X like that of everyone else who cannot write. She makes her mark as a big O.

"Do O's count?" José says to me.

"Of course," says Gabito, who makes up his own rules.

"Of course," I say, since I also make up my own rules.

José exhales with a long breath. "Thank you, Mamá."

He grabs the stiff brown paper and blows on the O.

"One bucket a week for as long as the children are married?" says Fecunda.

Her eyes are filling with all her snail sales.

"Yes," I say. "From now on let us be good neighbors and good in-laws, Fecunda. I bear you and Miguel no ill will."

"You hate us," says Fecunda.

"Aside from that," I say, "I bear you no ill will."

Fecunda grins and shouts at the beaded doorway.

"Pilar, get your holy little ass in here!"

José turns red with anger again. When Pilar parts the waterfall-blue curtain of beads, he blushes an even deeper shade.

Pilar has taken care with her tight bun. A small dried flower in her hair signals "virgin," though most virgins choose a lush, open variety. Her pale face does not look at José.

"Pilar, my beloved," says José, holding out the contract. "Your mother has given permission for us to become man and wife."

Pilar's hands flutter like a vesper sparrow above her breasts. She hiccups. And she hiccups.

"You'll get used to that," says Fecunda.

José steps toward her suddenly and yells, "Boo!"

Pilar gulps, shudders, and the hiccups stop. "You see? I will be a good husband, Pilar," says José. "Will you marry me?"

Pilar's nun-whisper is easily heard by us all. "I will honor the memory of my dead father, Domingo, by joining the convent."

The dark oleander look seeps back into José's face.

I walk over to Pilar and grab her by both shoulders.

"Pilar, you are a mean, frightened, dull girl! But if José wants you, you will honor your mother, your father, the contract, and me. You will wed José!"

Pilar's eyes are wide enough to see white around the edges. Gabito floats next to me. His strong hands smooth my back.

"Gently, Tortugina," says Gabito. "She will be our daughter soon."

"Pilar, welcome to the family," I say, and press a dry kiss on her cheek.

Her skin is softer than I could have imagined. She smells like beeswax candles. The white edge of fear remains in Pilar's eyes.

"I will only marry Jesus. You can kill me if you like. It only means that I will meet my Savior sooner and be welcomed by the immaculate kiss of Jesus."

Her hand slowly brushes her cheek where I kissed her.

"Pilar, marry me!" José steps so close to her that his boots crush her delicate sandaled toes.

"My feet! Get off my feet!" she screams.

José trips against Pilar. They fall together and then apart as she pushes him away, and then together again for balance. They are like mating dragonflies, with her frantic loops to escape and his pressing into her. But for the layers of clothing, their bodies touch for the first time.

"Pilar," José whispers, "I love you."

Pilar would make a fiddler's taut bow look slack. Even her ears angle away from his lips.

"Let me go!"

"I cannot let you out of my arms now," he says. "I will never get you back."

He holds her as though he were wrestling a steer, not a girl with a rib cage.

"Let her go, José," I say. "Love cannot be squeezed into existence. You will court again tomorrow."

"Do not be so quick to end the visit, Tortugina," says Gabito.

Gabito lowers his mouth to the half-finished Italian wine bottle and blows across the neck. A sound of lusty trumpets is followed by a purple mist that engulfs José and Pilar.

"Mamá," José says silently to me. "What are you doing?"

"It is not me, José," I answer silently. "It is your father, the ghost you do not believe in. He is here to help you win your bride."

"Mamá, of all days," he says to me. "Do not be insane now."

Gabito stares at José and Pilar with a strong gaze that I have never seen.

"What are you doing?" gasps José.

The purple cloudbank lifts José and a stunned Pilar slowly toward the ceiling. Surrounded by the breath of romance, their bodies glow as though a sunrise glistened beneath their skins. They are standing in an ancient vineyard. A deep orange sunset reflects on rows of grapes coiling out of rich topsoil.

Fecunda pounds my shoulder.

"Tortugina, are you a witch?" she says, staring at the children on her ceiling.

When their heads reach the rafters, Pilar throws her thin arms around José's neck.

"José, put me down! Mamá! Help!" says Pilar.

Albino jumps and grabs at Pilar's foot, but she is too high, so he stares straight up her skirt.

"Albino! Stop that," says Fecunda. "Tortugina, bring her down."

"I have nothing to do with this!" I say.

Pilar clings to José's shoulders. A grin spreads slowly across his face. His eyes tell me he is as close to heaven as a boy in love can be. He strokes Pilar's trembling back.

"You are safe with me, Pilar," says José.

Gabito has still not taken his eyes off José.

"Gabito," I speak silently to him. "Levitation is not seduction. Now what?"

"Improvise," says Gabito.

The two children cling to each other above us. Pilar is as pale as a star.

"Please," says Pilar. "Please put me down, José."

"Mamá," José says silently. "What do I do now?"

"Tortugina, help him and hurry," says Gabito, in a voice that betrays the strain of holding the two children on the ceiling.

Watching the little nun's teeth begin to chatter, I am struck by a wicked thought.

"José," I say, "tell her…tell her you are Jesus."

José stares down at me. He blinks, turning my suggestion over in his mind.

Finally he says silently, "But Mamá, what happens when we are married and she finds I am not what I claim to be?"

"That is the way of all marriages, José," I say.

José gazes into Pilar's flat black eyes and says in a tentative whisper, "Pilar, would you believe me if I told you that I am your savior, Jesus?"

Fecunda's belly shakes with laughter. "Even she is not that stupid."

I fold my arms and sit back on the chair next to Gabito, who is beginning to sweat with the effort of the miracle.

"Fecunda," I say, "if he is not Jesus, then why are there two people floating on your ceiling? And remember the snails."

Fecunda cuts her laughter short.

"Yes, Pilar, why are you on my ceiling with José if he is not God's messenger? Accept him on blind faith so I can get my snails."

Pilar pulls as far back as she can from José. "Can you prove you are Jesus?"

Almost without hesitation, José says, "Has anyone else taken you up for a float?"

He looks down at me, proud of himself.

"But," says Pilar, "I want to serve God as a nun."

With newfound confidence, José spins an even bigger lie. "Pilar, it is because of your strong heart and devotion that you have been chosen above all other women to give the world a new baby Jesus, with me."

Gabito smiles, but I am worried that José seems to enjoy this lying too much.

Fecunda stifles one of her giggles. “Pilar, why do you hesitate? It is a big honor to marry into God’s bloodline.”

Pilar considers slowly. “Then I would be like the Madonna?”

José squeezes Pilar’s waist with tenderness. “I will make all your prayers come true, my love.”

Blood pumps into her pale cheeks. Her lips curve into a smiling row of small, kernel teeth. She looks down at Fecunda, her shy face turned away from José.

“I will be your wife,” whispers Pilar.

The dried virgin flower behind Pilar’s ear falls to the floor.

“Beloved, you have made me the happiest man in the world!” José’s face is caught between heaven and the hell of his lie.

“What have I done, Mamá?” he says only to me.

“You have won a lifetime of joy, José,” I say, without believing it.

Fecunda raises her glass.

“That was a true miracle, Tortugina. To our children.”

“There is one condition,” Pilar says. “You must remove the curse on the house of Svendik. I want to be happy and have children who are happy.”

José blinks. “Of course, my love, we will make lots of happy children.” Silently he says, “Mamá, help.”

Once again my son calls upon me to fix his life, but I have no idea what to tell him.

Fecunda looks up at her daughter.

“Pilar,” says Fecunda, “may I remind you what Miguel said. José is a bastard. José is not a Svendik, so there is no problem.”

Pilar is not content with her mother's answer. She faces José.

"If you bear the Svendik name, you may bear the Svendik curse. I will not take a chance with my happiness or that of my children, even if you are the son of God."

Gabito chews the edge of his snail-shaped hat. "She is not coming down unless she weds him." His eyes strained upward, he keeps the children aloft. "That is my promise to my son."

"Tortugina," says Fecunda, "the Hermit can stir up solutions to difficult problems. He could not help me, but perhaps he can help you."

There is a warning in her eyes.

"Pilar," I say, "I will go to the Hermit. I promise you, I will make him remove the curse."

Pilar seems convinced enough to say, "When that happens, we will wed and I will accept my destiny."

She allows José to brush her lips with the barest touch that could still be considered a kiss. With a regal flick of her hand, she says, "José, you may put me down now."

Gabito takes quick inhaling breaths, and the purple mist descends with our new deities. When their feet touch the hard planks of Fecunda's kitchen, the mist evaporates completely. José and Pilar ascended as children and returned as adults.

"You did that very well," I say silently to Gabito.

He looks so pleased with himself that I want to kiss him.

Pilar bows her head. "Let us pray."

We bow our heads. José cannot keep his eyes off the curve of her tiny breasts.

"Dear God," says Pilar, "bless my union with your son, who, for reasons known only to You, has manifested as José

Svendik. Until the Svendik curse is removed, we will be as brother and sister in your light and prayer. Beloved Virgin, please allow José and me to conceive our holy children as you did, through the chaste union of Immaculate Conception."

José chokes on "Immaculate Conception."

"Amen," says Pilar.

CHAPTER 29

BENEATH A FULL moon, the tide stretches up the sand in wide sheets of silver. Tumbling moonstruck crabs quickly bury themselves in the rushing water.

Ahead of us under a tall pine, the Hermit's hut glows from within. It is made of smooth driftwood logs stuck in the sand and fastened side by side like a fort. Between the bleached logs is the glow of a cookfire, where the shadow of the Hermit's body passes back and forth.

José and I try to keep up with Pilar's pace, her small sandals churning through sand toward the hut. The stiff new dress scrapes my legs, thanks to Pilar, who would not give me a moment to change.

Gabito floats beside me over the sand as though he were stretched out in a hammock.

"Most girls would sit quietly after a proposal and weep with gratitude," I say silently to him. "But not this little nun. All her questions have to be answered tonight: 'Can the Hermit remove the curse? What if the Hermit can't remove the curse?' Gabito, we are doing an evil charade. The Hermit cannot remove the curse or he would have done it by now. Poor José."

Gabito turns in the moist night air. "Tortugina, do not be so quick to see the dark side of life."

The dead can afford to be optimistic. And Gabito does not live inside José the way I do.

Only a few feet from the Hermit's front door, our sandals crack on hundreds of brittle clamshells covering the sand. This popping is a good alarm for the old Hermit to hear our approach.

The Hermit pulls back a heavy carpet that hangs across his doorway. His uncombed hair has worked itself into long, thick tangles that would scare a tarantula. It is said that he never bathes, and when his ragged tunic of animal skins rips, he simply sews on another loose piece. He moves toward us in layers, like a molting beast without all its fur truly attached.

In the moonlight, I hold my breath against the combined stench of his sweat and badly cured hides. His ragged beard glistens with animal fat.

"Speak," says the Hermit, "and hurry. I left my potion bubbling."

His amber eyes glow under a protruding brow.

Pilar approaches. "Señor Hermit, I want you to remove the ancient curse on the house of Svendik so that I may marry José Svendik."

His lips part in the moonlight, revealing a crooked smile.

"Marriage?" he says. "Marriage is a dangerous journey that only fools take."

"What does it cost?" asks Pilar.

She is practical as well as relentless. Good traits for our dreamers' bloodline.

The Hermit's prodding tongue loosens fish bits from the gaps in his teeth. He spits and small shots of white fish hit the sand.

"Death is one cost," says the Hermit. "Death is common among people who seek to change the past. Think of that before you volunteer, Señora Tortugina."

"Me?" I say. "This little nun is the seeker."

"Señor Hermit," says José. His face is a shield in the silver moonlight. "It is I who will face death for Pilar's love, not my mother."

The Hermit's eyes glow like his cookfire as he circles José.

"You?" he asks. The old shaman pokes José in the chest. "Are you telling me my business? It is only the wife of the senior Svendik who can lift the curse. That is Señora Tortugina."

The Hermit's amber eyes leave a cold chill in my chest.

"I will divorce Miguel and let Fecunda marry him. Then she will be the number one Svendik wife."

"Do not argue with me," says the Hermit. "Fecunda asked me, and I told her the same thing. As curses go, you are Miguel's wife now, his only wife, the one who can lift the curse."

At the risk of angering him, I ask, "But in all these generations of Svendiks, why is it another wife did not come to you for uncursing?"

He turns to sniff his potion. It smells like something is burning.

Chapter 29

"Most people lack imagination, Señora. They do not want to change things. That is why the world is the way it is. But you are here."

Gabito wets my ear with a kiss. "If you do not survive, we will be together sooner. There does not appear to be a downside to this arrangement."

The chill has taken hold of my bones. I pull my shawl tighter and thread my arm through José's arm. Love never leaves a choice, and that is unfair.

"Do you really want this little nun?" I say to José silently.

He nods. I give him the answer he wants.

"I will do it for you, José."

There are no happy endings for martyrs. José takes my hand.

"But Mamá, I cannot let you risk your life for me. I love you too much."

Thank God. I inhale deeply, safe in my son's love. It was a hard choice, but my José has spoken. The little nun loses.

Pilar wraps her white fingers around José's other arm.

"José, we must allow your mother her sacrifice." There is an edge to her voice. "It is for our children's sake."

My fingers tighten around José's hand.

José stands between the two of us and looks up at the night sky. When he turns to me, his eyes glisten.

"I am sorry, Mamá. You are my soul, but Pilar is my heart. What is a man if he does not listen to his heart?"

I should make this easy for him, but I do not.

"What do we call the wise son who carries his mother first in his heart?"

"Single," says Pilar.

Gabito knocks my shoulder. "Tortugina, stop torturing the boy."

The Hermit rubs his black fingertips in front of my face.

"Ten chickens and I will be gentle," he says.

"No one pays ten chickens, except for a burro. Five," I say.

"Uncurses take all night," says the Hermit. "Eight."

His sour smell is beginning to make my eyes water.

"Five or we go home," I say.

The Hermit's square fingers pluck a pine needle from my hair. "Seven is my last offer."

Pilar pushes José forward. "I will return with seven chickens," he says and quickly puts out his hand.

The Hermit shakes José's hand. "Return as quickly as you can, José," says the Hermit. "Once I begin, there is little time left for the uncursing, and I need you here for that."

The Hermit pulls out a knife and whacks a strand of José's hair off of his forehead.

"Why did you do that, Señor Hermit?"

The Hermit moves his arms up and down like a rooster. "Roll the bones, suck an egg. I am a busy man. I do not explain my magic, boy."

He gestures toward the hut. "Señora Tortugina?"

José starts to embrace me. The Hermit steps between us. "Your mother is mine now. Go get my chickens!"

José allows Pilar to steer him back to the village. Their sandals sink to the same depth in the dune. This may be my last sight of him.

The Hermit holds the rug door open for me with a most courteous bow.

"Señora Tortugina," says the Hermit.

His voice has turned musical and creates a soft lure. I

step inside the hut onto woven rugs thrown two and three deep across the sand floor. A small cauldron bubbles on rosy embers. It smells like burning seaweed. The scent of heavy smoke and many meals rises from the wool carpets.

Gabito floats to an ancient loom strung with crimson threads and pretends it is a harp. He wants to entertain me before I die.

I catch the Hermit's gaze on my breasts. His eyes travel down my legs.

Gabito's eyes snap. "Smelly beast!"

"Señora Tortugina, you are aging well," says the Hermit.

I edge as far away from him as the hut allows. "It is the new dress," I say.

He slaps the bed covered in red blankets. "Lie down, Señora."

Gabito plucks the strings of the loom nervously. I step around the embers and sit on the bed.

The Hermit slips the shawl off my shoulders and pushes me back onto the red blanket that reeks with sweat. With a humming-bird touch, he unstraps the buckles of my sandals.

"I am starting to be frightened, Gabito," I say silently. Gabito swings his legs over the loom and hunches toward us. "Me too."

The old man moves to a low table covered with colored bottles. He pours a blue and then a green oil over a fresh bird fetus lying in a dish. Using the oil-covered bird like a bar of soap, he washes his hands with it. Then he presses his fingers onto my feet in a gentle massage. It reminds me of rubbing Papá's calloused feet, "onions and bunions and carrots and tomatoes."

"Be tranquil, Señora Tortugina," he says.

The Hermit's fingers slip between the tender valleys of my dry toes. A sweet warmth invades my skin. The fetus oil, his touch, are a soft narcotic. I feel suspended in warm honey, drugged by the rhythm of his fingers releasing muscles that have been clenched for a lifetime. My body loosens like an old robe falling open.

Out of the corner of my eye, I see Gabito rise off the loom. He turns his head away, his face as red as the blankets. "I will go crazy if I watch this."

"Please," I whisper. But the Hermit's hypnotic touch and the calming oil lull me to sleep.

I am half-awakened by the sound of the Hermit chopping the lock of José's hair into small pieces that he brushes into a dirty white bowl. Adding purple powder from a rusted box, a pinch of something scaly-green, and a small handful of tiny dark beans, he throws it all into the hot, black, soupy potion bubbling over the fire.

Pouring the soup into a small bowl, stirring the potion with his knife, he holds the steaming bowl to my lips.

"Drink this, Señora Tortugina."

A strong, sweet smell like black molé rises from the soup. A few beans floating on the top appear to have legs. I turn my face away.

The Hermit speaks slowly, or I am listening slowly.

"When you drink this potion, it will make your blood go backwards. Then Señora Sepulchura, whom I have summoned from the grave, will enter your body. Your body will become hers for a short while. José must persuade her to lift the curse. There is very little time to make this work."

The Hermit presses the bowl to my lips.

Chapter 29

"For José," I say, and swallow the muddy grit that fizzes in my teeth. The hairs cling in my throat. Coughing and choking with the last swallow, I gulp hard against the awful prickling. The Hermit forces a mild wine down my throat. A few swallows cure the gagging.

"Has anyone actually survived this?" I cough.

"You are my first uncursing," says the Hermit. "I am using my great-grandfather's formula." He pauses and feels my forehead. "And now it begins."

I inhale and my breath is on fire. I exhale and my breath is like ice. I know that I am going to die.

"Courage," he says.

Time is pouring backwards. Cold sand slips through my heart that has become an hourglass.

"Gabito!" I scream in terror. My hinges creak. My spine is made of wood. I am a coffin.

"Tortugina," says Gabito. "All we can do now is think of our son."

What I think of José at this moment, is the same thing Mamá said to me: "I should have killed you before puberty."

The Hermit shakes my shoulder. "What do you see, Tortugina?"

An old woman comes toward me out of a long tunnel. She is dressed in the dark clothes of another century. I recognize her from the ugly portrait in the church where I prayed to Saint Uncumber. It is the ancient Señora Sepulchura, Miguel's great-grandmother, the one who laid the awful curse on her family.

The old woman holds her swollen belly as though she were pregnant. Her filmy eyes look down at me. She bends slowly to sit on the bed then lies down on top of me, the coffin that I have become, and sinks into my flesh. My body rumbles, shaking bones begin to crumble, my skin shrinks with decay until I am the ancient Señora Sepulchura.

The Hermit steadies a piece of rusted mirror in front of my face. My breath clouds the edges. Señora Sepulchura looks back at me from the mirror.

"Holy Mother of God!" I try to yell, but my mouth is full of her yellowed ivory dentures. They chop my words to bits.

I blink in the mirror. She blinks. She is me! I am her! It happened so quickly. The old woman is even uglier than her portrait in the church alcove. Silver hair halos a sunken face. Her quivering neck is anchored to a sunless chest. Terrible stained-laundry flesh, yellow fingers curled with arthritis. I pull a layer of creped skin out from my cheek. Skin as dry as peanut shells recedes slowly back to the bone. Even that small movement is painful with these swollen joints.

The Hermit covers me with a blanket. The pressure of the weave is too much. I try to look up into his eyes. My ancient vision is smeared with jagged dark forms floating across a gray-white sea.

"Do not worry, Señora Tortugina," he says. "A softer vision of life compensates for the hardening of arteries. Accept your new limitations with grace."

He massages my bony shoulder.

"You must go now. Sleep and make room for our guest. I hope you can avoid whatever pain she brings with her."

"Wait!" I want to yell. I try to inhale deeply, but the old woman's lungs are fragile from so many years in the grave.

The Hermit shouts into the old woman's ears. "Señora Sepulchura! Wake up!"

Chapter 29

She crowds me out behind the watery eyes we share. I am a woman trapped in another woman's body. I am a wanderer in her petrified landscape. This is a preview of death. Will I ever return to the contours of Tortugina? A gurgling moan rises in our throat.

"Señora Sepulchura?" The Hermit bobs close to my face/her face. Her awakening brings a sudden sharp pain in my belly. The old Señora pushes her tongue against the ivory teeth.

"Wuh," says Señora Sepulchura.

She uses the heels of my palms to push on the blanket. The hot pain in her womb spasms.

"What!" The old Señora inhales. "What infidel dares to wake the dead?"

Her voice scratches like a branch rubbing against closed shutters.

The Hermit leans toward us. "Señora Sepulchura. I am the Hermit. My great-grandfather was the Hermit in your time. You knew him well for his erotic potions."

The old-woman voice sniffs, "You smell as foul as your ancestors. Send me back to the arms of death now, you evil animal. This is my time to sleep my pain to ash."

Reaching her gnarled fingers under the blanket, the old Señora feels my stiff dress. "Who dressed me in these horrible clothes? I was buried in my blue silk dress, a lace mantilla, and silk underwear." Her trembling fingers knead her swollen womb. The Hermit places his palm over the same spot, and the pain recedes to a dull ache.

"I brought you and your evil disposition back," says the Hermit, "to remove your curse from the house of Svendik."

The Señora releases what little air is left in our lungs. It sounds like laughter.

"Remove the curse? Thor Svendik murdered me with his seed. Mounted me like a stallion! I would never help a Svendik! I want to die!"

I taste salty blood as her ivory dentures grind against our gums.

The Hermit speaks with impatience. "Señora, we are short of time. When you remove the curse, I will let you return to the hell that you deserve. They are paying me seven chickens."

The Señora raises her eyebrows. "Seven?"

She closes her watering eyes and folds her hands across her chest as if in prayer. Under the darkness of her paper eyelids, the old Señora says, "I died once without your help, Hermit. I will do it again."

We are awakened in the dark of early morning by clamshells splintering under a hurried tread. Outside the hut, the sound comes closer and closer. A chicken squawks, then another.

Señora Sepulchura opens our thin eyelids. Her tears blur sight. She presses her fingers into our tender belly and moans, "I did not die."

A breeze carries José into the hut.

"Señor Hermit!" he says. "I have brought you seven chickens. How is my mother?"

José is a smeary silhouette at the edge of our sight. He holds flapping chickens by their bound legs, lowering the bouquet of brown wings to the Hermit's red carpet.

Chapter 29

The Hermit's voice rumbles like the earth turning.

"José, this woman is, by marriage, not blood, your great-great-grandmother, Señora Sepulchura. Your mother is asleep inside the old Señora."

"Mamá?" José steps forward and looks down at our old face.

"She will return good as new when we are finished," says the Hermit, "if all goes well."

The Hermit wraps us cigar-tight in a red blanket.

"Here, take her. Take them. I have done my part."

He places us gently in José's arms.

"What do I do?" says José.

"Carry her to the Square of Don Pedro the Cruel and the Just," says the Hermit. "Lay her on the steps of the Illustrious Victims Church, where she made the original curse, and ask her to remove it. It is simple."

"Mamá," says José. "What have I done to you?"

His falling tears are quickly absorbed into our parched skin.

The Hermit gestures toward the village with a chicken. "Hurry, boy. You only have a half-hour left. Do not waste your mother's sacrifice."

José has never looked at me as he does now, as a stranger. I feel the loneliness of burial inside the old woman.

I know he cannot hear me, but I shout as loud as I can, "José, I love you!"

José's fast stride toward the Square of Don Pedro the Cruel and the Just jolts the old woman's spine. Roof dogs bark down at us as we pass. Through the Señora's blurred vision, the village looks completely different, as though it had turned to liquid. Purple bougainvillea pours down a wall like wine. A plot of white chrysanthemums is spilt milk. Trees are leafy green splashes against a blue wash of sky.

The clang of beating, metal on metal, signals the garbage wagon's early morning passage through the streets. Piquante, the tiny mayor's son who is never without a question, clings to the wagon and shouts, "Is that a corpse you are carrying, José?"

He jumps off the back and runs after us. "Let me see!"

"No, Piquante, she is not dead."

José lifts us higher in his arms.

José's sandals slap faster and faster against the street stones. Finally he turns the corner into the gray morning light of the Square of Don Pedro the Cruel and the Just.

José's long-legged strides take us past the scent of freshly brewed coffee from Señora Nauseobondo's taverna. After one hundred years without so much as a sip, Señora Sepulchura's senses turn lucid just from the smell. She awakens her long-dead nerve endings by inhaling.

"Coffee. Now!" whispers the Señora. "Or I cannot lift my head, much less consider lifting a curse."

"Señora, we must hurry," answers José.

"Get me a cup!" she says.

José returns quickly to the taverna and lowers our stiff body onto one of Señora Nauseobondo's empty tabletops. The old vertebrae crackle like fireworks on the table's flat surface. José covers our face with the red blanket.

Señora Nauseobondo's high heels click toward us. "Who is that person?"

Even under the blanket, I can smell the strange eucalyptus perfume of Señora Nauseobondo. It is a sex-smell that always tumbles before her in the breeze.

"Please hurry, Señora," pleads José. "A cup of coffee for the old woman."

Chapter 29

Piquante jumps for a peek. José pulls the blanket completely over the old woman's face.

"José has a corpse!" yells Piquante.

"She is not dead," says José.

"José," asks Señora Nauseobondo, "you lay a corpse on my table?"

Chairs scrape against the cobblestones. The villagers rise out of their coffee conversations.

"José," says Mayor Perfecciona. "As mayor, I must point out that it is bad luck for the dead and the living to share commercial property!"

The deeper voice of Sheriff Nina speaks over us. "José, are you involved in a crime?"

"No, no, the old woman is not dead," José says.

The villagers press shoulder to shoulder around the table. Señora Nauseobondo pulls the blanket back. Our watery eyes blink up into an umbrella of brown faces.

"Where is my coffee?" says Señora Sepulchura.

Piquante jumps up and down and screams like a parrot. "She is alive! She is alive!"

"Who are you, Señora?" asks Señora Nauseobondo, as she tilts the coffee into the old woman's mouth. The thick, sweet Arab gruel of Señora Nauseobondo's coffee eats its way down to our empty belly. The old woman clamps her ivory teeth on the rim of the cup from pain.

"Who is she, José?" says Señora Nauseobondo.

"I am Señora Sepulchura," she says, clearing her throat.

"La Scorpion?" whispers the little mayor. "Can that be true, José?"

José coughs and nods. "The Hermit did it."

Mayor Perfecciona crosses herself. "Piquante, go find

Padre Monástico!" she says. "This is not a civil matter."

Piquante turns away from the table and shoves his way through the stand of legs. The villagers pull noisy prayer beads out of their pockets and stare at us.

"Look at all of you," says the old Señora. "Your ancestors were as dull as a poor man's plow, and your faces bear the same stamp."

Señora Nauseobondo's face hangs over us and looks more fleshy than usual under her dense cinnamon hair.

"Señora Scorpion, death has not tempered your sting," she says.

"You," says Señora Sepulchura, "must be descended from that circus fur-piece, Señora Peluda. She, at least, would have had the good manners to feed me."

Señora Nauseobondo dips her fingers into the yellow brine of her olive jar. She slips a hot green olive through the old woman's elephant-ivory teeth as though her mouth were a mail slot. The old woman chews, and her gums bleed. She spits the bloody pit out on the table.

"José," says Mayor Perfecciona. "With all due respect, why would the Hermit bring back this piece of trouble?"

José's face is as red as the old woman's blood.

"I hired him," he says, "to bring Señora Sepulchura back from the grave to lift her ancient curse, so that Pilar Peres will accept me as her husband."

"Ahhhh, yes, love," sigh the villagers.

Señora Nauseobondo pinches José's cheek and smiles her red lipstick smile.

"Romance. A groom without a curse is much better than a bachelor with a curse!"

"What is happening to her?" says Sheriff Nina.

Chapter 29

The old woman screams, and I scream inside the horror of her flesh. Señora's womb is under siege again. Nerves flay and spark.

"Oh, God, help me!" She holds her womb with bent fingers. Her tears run to drool. "I cannot die this way again!" she screams.

José picks her up off the table. "Please do not die yet, Señora." He runs as fast as he can over the cobblestones.

The villagers follow her wailing across the square to the Illustrious Victims Church. José lays her gently on the top step. The old woman pushes José's hand into the blanket between her legs. He leans close to the old woman's chattering teeth.

"What do you want me to do?" says José.

"Oooww!" she screams. "Take it out! Take it out and I will recant the curse!"

José's eyes are trapped animals running back and forth. "Take what out?"

The old lady wraps her snake-blue fingers around José's wrist.

"Put your hand inside me. You are my great-great-grandson. You are the one to pull it out!"

José gags. "Put my hand inside you?"

"Hurry!"

Poor José. I cannot help him in my silent tomb.

The villagers whisper, "No, no, no."

José wrenches his hand free. "Reach inside my own mother, my great-great-grandmother?"

My heart cracks a little at the horror in his eyes. José has never looked at me with such repulsion.

The old Señora's thick yellow nails press into the blanket.

"Hurry! I will be dead before you get your wish," says Señora Sepulchura. "Close your eyes. Think of your beloved bride. Reach in and pull it out."

"Pull out what?" says José.

Prayers cannot shield him from this.

"Do it, José!" Perhaps he hears me, because he takes several deep breaths as I have taught him to do when he panics. He allows the old woman to guide his hand under the blanket.

Sheriff Nina shushes the crowd of villagers. Señora Sepulchura breathes as deeply as she can.

José wrinkles his nose against a stench even I can smell. His hand jerks back at first contact with her clotted thigh. He turns his head farther away the closer he gets. The Señora gags on her drool and spreads her rusty bones for him.

Señora Nauseobondo, still carrying her jar of olives, kneels beside José.

"It is all right, José. You can always go to confession."

José chants, "I love you Pilar! I love you Pilar!" His hand enters curtains of dry flesh.

"Further, José," whispers Señora Sepulchura.

Her legs are spread as far as the old joints are willing to part. Tears pour out of José's eyes.

"Still further," she whispers. "You are almost there."

Poor José's arm is so far under the blanket that his chin rests on her stomach. His nostrils are turning white.

"I feel something," he chokes.

His clawing finally grasps something hard.

"Pilar! Pilar! Pilar!" he shouts.

Señora Sepulchura screams.

Chapter 29

José's fingers yank the lump out. He drags it up and lays it on the blanket for all to see.

It is a calcified child, long dead, no bigger than a large bun and sticky with blood.

The old Señora releases a sigh she has saved up for a century.

The villagers step back, holding their noses.

Señora Nauseobondo quickly slips off her wine-stained tavern apron and wraps the bloody relic with so many layers of generous cotton there is no way to tell if it had a human destiny.

José plunges his hand into Señora Nauseobondo's big olive jar. Green olives roll as he froths the yellow brine red with a vigorous washing. He dries his hand on his dirty white shirt. The smell of José's briny skin is a relief from the womb stench.

The little mayor tucks the red blanket around the old lady's brittle shoulders.

"Ahhh," sighs Señora Sepulchura. "It was worth coming back just to die without that pain."

She sucks contentedly on her loose teeth. In and out, in and out against her bloody gums. Her heartbeat is as subdued as a glassy tide. I am sleepy with relief.

With Piquante leading the way, Padre Monástico pushes through the villagers. The old priest is winded from running. Señora Nauseobondo holds the smelly bundle at arm's length and tells the brief story of the apron-wrapped fetus. Padre Monástico nods.

"Et Spiritus Sancti," says Padre Monástico. "I will christen it, and then we will bury it in the graveyard. Señora Sepulchura, what do you want to call it?"

The old Señora, weakened by the birth, whispers, "José.

Call my baby José, after my great-great-grandson."

At least she appreciates one man in her life.

"I will relieve you of this one curse, José," the old woman says. "But it hardly matters. No one can escape the terrible curse of life itself."

José is ready to spit with anger. He leans close, and for the first time in my life, his face frightens me.

"It is you who cause your own suffering, old woman," says José. "I will bury your ugly words with your dead baby. Recant the curse now. I want to see my mother, who is worth loving!"

The village is quiet. Not a dog barks or a child cries. The only sound is the old woman's quiet breath.

"The curse," she whispers, "of all Svendik men to know only the suffering of love, without the joy of love, is over. From this day forward, the House of Svendik, its women and its men, shall know everlasting love. If there is such a thing."

José slumps with relief. Then he jumps to his feet, raising dust off the stones. He jumps even higher than Piquante's head. His fists are triumph-high in the air. Sheriff Nina catches him in her giant arms and hugs him. When she sets him back on the steps, Señora Nauseobondo kisses him on the mouth. Piquante jumps on his back. Villagers pound him and kiss him.

"I love you all!" he cries. José frees himself from their hugs and kneels beside me.

"Mamá, thank you! Come back! Mamá, wake up! It is over!"

He shakes my shoulders. The old woman's pulse slows and finally stops. I am caught below the surface of her dying flesh.

Chapter 29

José, my last look at you is through a spiderweb of veins and faraway light.

CHAPTER 30

A GUITAR BECKONS me down a long dark tunnel. My skin is as smooth as moonstone. Shadows cut across the light. When Gabito whispers my name, I step out of the dry husk of Señora Sepulchura's body and move with a luminous step.

"Tortugina, wake up," says Gabito. A candle flickers. A warm quilt of air spreads when I move my fingers. Someone strums a mariachi chord.

I open my eyes and break the thread of dreams. A bowl filled with steaming soup sits on a low table next to the bed. A flying beetle clicks its castanet wings and lands on an island of potato. In a pitcher of water floats a thick slice of fresh lime.

Gabito is nestled on the bed with me. "Tortugina, my little turtle. Thank God, you are awake."

"Do I look like me, Gabito?" I ask.

"Yes, my love," he says and kisses me. "Not a wrinkle left."

Chapter 30

Sweat soaks the sheet. My head feels weighted to the pillow. The music is so loud in this little room. I turn and look past Gabito at the open door. Now I recognize where I am. More of an alcove than a bedroom, it is Señora Nauseobondo's guestroom for travelers. The door is opened wide into the main taverna, where Rosa, Mimosa, and Auntie Patina pass by carrying large platters of steaming tamales. Señora Nauseobondo hurries across the dance floor with a tray of dripping beer glasses.

A drunken José in a suit of ink-black formality is carried on the bucking shoulders of the men. He does not see me in Señora Nauseobondo's little guestroom.

From a distant corner of the room villagers yell, "To the marriage of José and Pilar!"

"José married without me?"

"Tortugina," Gabito says, "you have been asleep for three weeks." Gabito wipes my face with a damp cloth then wipes away his own tears. "How do you feel?"

"Three weeks?" I say.

The candle begins to waltz around the room. Three weeks. My son has been in the world without me for three weeks. Who fed him?

"You must eat something," says Gabito.

He helps me wedge myself up against the pillows. He spoons hot chicken soup into my mouth. My landscape gurgles. I will be in bloom again soon.

Church bells ring. It is not the steady clang of the hour, but the wild ring of celebration.

"As always, I am left outside," I say.

"Tortugina," says Gabito, "you were there at the wedding. José carried you to the church and tied you to a chair so that you sat by his side when he and Pilar exchanged rings. You nodded and drooled a little, but you were there. No son could be more devoted. José slept by your side, cleaned the house, fed you and cared for you. If you were one of his statues, you would not have received more attention.

I sniff for José's fingerprints on my skin and wipe my tears. My baby can survive without me. This is the destiny of all healthy children, but it is not a pleasant feeling for a mother. I will not believe it until I see it for myself.

A wild shout from a hundred throats rattles my soup bowl. Gabito floats to the door for a peek.

"José and Pilar are climbing the stairs to the Poke Room."

My baby is mounting the stairs to become a man in the chamber that Señora Nauseobondo decorated from catalogues and rents by the hour.

"Having been a virgin myself," I say, "I have much to tell José about breaking her little hyacinth."

Gabito's lips crack into his uneven smile. "Tortugina, any son of mine will make us proud in the bedroom."

I know Gabito is thinking of our sweet sex together. But do boys inherit their father's skill? Or if they do, is it like a diving talent that must be developed?

Above our heads, there are thuds as José's heavy boots drop on the chamber floor. They might as well have landed on my stomach.

"Gabito, I am worried," I say. "Pilar is a girl who expects miracles, even in the bedroom. If he frightens her and she sucks in her little clam, there will be no stained sheet. José will start his marriage under a cloud of disgrace."

In the candlelight Gabito smooths my quilt. "Leave him alone, Tortugina, or you will make an enemy of them both."

Chapter 30

There are sounds of shifting from the room overhead. I nibble at cheese grown hard at the edges. The villagers begin to pound steadily on the tables with spoons, knives, and bottles. It hurts my poor head. Señora Nauseobondo twirls into the middle of the floor, clapping her hands above her head. "Everyone sing!" she shouts:

Hurry! Hurry! Hurry!
The Bride's been wed. She's in her bed. The gate's been spread.
She's off her feet.
Show us the sheet! Show us the sheet! Show us the sheet!

Fecunda beats two large metal trays together. Rosa, Mimosa, and Auntie Patina rap their knives against bottles as they join the dancers around Señora Nauseobondo.

"Show us the sheet!"

At least they drown out the sounds overhead, but it is going to be a long night.

"Gabito, find me a poultice for the pain in my head."

When he is gone, I shut my eyes so tightly that red and white veins float past in the darkness. I will just peek, to make sure everything is going well. Children always protest a mother's guiding hand, but in the long run of life, my son will thank me.

Little by little, I sense where José is in the wedding suite and allow my mind to snake upward through the plank ceiling, past the plank floor.

Through José's eyes, I see Pilar hiccupping badly, one right after the other. Her face is pale, almost blue. José sneaks up behind her and screams, "BOO!"

"H-help me," she hiccups.

José considers what to do, then grabs Pilar and throws her on the bridal bed. She screams. Her white bridal gown flips over her head, and a great gasp is heard from the crinoline pile. Her hiccups stop.

"It worked!" says José.

He helps Pilar sit up and straighten her dress.

"Thank you, José," she says.

Her eyes water. José sits next to her on the field-sized bridal bed and wipes away her tears with the sheet.

"You are just frightened, Pilar," he says. "I am too."

She lets him stroke her hair.

"I dropped the Madonna statue on your head," she says, "so you would go away and leave me alone. I wanted to hide inside God's love. It is the only place I feel safe."

She lets José touch her shoulder.

"I saved you from hiccups, twice," he says. "Do you feel safe with me now?"

She lets him kiss her shoulder.

The villagers' drunken singing from below is too loud for romance. "Show us the sheet! Show us the sheet!"

If I were José, I would tell them to quiet down. But he just sits with his bottom clenched on the freshly ironed sheet and inhales the body-scented air. Even I can smell her fear disappearing. He takes Pilar's hand gently and kisses her fingertips.

"Your tiny nails are pure and hard like you. I have saved myself for this night, for you, Pilar. I too am pure."

She blinks at him but does not speak. I am speechless too. José a virgin? I assumed since so many women wanted him that he had gone with at least one. What about little

Julia with the big breasts? Then there was María with all that hair, and Estrella, who blew him kisses from her pew. This is worse than I thought.

"It is a good thing to be pure, José," says Pilar. "I am happy you are like me."

José and Pilar sit on the edge of the bed and look at themselves in the mirror. They look like two-year-olds, their legs dangling off the mattress.

"I am so lucky," he says, "to sleep beside your beauty for the rest of my life."

"I never cared that I am ugly," she says, "until you attacked my mother with your flowers and nailed poetry to our door. Then I wanted to be beautiful for you, but I wasn't sure how."

Pilar touches José's face with her small white hand for the first time. He almost faints from joy.

From below the drunken crowd shouts impatiently. "Show us the sheet! Show us the sheet!"

"That custom is so vulgar," says Pilar.

José frowns at the door.

"Pilar, I do not care what anyone chants. We will do whatever you say. You are all that is important to me in the world."

He gently kisses the tears on her cheek. Pilar's trembling whiteness is like a halo. She looks up at him with big dark eyes.

If I had José's body and a man's desire, I would have difficulty not touching this soft, surrendered pale thing that Pilar has become.

"I know you are not Jesus, José," she says, "but you are as kind as Jesus."

She kisses José's unprepared mouth. José's face heats to match the rest of his body. He clutches the sheets to keep from throwing himself on the mound of her snow-white petticoats.

Pilar slides back into the middle of the enormous bed and lifts the mountainous folds of her gown. José squints. Even in candlelight, the skin of her thighs is as blinding as a hard winter star.

"You are made of silver moonbeams," he says.

"José, my husband," she says. "Let us make a little angel."

Over snow-white sheets, José makes the longest journey of his life, the hesitant crawl of his hungry manhood toward that dazzling crystal cave. I will leave them now. José will never know of my devotion in these pre-consummate moments.

But I am held by the rush of heat between them before their bodies meet. José collides with the pale mist of her. With bone-thin fingers, Pilar frees him from his clothes. She lies back, and his loins sink between her snow-bank thighs.

Now it is really time for me to go before Gabito returns. I steal one last glance as Pilar rubs her damp little clam against him and his chico gigante grows into a soft carrot. He slides up and down against her growing wetness. The carrot is gradually hardening. He just needs to relax.

"José," says Pilar, "am I doing it right?"

José the virgin, without a practical suggestion, can only strain against her. His body is sweating before he has begun. I feel the panic in him. He is not quite hard enough. Should I remind him to breathe and relax?

Gabito rises through the foot of the bridal bed. His epaulettes shake.

"Tortugina!" he screams silently to me. "Get back down through those cracks!"

His fury startles me so badly that I forget to answer only to Gabito.

"I was just leaving!" I say, and José hears me.

He freezes as though he has been slapped. "Mamá?"

"Oh my God, Tortugina!" Gabito says only to me. "He heard you!"

Pilar's gentle rhythm stops. "Why did you call me 'Mamá'?"

"Sorry. Sorry, José," I say. "Go back to what you are doing."

José's heart pumps wildly. He remembers to speak only to me.

"Mamá!" he says. "I am glad you have recovered, but you have to get out of my head right now!"

José's sweat drips onto Pilar's lips. Her face turns even paler.

"José?" she asks. "What is wrong?"

José's carrot wilts. He moans.

"José, I am so sorry," I say.

The little nun's face colors with a terrible blue-veined hurt. José hits the pillows on either side of Pilar's head. He screams into the darkness for all to hear.

"How could you do this to me? This is my wedding night!"

The crowd outside screams, "Show us the sheet! Show us the sheet!"

"José," I say. "Calm down. I was just leaving."

"Get out! Get out!" he screams.

Pilar pulls her dress down and scuttles out from under him.

"No, Pilar, not you," he says.

She cowers next to the mirror.

"José, what is wrong with you?" she sobs.

He slaps his head to get at me, furiously, as though he were slapping at stinging hornets.

"I hate you, Mamá!"

He slides out of bed, shaking with humiliation, and bangs his head on the wall mirror so hard that it cracks and bloodies his forehead.

"You are a madman!" cries Pilar.

She disappears inside the closet and slams the door shut.

"Pilar!" he yells.

José beats a pillow against the mirror. The feathery down scatters like snow around the room. Down sticks to his wet cheeks. He quickly pulls on his clothes and boots. Blood drips from his forehead down his cheek.

Gabito looks like he is going to strangle me.

"I am dressed now, Pilar!" says José. "I can explain. Come out. Please."

There are muffled sobs.

"Leave me alone! My mother was right! You are crazy, José. I never want to see you again!"

José wipes his bleeding forehead with the sheet.

Downstairs the men and women of the village scream.

"Show us the sheet! Show us the sheet!"

Gabito moans.

"José," I say. "Throw them the sheet. Tell them it is her blood."

José looks down at the stained sheet.

"What kind of man dishonors his wife with lies, Mamá? Go back to your coma." His voice is so bitter I do not recognize it. He throws the sheet at the mirror. "What kind of man cannot make love to his own wife?"

He climbs out the back window and slides off the roof. I hear his boots running, running away from me.

CHAPTER 31

THE SQUARE OF Don Pedro the Cruel and the Just sends shimmers of unbearable summer heat off the cobblestones.

Gabito and I wait inside the dark taverna of Señora Nauseobondo. Since José's disappearance a year ago, there is little to do but sip the icy emerald mint tea. I take a long ice-cube-cold swallow. The sides of my head freeze into a silent scream.

Gabito sits in the open window of the taverna with his heart frozen. He is balanced between sun and shade, the solitude of a silhouette. We are not a pretty couple.

Across the square Pilar carries a full bag from the Sweets and Curables Store now owned by Fecunda with her green snail money. Everything Pilar eats is for consolation or curing some kind of pain, and it has put meat on her bones.

"Gabito," I say only to him, "here comes Pilar. There is an unusual lightness to her step. Shall I ask her again if she has heard from José?"

Chapter 31

Gabito does not lift his cracked skull. His dark eyes are bright with tears. He watches Pilar walking toward the taverna and sighs.

"Tortugina," says Gabito, "you have tracked Pilar like a vigilante. Her steps are as measured today as they were yesterday, as they have been every day since José left. Our son is gone forever and rightly so. Let me suffer in peace."

"How many times can I apologize, Gabito?" I say silently to him.

Rosa, Mimosa, and Auntie Patina weave through the crowd, rolling their hips to my table.

"Mail brigade, mail brigade," says Auntie Patina.

They are fresh from the market, their handbaskets full of red tomatoes, small bitter melons, and flush summer squash. They hold their sad smiles out as an offering to me. Since José disappeared, the women of the wet chichis and the Deep Diving Cooperative have been my handkerchiefs, my waiting companions.

They also hope I will give them green snails, as I do to Fecunda.

"Tortugina," says Mimosa. "No mail? No word?"

The women put their baskets next to the table and sit in the heavy wooden chairs. The only solace of waiting is the routine of waiting with friends. Month after month after month, hoping the honey-colored mailman, Augustine, will bring me a letter from José.

The ice-pain in my head is draining. "Perhaps today," I say.

Rosa loosens her scarf. "What would make a boy so cruel to his mother, and to little Pilar?"

"Pilar keeps her wedding night a secret," I say. "I do not know what happened."

Gabito glowers at my lie.

From the heat of the square, Pilar breezes in, wearing her new blue sandals. Every week she selects the same chair, facing the window, and passes around her chewy, medicinal ginger candy. Since José disappeared, her black eyes have always been rimmed in red, but not today. She sits next to Rosa with a new kind of confidence.

So many things about Pilar have changed since José left. Her skin has filled out from the bone with fat to spare. A few more months of ginger candy, and she will be our little puffer fish. She has lost her girlish death-pallor. Her new dress, blue and orange instead of the usual grays, and those delicate sandals make her almost beautiful.

"Is that rouge on your cheeks?" I ask.

She pushes her long brown hair back from her neck.

"Yes. Señora Nauseobondo is helping me to become the kind of woman that a man would not leave," she says. Inside the new dress she wiggles her shoulders with pleasure, and I notice, for the first time, she has cleavage.

Gabito hisses at me. "Tell her the truth." He gives me such a look that I am forced to speak.

"Pilar, I want you to know, the wedding night was not your fault."

Pilar stops chewing the ginger candy. Under the rouge, she turns back to her old pale.

"How do you know? Were you there?" she says.

Perhaps she is thinking of how José called my name in bed. I stroke my sweating tea glass.

"It is always the man's fault," I say. "We women are the innocents."

The women laugh and nod, but Gabito rolls his tired eyes.

Chapter 31

"Coffee for the mail brigade," says Señora Nauseobondo.

She slides a wood tray onto our table with six tall glasses of her strong-brewed coffee over shaved ice topped white with cream. Her plate of sugar cookies nearly slides off the tray.

"And one glass for our loyal mailman, Augustine," she says. "When he gets here."

Señora Nauseobondo pulls a creaky chair from another table and sits with us. She drops a bright green pair of silk underwear on the table in front of Pilar.

"Here, Pilar, a little something for when José returns."

Rosa, Mimosa, and Auntie Patina clap. Gabito's face reddens, and he looks away. Pilar modestly crumples the shiny little pants into her pocket. She looks up at Señora Nauseobondo as though she were in love with her.

"Thank you, Señora," says Pilar.

I put aside my tea. The iced coffee slides more sweetly down my throat. I try to ignore the church bells clanging all twelve loud notes of noon. A mint-green headache slides all the way down my neck.

Through the window we watch Augustine trot his lathered Andalusian across the cobblestone square. For a few precious moments I allow myself to believe that a letter from José is arriving. My boy was always good at forgiveness. He must know I am not the enemy of love.

"Mail delivery," shouts Augustine.

Hundreds of miles of dry dust are etched into his voice. Villagers turn away from their food stands, abandon their municipal concerns, and make a slow parade toward the taverna. Like me, they hope for letters of their own. Everyone will share news from relatives along the coast.

Even Gabito leans out the window, watching Augustine tether his mount in front of the taverna.

"Only an hour late," says Rosa.

The postman's long bowed legs swing off his Spanish saddle. With his wide sombrero, Augustine beats his shirt and pants until a cloud of dust rises around him. He walks toward the door shaking out his long pirate hair. The villagers follow him and his precious saddlebags to our table.

"May I sit down among you?" he says.

We nod as we do every week.

"Señor Augustine," says Señora Nauseobondo in a voice as sweet as the coffee.

Standing before the charm of her smile, he always bows with his hat sweeping the floor.

He sits in one of the heavy chairs, and we all wait silently while he swallows the glass of iced coffee down to its last swirl.

"Ah," he says. "It is that first bite of cold."

He clears the dust and cream from his throat with a smoker's cough. The villagers crowd close as he empties the mail in front of Señora Nauseobondo. Her fingers sort quickly. Gabito floats nervously above the table and watches over the Señora's shoulder.

"Here's one for you, Mimosa." Señora Nauseobondo slings it over the frosted glasses into Mimosa's hands. She holds up a blue letter. "Sheriff Nina!" Villagers hand it back to Sheriff Nina.

"My daughter!" shrieks the sheriff.

I lean close enough to Augustine to smell his coffee breath.

"Augustine," I say, "is there a letter from José?"

Chapter 31

Augustine repeats what he has been saying for a year, but this time he cannot bring himself to look at me.

"I have no letter for you, Señora Tortugina."

Gabito floats back to his perch on the window. Each week it is harder to hold back my tears.

Gabito and I are like badly fermented wine, poorly corked and ready to explode. I give Augustine two coins for his trouble, one for me, one for Pilar. Augustine drops the coins into a leather pouch at his waist.

While Señora Nauseobondo passes out the mail, Augustine sighs and draws a mango from his lunch bag. As he slices it, the juice coats the tips of his fingers. He holds a dripping orange piece toward me. His light gray eyes watch my lips moisten as I chew his orange, pulpy gift. Gabito's silhouette hovers near the windowsill.

Augustine finishes his lunch and cleans his hands on a wet towel.

"Sons come and go, Señora Tortugina," he says. "My oldest son is gone fourteen years. Then last year, a letter comes from India. He is married and I am a grandfather five times. One day you will receive a letter with good news."

There is sweet hope in Augustine's gray eyes. For a moment I see José walking through the taverna door, healthy and full of love for me. But the shadow of hope quickly disappears as the mail has all been given out.

Augustine flips his long hair and pulls it back into a horsetail.

"Who is sending post, my friends? Quickly, I am on a schedule."

Señora Nauseobondo drops a white envelope into his saddlebag with coins for delivery and passes the bag back to the villagers. Pilar slides out of her seat and disappears into the crush of the crowd. I stand up, but I cannot see her.

Señora Nauseobondo hands the heavy saddlebags to Augustine and presses her dress against his dusty canvas chaps.

"Good journey, Señor Augustine."

It is a lover's good-bye. Augustine smiles at her with long yellow teeth, tucks the saddlebag over his shoulder, and pushes through the villagers who slip their letters and their coins into his bag.

Gabito floats above my head.

"Pilar put a pink envelope in the bag, Tortugina." Gabito pokes me. "She is taking care that you do not see her. We have to see what it says!"

Gabito has come to life with new hope. This is the most animated he has been in a year. I follow Augustine and watch him throw his saddlebags across the Andalusian's haunches.

"Wait, Señor Augustine," I say. "I want to ride with you to the edge of town. I must speak to you about a personal matter."

"I am on a schedule, Señora Tortugina," he says.

"I will pay you for your time. I will pay you extra," I say.

Augustine pulls himself onto the Andalusian's back and settles into the Spanish leather. His kind gray eyes look down at me.

"For money, I will let you win my race against time."

He bends forward as though to kiss me and pulls me up behind him. My arms seem to fall naturally around the hard muscles of his waist.

Pilar is left shading her eyes against the sun. Whether she is suspicious or not, she cannot catch up with the horse's hurried trot. As we trot out of the square, Gabito floats up to eye-level.

"Tortugina, you do not need to hold on that tightly."

"Gabito," I say, "the trotting is loosening my teeth."

When we reach the edge of town, I lean forward and whisper, "Augustine."

The deep lines of Augustine's neck twist as he turns.

"All I wish is to see the address on Pilar's letter," I say.

I hold up some coins and jingle them in front of his face.

Under the shadows of his sombrero, Augustine's eyes shift back and forth, and with a shameless shrug he says, "Señora, for good money you may read all my envelopes."

I shuffle through the letters until I find Pilar's. Gabito breathes heavily on my shoulder. The address reads: *To José Svendik, the Artisan of El Pulpo.*

El Pulpo! I almost fall off the horse. "He went home, Gabito! He went back to Mamá. Thank God, he was safe all this time."

Gabito spins in a joyful haze of epaulettes. "El Pulpo! Tortugina! We are going home!"

The horse dances in place under us. My fists pound against the hard muscles of the mailman's back.

"Augustine! You knew all this time! You let me worry for nothing!"

A year's worth of tears wet the back of his shirt.

"How could you be such a bad friend?"

His face looks a little uncomfortable, but nothing more. "José pays well for silence. Rejoice that he is well, like my son."

I start to tear open Pilar's pink love note, but Augustine snatches it out of my hands.

"That is an offense against the government. I will have to ask you to leave the horse, Señora."

Gabito clamps his legs behind mine. "Tortugina, do not get off. It is our fastest way to El Pulpo."

I slide my arms tightly around Augustine's muscled waist and drop the rest of my coins between his thighs. With my nose close to his dusty ear, I whisper, "Take all my coins. I'm coming with you to El Pulpo, Señor Augustine. That much you owe me."

CHAPTER 32

AUGUSTINE REINS IN the white Andalusian under El Pulpo's thousand-year-old cypress. The animal bows its dusty head and drinks from the small stream that runs to the sea. Across the coast road, lit by the moon, is my many tiered wedding-cake village. It no longer looks as stale as old bread. The white homes of El Pulpo shine with a smile-bright welcome.

"Our home, Gabito," I say to him as he slides off the rump of the Andalusian.

This place, I had almost forgotten in the small lifetime since I have seen Mamá and Papá.

With a groan from the feet up, I slip off the Andalusian's broad back. My legs are bowed and weak from gripping the hard leather mailbags that have rubbed my thighs burning raw. The chafing journey to El Pulpo has prepared me for the worst. But at least I am warm under Augustine's wool serape.

Chapter 32

I lean with quaking knees against the old tree. Its ancient bark is puckered around generations of rusty nails and splintered pegs for posting hand-printed messages.

Sea-worn papers flutter in the cold breeze: "Fresh octopus," "My pig is missing," "Ramón please come home."

Old, red-veined Ramón causing the usual heartache. It is nice to know that nothing in El Pulpo changes. His poor Luisa is still paying the priest good money to pencil a message for her drunk husband who cannot read.

A sudden, cold breeze from the sea lifts the squares of paper in one silent breath. Augustine's lined face looks down at me with warmth beyond friendship, as if he had never betrayed me with his silence. He hands me Pilar's pink envelope.

"I will miss your little arms around me," he says with a tired smile. "But for now, you may keep the serape. I will find you after dinner and retrieve it then."

He kicks the Andalusian closer and reaches down to kiss me. Before Gabito can harm him, I wobble across the coast road out of reach.

"You will find your serape at my mother's house," I say. "Do not ask for me."

"Next time I want a kiss. Ssst! Ssst!" he says.

The horse's hooves spark wet stones in its graceful trot past me to deliver the mail.

Gabito holds my arm and helps me with my chafed, bowlegged walk down Calle de Serpiente, white slate roofs, powdered oyster shells distilling in the pale air, the familiar path to home. The smells of salt and sea are the aromas of our childhood. How different things would have been if I had not killed him on the cliffs. We would never have left

El Pulpo. I would have become a diver and made Mamá proud. Now all I can do is tremble at the thought of seeing the disappointment in her eyes again.

"Easy, my love," says Gabito, helping me over the uneven cobblestones.

We pass the same winding rows of white houses, walls that are the white tunnels of memory. Windows of kerosene-bright curtains. I hear the faint laughter of the families inside and remember the insults.

Two new roof dogs on the Riveras' house lean over and bark strangled sounds like they are coughing up spinach. Their small teeth snap against the starry sky.

"Gabito, look," I whisper, and point to the old tortilleria.

The old tortilleria where Gabito and I breathed the same air every morning as children. At first I had not recognized my moonlit reflection in the window. I am thinner in the face. My jaw is hard from chewing and dreaming. My hair is up in a crooked bun just like Mamá's. Some fat has settled on my hips. The village will see my mother in me. There is no excuse not to have become something, anything, different. Over the years I have grown softer and harder, but not much else.

"Everything seems changed," says Gabito.

"Yes," I say, "except us."

Gabito floats through the low entrance of the tortilleria. A kerosene lamp blossoms orange on the tile counter. El Fuerte's gasoline motor still stinks, mingling with the heated smell of corn tortillas.

Gabito startles me out of my thoughts by touching my hand.

"Open the letter," he says.

Chapter 32

I draw the pink envelope out of my skirt pocket and hold the envelope on the hot glass to melt the glue. He blows on the fragile pink paper so it will not ignite. Our invasion into Pilar's wifely words is almost repugnant, but it is for José that we do this.

Gabito snorts impatiently. Finally, the flap of the envelope curls back, and I draw Pilar's letter out. Her blue-ink handwriting is so precise, it is like the watertight weave of basketry.

Dear José,

I prayed every day to the Virgin of Guadalupe for your safety. Thank the good Lord that you wrote at last. Please do not say good-bye forever. Stay alive until we talk. I am wiser. I understand now what happened. It happens to many men on their wedding night. I love you. I am coming to be with you forever. I did not tell your mother where you are, as you asked. Please forgive me and wait.

Your loving wife, Pilar

PS. I am much prettier now.

The page trembles in my fingers. "He still wants to kill himself, Gabito."

And the little nun will arrive in time to be a widow. I spread the letter on the blue tile counter to stop my shaking hands.

"José does not want me to find him."

"Tortugina," says Gabito, "we will find him and save him."

A young dark-haired boy stands in the distant shadow of the back door. His hands hold a broom that is too big for him. For an instant, I see José returning as the child he once was, pushing the hair out of his eyes.

"Who are you?" he says. "I am Alfredo."

With no fear of strangers, he comes to the counter, and I turn up the wick of the kerosene lamp to show him my smile.

"I am Señora Tortugina, daughter of Señor Gomez who owns the store in the plaza. Are Señor Gomez and his wife at home?"

The boy merely stares at me as if I were a ghost. A silent stare from a child can mean many things. In this case, I hope it means nothing. Then he points silently in the direction of the plaza.

"Thank you, Alfredo," I say.

I stuff Pilar's opened envelope into my pocket. Gabito holds my arm and helps me hurry as I try to ignore my burning thighs. Down Calle de Serpiente the switch-back, where I barely catch a glimpse of the small shops on either side that are still in the same place, the lavanderia, the pollo restaurant.

Finally we arrive at the Plaza de Allende. Every closed shop is painted the same bloodless white. Trimmed trees are dark against lighted windows. Sounds from the past are loud in the silence: grackles chirping and screaming. The old ones are dead. The new generation shriek like a hundred rusty doors. I can still hear my blood pumping with the rhythm of the dances, memories of old tunes played from the iron bandstand.

Gabito and I stop in front of Papá's store. The wooden threshold has worn deeper. The shutters are closed, but there is light upstairs. The two-story façade is colorless in the moonlight. Without the heavy hues of Las Mujeres to inhale, my blood feels thin.

I close my eyes and breathe deeply until my blood feels strong again.

The breeze brings the smell of a cooked dinner from Mamá's iron skillet, handfuls of cilantro, leeks, garlic, tomatoes, octopus, and chilies fried crisp. I can even smell Papá's pipe smoke, Amanda's baby powder, and Véronica's rancid olive-oiled shoes. My sisters will have husbands who smoke cigars. I will have candy-scented nephews and nieces. José is eating up there with them. They are one big happy family. And I am on the outside, as always.

My fists pound on the bolted door. I want it to hurt, but that is not why I am crying. What I truly want is to press myself into the sweet scent of Mamá's flesh and let go of myself, let her heavy arms hold me up, let her heat close around me. The two of us as we used to be, together in the warm womb of her kitchen.

I have tried motherhood. I have been an adult. Now I want to come home.

"Mamá," I yell. "Let me in!"

The neighbors' shutters are cracking light. I tremble as the heavy steps on the other side of the door come closer.

"Mamá, Mamá! It is me!"

The door in front of me opens, and there is Papá with his dinner napkin still in the neck of his brown shirt. He does not seem to recognize me.

"Papá, it is Tortugina!"

He steps back from the door, blinking as though I were a bad dream, rips the napkin from his collar, and shouts up the stairs. "Celia, come quick, it is our outlaw!"

Mamá puffs down the stairs, soft body unchanged, but without her big smile.

"Mamá, I missed you so much!" I try to come in, but Mamá blocks the door.

"You!" says Mamá and bursts into tears. She takes a moment to breathe and says, "All these years, Tortugina, no word from you. Then you send us your son who made us crazy! He has disgraced us worse than you!"

This is so much worse than I expected. I can barely breathe in the heated space between us.

"What did José do?" I whisper.

Papá puts his arm around Mamá's shuddering shoulders.

"The village paid him to make a statue of the Blessed Virgin on the cliffs," says Papá. "One that the fishermen could see."

Mamá wipes her eyes with her apron. "He refused to show it to us. After a year of wondering, some of the men tore off the tarp today to see what he made with our money."

Papá shakes his head. He too is nearly in tears.

"All that cost, and now the village has to tear it down."

I remember the beautiful, delicate statue José carved for Pilar.

"Mamá, José only knows how to make beauty with his hands. He is a master craftsman. He is even better than his father!"

Mamá raises her swollen eyes to look at me and begins to close the door.

"Go to the cliffs, Tortugina, and see for yourself," she says.

I press against the door to keep her from shutting it.

"You used to love me, Mamá," I whisper.

Her voice softens. "Little turtle, I do love you. Now, please, go away. It was bad enough when you lived here. But this son of yours…it is too much for my old heart."

She starts to sob. Papá gently pushes the door, and I step back as it closes against the worn threshold.

The cold breeze of El Pulpo whips my tears. Gabito takes my hand and pulls me as fast as I can run to the cliffs.

CHAPTER 33

WILD WIND AND moonlit spray whip my hair in a frantic dance. Below us, the dark waves thunder against volcanic spears. Currents cut at the ragged edges and spin into white foam that once carried Gabito's blood.

We shield our eyes from blinding gusts, squint through the mist. There it is, José's Blessed Virgin. I am awed by his monster of architecture. She is as tall as a lighthouse. Long curved shins and thighs pillar skyward. Her hands are lifted, a prayer that begins at the elbows and goes to the stars.

The body, made of hard bricks, has been plastered and sanded to look like skin, hair, fabric. José has carved the wind into the light weave of her fragile gown. The cloth clings to the molding of her body, one naked breast exposed to the lungs of the sea.

I cling to a stunted pine, and can barely contain my admiration. And then, my throat turns raw as I look up into the woman's face. My face! My pinched frown! My overbite like a canopy!

Chapter 33

A sudden sickness retches up my throat. No wonder Mamá and Papá shut me out. José has built an abomination.

"What kind of boy does this to his mother?" yells Gabito over the wind. "You appear naked in front of God and man!"

The great statue looks out at the waves with hollowed eyes.

"Have I been such a terrible mother, Gabito?" I yell back.

He avoids my eyes, but his silent expression tells me, yes.

A faint scent of kerosene is carried on a downward draft. Among the thin folds stretched across the Virgin's stomach, there is a flickering of orange from a hole, as though her bellybutton were on fire.

"José!" The wind tears his name from my lips.

"I will see if he is there," says Gabito.

Gabito's sandals rise past my eyes and up to navel height. I can only climb as high as the Virgin's adobe toenail, as big as a plate, her foot as large as José's single bed. Around the base of the Virgin's feet, bamboo scaffolding and a wooden ladder have been deliberately hacked to pieces.

Gabito descends so fast he almost misses the toe where I am sitting.

"Tortugina, hurry! He is sealing himself inside the Virgin!"

Gabito climbs behind me and wraps his arms around my waist.

"What are you doing?" I say.

My feet are suddenly off the ground.

"You have to get him out of there!" says Gabito.

Gabito's arms are as tight as rope. I try to settle comfortably into the hard nest of his muscles. It is not at all like being weightless in the sea. The wind tries to flatten us against the statue's solid shins. Cold air drafts up my dress. Gabito inches us up past the roundness of the Virgin's strong knees.

When we are eye-level with the square navel, I can see the orange flickering of a kerosene lamp inside. Gabito's heavy ghost breathing against my ear comes from so many holes in his head that it sounds like harmony.

"Hurry," Gabito says. "I cannot keep us both up forever!"

My fingers touch cold adobe, sanded to the imperfection of skin. I crawl into the small entrance that has not yet been sealed, jagged like crone's teeth, but wide enough for my hips. The short tunnel of bricks forms a tight girdle. Gabito nudges me from behind. I smell old tortillas, man-sweat, and the sharp, musty odor of mortar. My fingers touch freshly set bricks on the floor at the entrance to the womb. I climb over the bricks into a room rounded like a small cave by darkness and light from a lantern.

José's back is turned to me and his shadow is a giant spider on the curved wall. In a dusty pile around the base of a brick wall and crude planked floor are the basic items for such a life: a sleeping mat, a big skin of wine, a large tin of water, canned food, empty beer bottles and tins, building tools, a metal miner's hat, and curled ropes. A bucket of dirty water tilts next to a trough, and nearby are piles of brick, lye, and sand.

Unearthed in the deepest of all lairs, José hears my breathing and turns. He holds the kerosene lamp toward me and stares troubled, out of focus, perhaps drunk. José is a shirtless adobe statue, covered in brick dust and unshaven. His once shining curls are matted against his head. So many changes have passed beneath his skin in one hard year. I want to place my fingers over his tired, red eyes and help him sleep.

"José," I say softly, "look at you."

"Mamá," he cries. "Can I never escape you, even in death?"

José's body has put on muscle from the heavy labor of building a woman. Molded by deep light, he looks as if he were made to hold up the world. What do I say to my son in the womb of his creation? I pull the crumpled envelope out of my pocket, an offering in the palm of my hand.

"José, it is Pilar's letter. She loves you and begs you to forgive her. She will be here soon. There is no reason to shut yourself away."

He frowns as he takes the pink envelope and runs his finger along the unglued edge. His face turns as red as his eyes.

"You opened it?" he asks in disbelief.

"A mother's love made me do it," I say.

José stuffs the letter in his waistband and reaches for the leather wine bag.

"I never want to see the face of love again," he says. "Now please, go away."

He shoots a line of wine into his mouth. It streaks down the sides of his dusty face and chest. What can I say to delay leaving him?

"But we have much to discuss," I say.

José shakes his head. "No."

"Then give me some wine."

He seems startled, but hands me the wine skin. I lower my bottom onto the pile of curled rope and aim the wine into my mouth.

Gabito is inches from my ear.

"You are drinking?" he asks me silently. "While he is making a suicide?"

"I will get him so drunk he passes out," I say only to Gabito. "Then you can float him to earth. Do you have a better idea?"

I give the wine skin back to José. He takes another long mouthful. His eyes look bruised from the inside.

"If I had been a man with Pilar," he says, "I would have had the strength to shut you out, as I shut the world out when I carve. I should have focused on nothing but the body of my wife."

He drinks again, with pursed, wet lips that remind me of the harsh tug of his baby hunger.

"Get out, Mamá!"

Will I always be the culprit, the betrayer, to my son?

He turns away. With a perfectionist's eye, José pours lye, sand, and water into the trough and stirs.

"Entomb me for my sins, José," I say. "I will make the journey to hell with you."

He looks up at me with the wound of his wedding night still sharp in his eyes.

"I wanted to die as an old man in Pilar's arms, surrounded by my children and grandchildren."

José weighs the balance of the trowel in his hand as though he might strike me.

"Now I will die inside this womb with my mother!"

The word "mother" sounds like a curse.

"I thought I escaped you when I left, Mamá. But even my greatest creation looks more like you than like Pilar."

It looks exactly like me, I want to say. But I am silent as I watch José lather the brick and set it in the entrance to the womb. With the tapping of his wooden handle, the bricks slip perfectly into place. Gabito's whisper is harsh in my ear. "Tortugina, make him drink more, before the bricks set!"

"José," I say quickly. "Let us drink to the last sky we will see."

José squirts the wine into his mouth. Between each brick that he picks up with slower and slower deliberation, I propose a toast.

"To your statue, to your talents, to carpenters everywhere!"

He does not seem to notice that he is getting sloppy.

He holds the last brick, feels the weight as though it were precious. Wedging it into place, he shuts out the stars. José has built a woman, my nightmare woman, who is as complete as a destiny can be.

The wind is gone except for a small overhead draft.

We drink in silence.

We drink again.

Gabito hisses behind me, "The bricks are hardening!"

José leans back against the wall of the womb and lets his hand drop to Pilar's letter in his waistband.

"Mamá, you see where love has taken us." His words trail into the dust. "Why is there no happiness?"

The long muscles of his body slacken as he closes his eyes and passes out. With small snores, his purple-stained chest moves up and down.

"Quick, Tortugina," says Gabito. "Pull down the wall!"

Red chips fly as I beat the bricks with a hammer. The wall pocks but is unmoved. José snores in his coma-drunk sleep, curled around Pilar's letter.

"Hurry, Tortugina," says Gabito.

Desperate, I begin to throw unused bricks at the entrance. I gasp for air in the red dust. Panic settles deep in my chest. Gabito tries a little magic, but a purple haze and a few hand movements do nothing. I shake José, the first time I have touched my son in a year.

"José! Wake up!" I say.

He cannot hold up his head from the burden of wine. José shivers from a cool draft somewhere above us.

"Gabito, do you feel cold air from the outside?"

Without a word, Gabito shoots upward out of the lantern light and into the darkness.

I throw water from the bucket over José's head. He wakes up with his face wet, as though it has been cut from fruit.

José sits up. "Mamá," he moans, "leave me alone!"

He shakes water off his head like a puppy.

"José," I say, "you are no longer my insatiable infant. You are a man hungry to know his manhood. Your heart is full enough. Your wife loves you for reasons beyond your chico gigante. And if you do not learn from my words, you deserve to die in a sealed womb. Now get me out of here!"

When I turn up the orange light of the lamp, it burns higher into the darkness. José's cheekbones are defined by ancient shadows. But his eyes look new, as though he opened them for the first time. These are the eyes of a boy who would not let his mother die.

José leans forward until his brow touches mine. His head is fever-hot. He cries wine tears. Our minds are so close we smell each other's thoughts.

"Mamá," whispers José, "I will help you."

He places my palm flat against his chest. José's hands are weighted with such beauty.

"José," I whisper, "I love you, perhaps not well, but with my whole heart."

We hold each other in the drafty stillness of the womb. When I raise my hand off his chest, I have left my handprint in dust and wine.

CHAPTER 34

JOSÉ LOOKS UP into the cavern of darkness above us and scratches his matted hair.

"There is one way out," says José, "but it will be dangerous for you."

As José waits for my reaction, Gabito drops into the dust beside me.

"Tortugina," says Gabito. "The Virgin's eyes are open holes. You can escape!"

"Your father is here," I say to José. "He says the eyes are the way out."

"Yes," says José. "Where is Papá? I want to see him."

"He is standing next to me," I say.

"Papá?" he says. José stretches his hand in the space beside me. "I just feel air."

Gabito blinks as José's fingers slide through his transparent face. José is shaking from the excess of wine and too little food. "Papá, help me save Mamá."

Chapter 34

"He will help us, José," I say. "Tell us what you want us to do."

José takes a deep breath and slaps his cheeks to sober himself. Retrieving a dusty old rope, he ties it around his waist and mine, like the umbilical cord that once bound us.

José lights the candle on the miner's hat and adjusts it, but it is too small and sits high on his head. He looks up, shifting the pale candlelight along the brick walls so that we can see a little more of the journey that awaits us.

Long, narrow shadows waver up the walls. It will be like climbing the inside of a lighthouse. The candlelight from José's miner's hat illuminates a slight outward curve of bricks that must describe the woman's hips.

"Mamá," says José. "There is scaffolding above us, at the waist and breasts, just a few logs across, not a solid floor like this one." He stomps on the floor of the womb, and dust rises. "If we make it as far as the neck, you can rest on the inside of her chin."

If?

"Stay very close to me," I say silently to Gabito.

We follow José to his finely built wall. He shines his lamp on an iron spike jutting out from the bricks. It sticks out far enough for a handhold or a footrest. And there is one above it. José moves his light upward, showing a ladder of spikes that rise up the Virgin's spine like iron vertebrae.

"This is how I moved up and down her body as I built the woman," he says proudly. "I am used to it, but you must climb very carefully."

He waits as I tighten my loose sandals then slips his fingers around the first spike, then the next, one hand reaching over the next as he starts our journey. I pull myself up after him in jerks. Through the long rope, I feel the tremor of José's straining body. The bottom of José's sandal slips, sprinkling my hair and eyes with loose dust.

"Slowly, José," I say.

Gabito hovers at my elbow. The three of us form our own little ascension: father, son, and the unholy little turtle.

We climb, our toes taking the place of our fingers. The iron is rough and cold against my fingers. The rope tension slackens, and we find a rhythm.

On the floor of the womb, the kerosene lamp sputters in a wavering pool of orange, growing smaller as we make our way upward.

José's miner's candle spreads light against the smallest, gentlest of curves inward at the Virgin's waist. Two rough, rounded logs span the slightly narrowed space. But there is no place to rest and catch my breath. The spikes leave small cuts on my fingers as we climb up the spine, through the Virgin's invisible stomach without a pause, and with no intestinal rumblings but mine.

By the time we reach the breasts, my arms and legs tremble so badly from the strain that Gabito is practically pushing me up. From the spine, we can look across a support log to the Virgin's dry chichis.

Gabito's breath warms my neck against the cool drafty air. Failing muscles and cut fingers make the climb endless. When my foot slips again from weariness, Gabito replaces it on the iron spike.

Echoes of our blood pumping fill the silence as we forge upward through the barren space where the Virgin's giant heart would be.

Chapter 34

José's hat lights the logs across a narrower, tunnel-like structure above us.

"Once we pass through these neck beams," José says breathlessly, "there is a flat platform where the chin juts out. Soon you will rest, Mamá."

He pulls himself through the wooden beams and climbs onto the ledge of the Virgin's chin above me. He is safe, thank God.

José reels me in like an exhausted tuna. Every muscle is shaking. My fingers feel wet. It must be blood.

Kneeling near the edge of the chin platform, José reaches for my hand. The candle from his miner's hat shines in my eyes. With the help of the kerosene lamp from below, I can see through the beams, but I cannot reach José's fingers. He stretches a little farther. The metal miner's hat falls off his head. It strikes me between the eyes. A red slash of light.

"Mamá!" yells José.

The flame of the candle sears my eyelashes. I lose my foothold. "Gabito!" I reach for him in the air but he misses my hand.

As I fall past Gabito, José is jerked off the ledge by the rope attached to my waist.

In the faint orange light, the wild shadows of our bodies seem to slow into a dance as José and I plunge downward.

Our fall is cut short by the rope looping over the Virgin's breast beam. We swing side by side, like two pendulums. My body is the counterweight to José's dangling limbs. Above us, the wooden beam creaks.

The taut hemp cuts my waist, and blood flows backward, away from the sudden lasso of organs. José and I both pull upward on the rope to relieve the terrible pain. He grabs for an iron spike on the Virgin's spine, but it is just out of reach.

Gabito stops my swinging, wraps his arms around me, and carries me like a baby, upward. As my body rises, José, attached to the same rope, slides downward, descending toward the womb.

"Mamá?" he yells up to me. "What are you doing?"

"Patience!" I yell back.

Gabito carries me through the logs at the Virgin's neck and presses me over a raised crossbeam on the rim of the ledge that becomes her chin. I sit up, brace my feet against the beam, and straighten my legs. My waist is numb from José's weight. Gabito and I drag the dusty rope toward us. José is borne upward, inches at a time.

José hanging in space, supported only by the rope, by me, by Gabito whose life once hung by the waistband of his yellow goodluck swim shorts. The rip and the awful fall. In this family, someone is always at the end of a tether.

My legs start to buckle toward the neck hole. José's weight is too great. The rope slides away in jerks, burning my palms.

Suspended over the darkness, José screams, "Mamá! I do want to live! Please, please!"

Gabito and I find new strength to pull then lose it again. The strained rope see-saws back and forth over the rough wood crossbeam, back and forth, fraying the woven plaits, until the rope begins to unravel. I see it happening, but neither Gabito or I dare loosen our hold.

We yank with all our strength. The rope breaks and fires back at me. My spine slams flat back onto the ledge.

José's scream falls away from me into the womb.

Chapter 34

"OhBlessedVirginGodinHeavenhelpJosé!"

The past falls on my heart, as Gabito fell, as José falls!

I hear a distant echo from the womb. Strained, painful gasps that move closer, closer, and finally stop at the neck. I scoot to the dark shaft and lean over the crossbeam at the edge. Below me two heads rise into the dim light. Gabito ascends, puffing like the old tortilla machine, holding José with the torn rope dangling at his waist.

Gabito's fingers touch José's body in the way flesh meets flesh. They are two solid men with no transparency between them.

José stares at his father with wide eyes. Gabito pushes José's muscled body over the beam at the edge of the chin. José sits up beside me and reaches to help Gabito. Catching their breath, my two men sit on the solid beam at the rim of the Virgin's neck and trade winded smiles.

Gabito, beautiful in the dim light, leans his solid body toward José. He gingerly unties the rope around José's bloody waist.

"Papá, you saved my life," whispers José.

I unknot the tight rope around my bloodied belly.

"You let him see you, Gabito," I say out loud. "What miracle is this?"

Gabito puts his hand on José's shoulder and is careful to keep his good side toward his son. "It was my son's life," he says, as if it had always been that simple.

José places his hands lovingly on Gabito's face. Deliberately, he turns his father's face to him with the scarred and unscarred sides showing equally.

"It is all right, Papá," he says. "These are the wounds of living with Mamá. Yours are only on the outside."

Gabito is crying from so much happiness that his loose eye threatens to float onto his cheek. José lightly cups his hand over Gabito's socket so the eye cannot drop further then nudges it gently back into place.

Gabito's body shakes. "My boy! My boy!" he sobs.

Gabito pats José's hair, and as though it were a second thought, he uses a little magic to fluff José's filthy clothes, dissolve the brick dust off the boy's smooth face.

"Now, my son, you are better prepared to meet your wife," he says.

José reaches down to his waistband and extracts Pilar's letter, stained with his blood.

"Papá," says José, "I never thanked you for the gift of Pilar."

He holds her envelope in the dim light, slowly crushes it, and raises his fist as though he means to throw it back into the darkness he has just escaped. His eyes fill with tears.

"Papá," José whispers to Gabito. "I have disgraced my manhood with her."

Gabito wraps his arms solidly around José's strong body and they pound each other's backs.

"Never give up for a single failure," says Gabito. "Look at me. There is more magic in us than we know."

When they pull apart from the rough embrace, José stares for a long moment at Gabito, smooths Pilar's letter, and tucks it back into his waistband. He looks up at the blue light that shines through the Virgin's eyes, and his shoulders gradually soften as though a great weight is being lifted.

"José," I say. "I want to get out of this woman's body."

Chapter 34

His thoughts are broken by my voice, but he smiles sweetly at me and helps me to my feet.

Gabito and I follow him up the few spikes on the wall of the Virgin's cheek to the twin holes of light filled with sky. We climb onto a ledge and become the Virgin's eyes, witnessing the scene she sees every morning, the sunrise flattened across the sky.

From the cold draft inside her head, we climb outside onto a flat, narrow eyelid where we can barely keep our footing. Breathless from the height and the effort, I fill my lungs with the warm sweet air.

José shows me how to shuffle very gradually to the edge of the eye where I can step onto a ladder of iron spikes that leads to the top of her head.

Our movement up the Virgin's brow becomes reptilian, our bellies pressed against the curve of her forehead. At the peak of her head is a flat roof, and I gratefully rest in the morning breeze.

I had almost forgotten there was a world of such beauty out here. The red sea stretches out below us. The view is long both ways, the black Forbidden Cliffs to the right, the white village of El Pulpo to the left. José is on one side of me, Gabito on the other. I am filled with a peace that has been a long time in coming.

A voice I had been hoping for all night is carried up on the wind.

"José!"

Pilar stands at the feet of the Virgin in a tight, pink ruffled dress that flutters in the wind. She smiles and waves her big pink hat.

José can barely speak. He waves her letter.

"Pilar," he sighs. "My wife. She is so beautiful."

Pilar throws him a kiss. He throws her a dozen kisses. Perhaps he will have no fear now to lie with Pilar and grow his seed above her small hips. Beyond that, I hope they will live long lives and die with many grandchildren to mourn them. Death to life. The shift is always quick.

"Pilar! I love you!" shouts José. "I am coming. Don't move!"

Church bells ring the old alarm. The village is awake. Small groups of people tramp toward the Virgin with ladders and ropes. People point at us. Mamá and Papá are still in the distance. Is that sweet Amanda next to them? She looks so pregnant or so much fatter. If my arms were snakes I would send them winding down to my dear sister for one more hug.

"Tortugina," says Gabito, "we have done our job well."

He embraces José and says in his ear, "Never forget whose son you are."

Gabito steps to the edge of the Virgin's head and pumps his legs and arms as he used to on the cliffs so long ago.

José, horrified, watches his father's perfect dive. Arms and legs together, Gabito slices down the cliff through morning mist with such grace, his brown body looks unbroken as it turns back to ghost.

Gabito's voice, deep as eternity, is swept to me on the wind. "Dive, Tortugina!"

José moans. His dust-red fingers reach for me as I follow Gabito to stand on the edge.

"Mamá, no."

He moves behind me and holds on to my waist like Tomás held Gabito by his goodluck yellow swim trunks.

Chapter 34

"José, I love you. You are the best of sons. Now let me go."

José is crying behind me as he steps away. I pump my arms and legs to loosen kinks from our crawl up the womb and say silently to my son, "José, you are stronger than you know."

I lean forward into the warm air. The morning breeze is soft against my tears. The horizon blurs in endless waves.

"Mamá, what will I do without you?" says José.

The space between my mind and José's is stretched so thin we hang on to shredded air. "You will be a man, José."

With a push of my toes, I dive off the Virgin, arms together, legs together, toward the sea like a hollow-boned bird. This is the dive I have been waiting all my life to make.

Feather-bright, the air rushes through my skin, through my blood. I am tempted to soar. As dark cliffs slide past, I fall in the thin territory between life and death.

Let them all witness the diver I might have been.

The wind whips my damp hair against my head.

In the crimson sea below, Gabito's golden epaulettes shine as he treads the warm current and waits for me.

ACKNOWLEDGMENTS

MY GRATITUDE TO all the Dangerous Writers Group of Tom Spanbauer's workshops with whom I worked over the years. My undying gratitude to my writing mentor: Tom Spanbauer, a dangerous writer, who taught me the craft of writing. And to my original editor and teacher, Carolyn Altman, who was there for the long haul with compassion and humor, and showed me how, as Ray Bradbury once said, "to be drunk with writing." A special appreciation goes to my Fat Thursday critique group who cook as well as they write: Bonnie Comfort, Lily Gardner, Tamara Greenleaf, Peter Korn, Carolyn Kurtz, Diane Ponti, Liz Scott, Susan Whitter, Lynn Welsh.

Others who helped were Dave Cantrell, Joanne Tracy, Gage Mace, Robert Hill, Roger Larson, Ketzel Levine, Grace Paley, Pauline Peotter, Reed Mathis, and Lilia Trapága Tenney. Thanks also to Andrew Stuart of The Stuart Agency, New York, Elizabeth Udall of the Walden Fellowship, and the facilitators and participants of the following conferences: Willamette Writers Conference, Flight of the Mind, Squaw Valley Writers Conference, Santa Barbara Writers Conference, Fishtrap Writers Conference. And finally, thanks to the storytellers of my childhood: Bertha Seiferth Bannett, Lena Carlson, and my parents.

Ooligan Press

OOLIGAN PRESS takes its name from a Northwest Coast Native American word for the common smelt or candlefish, a source of wealth for millennia in the Pacific Northwest and likely origin of the word "Oregon." Ooligan is a general trade press rooted in the rich literary life of Portland and the Department of English at Portland State University. Besides publishing books that honor cultural and natural diversity, it is a unique teaching press staffed by students pursuing master's degrees in an apprenticeship program under the guidance of a core faculty of publishing professionals. By publishing real books in real markets, students combine theory with practice; the press and the classroom become one.

The following Portland State University students completed the primary editing, designing, and marketing for *José Builds a Woman:*

PROJECT MANAGER: David Cowsert

COVER DESIGN: Mark Insalaco

(the painting for the cover was created by Jan Baross)

INTERIOR DESIGN: Sherry Green

MARKETING LEAD: Monica Garcia

Colophon

Interior title: News Gothic Std. Bold
Interior type: 11 pt. Adobe Caslon Pro, Regular
Chapter heads: 13 pt. Gill Sans Ultra Bold
Running heads & folios: Adobe Caslon Pro Semibold
Glyphs: Adobe Caslon Pro and Minion Pro
Clip art: Public domain via wisegorilla.com
Paper: 60# white, pH balanced

Ordering Information

All Ooligan titles can be ordered directly from the publisher or from your favorite bookseller in the United States, Canada, and online. Booksellers, please contact us for distributor and wholesaler information. Educators, contact us for special discounts on classroom sets.

Ooligan Press
PO Box 751
Portland, OR 97207-0751
www.ooligan.pdx.edu
www.publishing.pdx.edu
503.725.9410
ooligan@pdx.edu